CAUTIOUS

Nancy,
Hope you enjoy
Marcus + Mia's Story!

xo
E.L. Monte

Also by E.L. Montes

DISASTROUS

What People are saying about Disastrous

"Five stars from me for a sequel brilliantly told! In my review of *Disastrous*, I said: 'Passion, heartache, laughter, tears, drama, intrigue. *Disastrous* had it ALL. In *Cautious* be prepared for the same!'"—Author Melissa L. Delgado on the *Disastrous* Series.

"I found myself laughing during this book at certain times. I found myself nervous during this book at certain times and also found my heart breaking for these characters as well." —Author Gail McHugh on *Disastrous*.

"*Disastrous* is about the angsty, emotional, intense relationship between a 1st year law student and a powerful, drop-dead sexy lawyer with a secret life. With such an original premise and relatable characters, I was sucked in, gutted, and completely captivated by Marcus and Mia's tragic love story."—Author S.L. Jennings on *Disastrous.*

CAUTIOUS

Sequel to Disastrous

E.L. Montes

CAUTIOUS

E.L. Montes

The following story contains mature themes, strong language, and sexual situations. It is intended for adult readers.

Cover designed by David Goldhahn

www.davidgoldhahn.com

Edited by Theresa Wegand

Proofread by Miranda Petrillo

This one is for the couple that started it all, Marcus and Mia. Thank you for allowing me to be a part of your story. After all, it is YOUR story. I just wrote it. It was quite a roller-coaster ride, but I enjoyed all the ups and downs. You will always have a special place in my heart.

Love,
The boss lady ;-)

PROLOGUE

As I entered the room, my blood was still pumping with adrenaline from what just happened. I blinked a few times as the cloud of smoke from the gunfire filled the room. My eyes searched for the one person I feared for the most. It was a rampage and guns continued to fire. I quickly ran around searching but could not find that familiar face.

My heart picked up its pace as I hovered over lifeless bodies and held a tight grip on the gun in my hand, ready for anyone who got in the way. As I continued my search, I finally spotted Jimmie. He was kneeling on the ground, hovering over someone. My throat closed, and my entire body stilled as I saw the person before him. For a mere second, I grew faint but managed to force my trembling legs toward them.

Jimmie quickly turned and aimed his gun at my approach. His mouth dropped opened in relief at the sight of me. Tears swelled in his bloodshot eyes, and breathing heavily, he stared at me, ready to break. "I'm so sorry. I tried, but I . . . *Fuck! I fuckin' tried . . .*" Immediately, he turned his attention back to the person before him. "Come on, don't do this to me." With bloody hands, he pressed against the wound as he grunted. My body shuddered, terrified as I leaned over his shoulder to have a closer look.

My heart was ripped out of my chest as I gasped. My mind was screaming and yelling, but I stood mute. I collapsed beside Jimmie, and the gun I held dropped onto the cement floor, making a distant clinking noise. Forcing Jimmie aside, I looked down and witnessed the one person that I loved more than anything in the world covered in blood. I couldn't breathe as my beloved was gasping for a last breath. I watched as the face of my truelove turned slightly blue while continuing to gulp for air, and then the eyes locked with mine before the lids shut closed and the jaw spread open.

Traumatized by what I was witnessing, my throat collapsed as fear coursed through my veins. Reaching down, I gathered the body and pulled it into mine. With a shaky hand, I tried to locate the gunshot wound.

I shook my head viciously. This could not be happening. This had to be another nightmare. *I'm not going to lose you. Come on, wake up. Come on, wake up!* My eyes blurred with tears, and I blinked them away as I brought that face against my chest. "Come on, baby . . . Come on, you need to get up." With bloody hands, I caressed the perfect skin. I tried to wipe the blood off, but it continued to smear along the perfect cheek bones.

I wanted to scream from the top of my lungs as I rocked back and forth, trying to keep myself from breaking down. I wanted so badly to be strong. There wasn't much I could do, but I needed to do something as I pressed my fingers along the soft eyelids. "Come on, baby, open your eyes. Just wake up for me." AHHH! I needed to do something. I was useless! The love of my life was motionless and helpless, and there was nothing I could do about it.

I felt a hand press firmly against my shoulder, pulling me away, telling me that help was close by.

But help wasn't there at that moment. Something needed to be done now! "No, I have to do something. I have to at least try." Still rocking, I pressed my lips against the frigid lips that I had kissed a thousand times before, those perfect lips that used to make my every worry and bit of stress disappear once they touched mine.

In between small gentle kisses, I began CPR. "Come on, baby, don't leave me. I need you."

CHAPTER ONE

Nine weeks earlier

MARCUS

Mia let out a slight moan as her back slammed against the wall. She was so fucking beautiful in every way. Her hair, still soaked from the rain, framed her face as strands lay along her collarbone. Her shirt clung to her body, exposing her breasts as she breathed heavily. I should have savored this very moment and taken things slowly, but the past three weeks without her had been nothing but excruciating. She was finally mine, and I was not going to let time slip away. Before I realized that moment might've been a dream, I attacked her with all I had. Forcing my body into her, I gripped her wrists and pinned them against the wall over her head.

With our faces mere inches away, her breath hitched, and my eyes traced from the most beautiful green eyes down to the perfect plump lips. Those lips I'd missed and wished to kiss over and over again. Before another moment was wasted, our mouths crushed into each other's. Her lips were still cold and moist from the rain. I devoured that kiss, breathing her in, tasting and remembering exactly how she felt.

Letting go of her wrists, I dug my fingers into her damp hair and wrestled my tongue with hers. The tiniest whimper escaped her. Fuck, I'd missed her so much. She was all I'd ever wanted and needed. There was no way I was ever letting her go again.

Mia arched into me as my name escaped her in a soft sigh. The way she said my name with so much yearning sent me over the fucking edge. Groaning, I shoved my tongue further into her mouth, forcing her to lift to her toes. She moaned again as her body fell weakly in my arms. Very slowly, she dragged her hands over my shoulders and made her way toward the back of my neck. Mia pulled me in closer, bit down on my bottom lip, and dragged her teeth along my flesh. *What the fuck?* That's when I lost control. Her sweet scent, the way she felt underneath my touch, her lips, everything about her made me go wild for her and only her.

"God, Mia, I want you so bad." My hips flexed into hers, and she flashed her eyes open with a pleasurable sigh. Her lips slightly parted as her breathing became heavier.

"I'm yours, Marcus. You just have to take me." She demanded as the burning desire in her eyes pierced into mine.

I did just that. I reached down, gripped her thighs, lifted her, and wrapped her legs around my waist. Screw the fucking stairs. I went straight into my office and sat her on top of my desk. I stood back to admire her. How could I have ever walked away from her?

With my hands, I framed her delicate face and lowered my head so that we were at eye level. "We're never going to be without each other like that again. Do you understand?" She simply nodded. I shook my head at her response and firmly held my grip on her face. A nod wasn't good enough for me. I needed to *hear* it. "Say it, Mia. We are never going to be without each other again. I won't be able to survive it another time."

Her emerald green eyes glistened with unshed tears. "I love you, Marcus." Was that all she could give me? It wasn't the promise I wanted, but hearing those words from her felt as if someone had dug into my chest and began tugging at the thrashing muscle. It was a painful but pleasurable feeling. How could she ever love a man like me?

"Come with me." I reached for her hand and dragged her out of the office.

"Where are we going?" She breathed out.

As I led her up the stairs, I dragged her along without responding. I just continued down the hall and into my bedroom. Mia didn't resist after that. As soon as I locked the door behind us, I lifted and tossed her over my shoulder.

She squealed and playfully kicked her legs. "Marcus! What are you doing? I could walk, you know!"

"Yeah, but this way is faster." She giggled after I tossed her onto the plush mattress. God, I never knew how much I could miss and adore such a simple sweet sound.

Kneeling on the edge of the bed, I sat there and watched her. I'd put her through so fucking much within the last four months. Yet here she was with me. Through it all, she still believed in us. If she didn't, she wouldn't be here. My key goal was to make up for the heartbreak I'd caused, every single tear she had shed because of me, and every single doubt she had harbored about us. I wanted them to be erased from her memory. I had no clue how I would make up for all of it, but I'd try my hardest to find out. I wanted to show her that there's a side to me that's worth fighting for.

Mia popped up on her elbows and tilted her head as she studied me with a wary expression. "Hey, what's wrong?"

My heartbeat grew rapid. Why was I so fucking nervous? I shook my head in response, but she wasn't convinced. Slowly rising, she made her way toward me. The both of us now kneeled before each other.

Mia reached up and cupped my face with her hands. Her thumbs rubbed my cheeks. I closed my eyes and exhaled into that familiar warm touch.

"I missed you, Marcus." My chest expanded as I let out a long draining breath. "Look at me, baby." She pleaded with a soft voice. I opened my eyes and searched hers. "I did. I missed you so much. I was broken without you, and as much as I was hurt, I thought if I painted a picture of my life without you, it wouldn't ache as much. I was wrong; it was painful."

Hearing her say that caused a bit of annoyance to surge through me. I knew I had no right to be pissed, but I had begged her to take me back for days on end, and she had refused me. "Mia, at one point, I thought you were completely done with us, even when I wouldn't give up and you wouldn't hear me out. I just thought maybe you didn't care enough to try anymore."

"Marcus, I . . ." Hesitantly, she let out a shaky breath as tears began to swell her eyes. "We still have a lot to work on. It's going to be hard. Our relationship was rocky from the beginning. What do you expect? For things to be as if the past few months had never existed?"

It was true. Our relationship wasn't fucking hearts and flowers. We weren't skipping around town holding hands. We argued all the time. At times, she frustrated me and drove me insane. At others, she made my heart swell, and I couldn't stay away. It was a fucking headache one minute, and the next it was perfect in this odd, fucked-up way. Mia had a hold on me that couldn't be broken, even if I fucking tried.

Nodding my head in agreement, I said, "I know we have a lot of straightening out to do." I traced my thumb along her moist cheekbones, wiping away the tears that fell. "It's going to take some time for things to be the way they were."

She quickly shook her head, "That's the thing, Marcus. I want things to be better than the way they were. We were a train wreck. All of the secrets and lies, I can't take that anymore." Mia leaned back to sit on the heels of her feet. She let out a deep breath and lowered her head. "I don't want it to be as it was. I don't think I'll be able to handle it. We need it to be better or it won't work." Peeking up through her long lashes, her eyes pleaded with mine. "Please, promise me. No more secrets or lies. From here on out, we are completely honest with each other one hundred percent."

"Mia." I placed two fingers under her chin and lifted, forcing her to fully look at me. "I know it's not easy to deal with all the baggage that comes with my lifestyle, and you've accepted me even when you should've left. There's no one in this world I trust more." Pausing, I let out a gulp of air before continuing. "I promise I will never lie to you again."

It pained me to witness tears run down her face, tears of uncertainty. I wanted to take all of her worries away, but I knew actions spoke louder than words, and soon she'd see that I meant every single word. Lowering my head, I pressed my lips against hers and kissed her hard and passionately.

***

The next morning, I was awakened by a loud buzzing noise. Moaning, I shifted to my side and exhaled deeply, thinking about how comfortable the bed felt. I couldn't remember the last time I had gotten a good night's sleep, and then Mia popped in my head. My eyes flashed open, and I caught sight of her beside me. Thank God. A slow smile crossed my face as I dropped my head back down to watch her sleep.

Mia was lying on her chest with the side of her face resting on top of her arms. Her hair was tangled and tossed down her back and over her shoulders, perfectly. Her bare, curvy body was tucked underneath the silk sheets. She looked peaceful and content as she breathed evenly in her sleep. Without being able to control my impulses, I reached out and grazed the side of her face with my fingertips. Her lips gently twitched to a smile, but she remained asleep.

The buzzing noise that had originally awoken me went off again. After I glided my fingers over Mia's lips, I turned and reached for my phone by the nightstand. There were a few text messages from Lou. Before taking a look, I sat up and leaned against the headboard.

Lou (2 hours ago, 8:00 a.m.): I need you at my office now.

Lou (1 hour ago, 9:00 a.m.): Was I not fucking clear about NOW!

Lou (10 mins ago, 9:50 a.m.): Either you get your ass to my office or I'll drag your ass here.

Lou (1 min ago 9:59 a.m.): You have ten seconds to respond to this text.

Me: Can I have a fucking life? What's so important?

Lou: My office in 30 mins.

Me: Yeah, I'll be there.

After several attempts of trying to wake Mia, I realized it was useless. She was in a deep sleep. I quickly threw on my clothes and left a note that read, "I'll be back soon. I love you." Then I ran out of my house. The rain from the night before had picked up again, and I was soaked by the time I reached my car. I didn't give a fuck at that moment. I just wanted to get this shit over and done with.

Lou Sorrento had known my father since they were kids. Both of their fathers together ran one of the largest crime organizations in Boston. Lou and my dad grew up knowing nothing else. It was something that was taught to them at a very young age. It was as if they had no choice but to choose that lifestyle.

My father wanted different lives for my brother Jimmie and me. He wanted us to have this successful life, full of the best education money could buy, but he forgot one thing: to leave that criminal life behind. So even though he wanted it to be different for Jimmie and me, we still were surrounded by it every fucking day: the drugs, the money, and the hits. In the end, it cost my father's life and turned out to be Jimmie's and my fates.

My father was in charge of the organization. I guess you could've called him a mob boss. After his death, Lou took over and became the ultimate boss of them all. He made deals with other mobsters and cartel groups with whom my father would've never dreamed of doing business. He gained enemies in the process. To make a statement that he was not one to be fucked with, he killed people, only Lou's were not simple, one-shot-to-the-head murders. No. Lou loved to make his enemies suffer, torturing them for days or even weeks. Once the word spread around about how Lou handled his business, he became indestructible. No one even thought to touch or even look at Lou Sorrento.

After finding parking, I entered the three-story brick building located in Dorchester Bay, an area of South Boston. This was the "finance business" my father and Lou started over thirty years ago. It was also a spot where we all met up when he wanted to speak with any of his men immediately. Anything that involved trades or deals was handled at my Club. We'd get together and hang around in the VIP room to discuss the details. Stacy, a longtime family friend and Lou's assistant, greeted me from the front desk. "Marky!" She slapped her hand against her hip as her bright red lips spread into a wide smile. "How's it possible that you grow even more handsome, every time I lay eyes on you?" She lifted her right hand, pressed her fingertips against her lips and blew a kiss. "Gorgeous! You're the spitting image of your father."

Smiling, I shook my head. That was a compliment I received a lot, especially from those who knew my father very well. I was told that I not only resembled him, but I also talked, walked, and thought like him, whatever that meant. Either way, I'd always felt privileged that I was left with those traits of his. "Thanks, Stace. I'm gonna check in with Lou."

Deciding to skip the elevator, I jogged up the staircase toward the third floor and barged into his office. The smell of burned cigar filled the room. Lou was seated behind his desk with a cigar in hand, surrounded by a cloud of smoke. The smirk on his face annoyed me, which caused me to snap. "What's so fuckin' important that I had to run down now?"

Lou's jaw tightened as his nostrils flared. I held back a smirk as he straightened his jacket after putting out the cigar. When Lou was about to lose his temper, he had a habit of flexing his neck from side to side and cracking it, which he just did, but with me and my brother for some reason, he kept his cool just a little longer than he would with others. "Why the fuck are you soaked?" His tone was low and grew with irritation.

Quickly looking down at my appearance, I snapped my head back at him as my arms flung in the air. "It's pouring out, what else could it be?"

"Don't you have a fuckin' umbrella?"

"What do you want, Lou?" I don't have time for this shit. I was ready to get out of here and go back to Mia.

His chest heaved as his breathing grew rapid. He was clearly irate. "I want to know," he hovered over his desk, and yelled from the top of his lungs, "WHO THE FUCKIN' RAT IS!" I just stared at him.

He had lost his fucking mind.

During the next five minutes, I simply nodded and listened to his instructions. My main focus was Mia at that moment, and I just said whatever he wanted to hear. Once we were done, I flew out of there and hopped back into my car.

***

As soon as I stormed through the front doors of my house, I jogged up a few of the steps, when a tiny voice stopped me in my tracks. "Uncle Marc?" I spun around, knowing already I would catch sight of my adorable niece at the bottom step.

She stood there with one hand on her hip and the other on the wooden railing. "Hey, Elle, what are you doing here? Aren't you supposed to be in school?" I swore I had the cutest niece ever. Her smile won me over every single time.

She rolled her eyes as she answered, "Um, it's Saturday, Uncle Marc. I don't have school today. *Jeez.*" Fuck, was it Saturday? My days usually tended to blend together. Elle perked up a little and lifted her hand in front of me. "Look at my nails, Uncle Marc. Mia took me to the mall, and we got mani-pedis yesterday. Do you like 'em?"

Bending down, I reached for her hand and humored her by inspecting her nails. "I think, hmmm." I brought my attention back to her light green eyes and gave her a serious expression. Her smile faded as her face mimicked mine. "I think . . . I love them." I winked, and, with that said, her face lit up with the biggest, most adorable smile.

"I knew you would love 'em!" She squealed. I kissed her forehead and ruffled her dark brown hair before she turned and ran in the direction of the living room. Shaking my head with a laugh, I turned on my feet and jogged back up the stairs.

When I swung the door open, Mia was seated on the bed. Her back and head were leaning against the headboard. The bed sheet was wrapped around her chest, revealing her shoulders, so I knew she was still naked underneath, but she didn't look happy.

"Not even twenty-four hours have passed since we made up and you run off." Shrugging a shoulder, she added, "Just like that."

What could I say to that? I closed the door behind me and made my way toward her. "I left a note." My tone was low as I looked by the nightstand, but the note was no longer there. She raised her hand, revealing the piece of torn paper she held.

"Thanks." She muttered in a sarcastic tone.

Letting out a deep breath, I sank down beside her on the bed. "Mia, I had to go. I wanted to wake you, but you looked too peaceful."

Mia turned her head to stare at me for a long time before responding. "Where did you go?"

I promised no more lying, and even though I knew the truth would do nothing but hurt her, this was what she wanted. "I had to see Lou." She shut her eyes, slightly pursed her lips, and shook her head.

"What did he want?" She whispered as her eyes focused back on mine again.

She wanted to know everything and not just what he wanted but everything in general. That required me to get comfortable, because we'd be there for a long time. After I flung my shoes off, I stripped down to my boxer briefs and slid underneath the comforter by her. She studied me with a wary expression. I smirked at her with a crooked grin and shook my head. So that I could fully face her, I twisted my body and raised a brow.

CHAPTER TWO

MIA

"What are you doing?" I studied Marcus as he sat half naked in front of me.

"I'm making myself comfortable so we can talk." He raised an eyebrow mockingly as if his motives were clearly obvious. I let out a sigh. I knew he promised that he'd be honest from here on out, but I knew differently. With what he was involved in, there was no way he could be one-hundred-percent honest with me. But I promised him a second chance, and our relationship deserved that more than anything. An outsider would have advised me to run like a bat out of hell, but sometimes you just had to crawl through the dark before you could see the light.

"Okay, let's talk."

Clearing his throat, he whispered, "Well, where do you want me to start?"

"What do you mean?" I thought it was clear that he was supposed to tell me what Lou wanted.

"You said you wanted to know everything, right? Or were you more curious about today's event? Either way, I'm not backing down. I'll tell you anything you want to know."

Shocked by that, I tried to gather my thoughts. I wanted to know everything, but I didn't want to force it out of him either. "I'm fine with wherever you want to start."

Nodding his head, he bit down on his lip and flopped back onto the mattress. Before he began, he exhaled deeply and then shoved a hand through his dark brown hair. "Have I ever told you that my father's death was pronounced a suicide?"

Oh my God. I moved over to lie beside him. Placing one hand on his chest, I held my head up with the other. Watching him carefully, I made sure not to distract him. He was lost in thought. If a glare could drill holes, he'd be drilling one into the ceiling at that moment. Leaning on my elbow, I patiently waited for him to go on.

"It's not something I love to talk about. I looked up to him in every way." He laughed once to himself as if that statement were a ridiculous one to make and then continued. "I even wanted to be just like him at one point in my life. It's funny how things turn out. How you end up getting what you want, though after you lived it, you'd give anything to have it taken away." Marcus turned his head toward me. I saw nothing but sadness deep within his dark chocolate eyes.

"Jimmie found him. He walked into my father's office one afternoon and found him slumped over his desk." He shook his head once and slowly wet his lips. "There was a gun in his hand." My heart swelled with pain for him, for them. I could only imagine what it must've felt like walking into something like that.

As I reached out and grabbed his face in a way to comfort him somehow, I bit down on my trembling lip. I didn't stop him. This was something he obviously had never spoken with anyone before, so I allowed him to go as far as he could. "It was hard for me to believe that a man so powerful, who had *everything*—a family that loved him, an entire empire with many admirers who bowed at his feet, and all the money that any man could only dream of—would want to give that all up.

"It wasn't until I grew the fuck up that I realized that even the most powerful man could only take so much. Maybe having everything was just too much to handle?" He looked at me for validation when he asked the question. "All the power, the money—all that comes with responsibility—and responsibility usually ends with a price."

He tilted his head and focused back on the ceiling. "When he died, I was only fifteen and confused by it all. I was fuckin' pissed off at him. On the day of his funeral, when everyone left, I was standing there alone . . ." Marcus took another unsteady breath. Whatever he was trying to say was difficult for him.

"Hey, we don't have to talk about this right now."

Lightly shaking his head, he muttered, "No, I want to." He glanced over at me again, and I saw the hurt in his eyes before he shut them again, remembering it all. "I stared at the pile of dirt where my father was buried six-feet under, and my thoughts were running wild with all the memories, especially the advice he had given me.

"One saying in particular was: 'You know, son, in life you're going to have some good days and some crappy ones. Maybe more crappy ones than good ones, but whatever you do, don't you ever give up. Make sure to push yourself the farthest you can go. If you want something bad enough, you have to fight for it. If you're not happy with your life, *you* and only *you* have to do something to change it.'" Marcus repeated his father's words mockingly and then his face grew serious. "The more I thought of that saying, the angrier I grew with him. I thought he didn't care for us enough, because he wouldn't have given up and killed himself after having a few crappy fuckin' days."

"Oh, Marcus, your father loved you. You have so many wonderful memories of him. Don't allow—"

Snapping his head toward me, his brows bunched together. "Mia, I know that, but what's fucked up is that I spent almost thirteen years hating my father because I thought he just gave up. I called him a coward at his grave site, for God's sake. For years, I thought he had killed himself. Later, I found out that the man whom I considered to be like a second father, the man that I looked up to at one point in my life, and the man that took me under his wing and taught me all I needed to know, was the same exact man who murdered my father."

Breathlessly, I blurted, "Why did he do it?"

"I don't know. Maybe he wanted it all. Now he has it, I guess."

We lay in silence for what seemed like a very long time. I watched him as he stared up at the ceiling. Marcus was not a man who expressed his feelings very well, so I was grateful that he let me in. Even if he hadn't told me everything in one shot, I was fine with getting bits and pieces at a time. I knew how it felt to have so many emotions bottled up, trying to stay strong for yourself, but it eventually took over your sanity.

"Marcus, thank you for opening up to me; it really means a lot."

Slightly twisting his head, he stared into my eyes. "Of course, Mia."

I wanted to lighten the mood and remove the negative vibe surrounding the room. So I jumped onto my knees, and with a huge smile, I poked his ribs. "I wanted to get to know you better, and learning some more about you just gave me an idea. Let's play a game."

With a raised brow, his lips twitched into a slight smile. "What kind of game?"

"Hmm." Shifting my gaze aside, I tapped my chin with a finger. "A get-to-know-you game."

"Huh?"

"You know. We ask each other questions to get to know each other better." A low raspy laugh escaped his lips. "What? Why are you laughing?" I demanded.

"Nothing, babe. Come here." He reached for my arm and pulled me in. It forced me to fall on top of him.

I stared into his dark brown eyes, and I took note that the sadness he'd held a few moments ago was now masked with lust and humor. "I'm serious, Marcus."

"Babe, I thought you meant another game." His brows wiggled.

"Do you have to turn everything into sex?"

"When you're involved? Yes." Rolling my eyes, I studied his clearly amused expression. "Keep rolling your eyes, and see what happens." His tone was stern, but his eyes were dancing with laughter.

"Ha, is that a threat?"

"Try me."

I did try him and dramatically rolled my eyes. A squeal escaped me as I was lifted and tossed back onto the fluffy mattress. Before I could recover, his hands attacked me, tickling every weak spot of mine. Bursting into laughter, my eyes swelled with tears, and my rib cage ached from laughing and screaming.

I was not sure how I managed it, but I pushed with my feet and tossed him back. Straddling him, I tightened my legs against the side his abdomen. With my hands fisted against my hips, I glared down at him.

"You know that all I have to do is flex my hips and you'll tip over right?" Marcus expressed with a raised brow.

"Hear me out. We need to focus on getting to know each other better."

Marcus traced his hands along my thighs, up the side of my torso, until he finally reached my breasts. His thumbs brushed across my nipples, causing goose bumps to form along my skin. Looking up at me, he sucked in air as he seductively whispered, "Mmmh, I think we can work on that."

Raising a brow at him, I studied him thoroughly. "You see what I mean, Marcus?" His grin grew wider. I bit back a smile. I wouldn't allow him to win me over with his charm. I needed to show him I wasn't joking. "I'm serious!" I tossed my arms in the air before jumping off the bed. I snatched the white, Egyptian bed sheet and hurriedly wrapped the soft fabric around my chest. There, hopefully I had his full attention.

"What are you doing? Get back in here." Swiftly, he reached out to grab me, although, I was faster than he was and able to take a few steps back. Tossing his head back onto the pillow, he let out a deep, raspy laugh. "Okay, okay." Caving in, he sat straight up, raised an eyebrow, and flashed that crooked grin. Oh, he knew what he was doing. That smile got me every time. Not then. "Talk." He instructed.

Clearing my throat, I straightened my shoulders and tightened the bed sheet around my breast. "Okay, as I was saying, you have a habit of transferring everything into sex, and . . ." His lips parted to say something, but I cut him off. "No, let me finish." He nodded in consent. "I feel that sex has become the basis of our relationship and that we need to focus on actually getting to know each other."

"Mia, you know me better than anyone, as I do you."

Narrowing my glare, I quizzed him on this. "Okay, what's my favorite color?"

The playful mask he held was instantly overshadowed with an unreadable one. "Well, why does that matter?"

"You can't answer it, can you?" After a few seconds of our eye-glaring contest, I felt as though I had the upper hand. Then my thoughts trailed to something that might be fun. "How about we make a bet?"

His perfect brows bunched together. "You want to make a bet?" Laughing once, he continued to play along. "What are the terms and conditions of this bet?" I hated it when he spoke in that sarcastic tone, but I wouldn't allow it to faze me.

On the outside, I held a poker face, but on the inside I was giggly like a teenage girl, super excited to begin this game. "I ask you three simple questions about me. You have to answer two out of three correctly. If you do, you can have me however you like."

Marcus's lips lifted into a slight smile. "And if I don't answer correctly?"

Now this was where it got good. "No sex for two weeks, ah, I'm not finished." I raised a finger at his dropped jaw. "And you have to take me out on proper dates within those two weeks, so we can work on really getting to know each other."

"Oh, this is ridiculous, Mia." He studied my expression, which had slightly broken from his dismissive statement, and then his face softened. "Does it mean that much to you?"

"Yes, it really does, Marcus."

Huffing like a child who was just told, "No," about watching his favorite cartoon, he breathed, "Go ahead then."

"Okay, I'll just ask all three questions in one shot, and you'll answer them in order." I waited for his nod and continued. "What's my favorite color, favorite genre of literature, and my favorite kind of flowers?"

He threw his head back in defeat. He didn't have a clue. I mentally flashed an evil grin. Looking back at me, he blurted, "Pink, romance, and, ugh, I don't know, roses?"

"Green, romance, and lilies." My lips curved into the biggest grin.

"So, I lost, what now?" he asked as he watched me take the sheet off and toss it back onto the bed. I walked over to where my clothes were thrown on the floor and put them on. After I was dressed, I walked over to him and kissed the tip of his nose.

"Now, you can start planning our dates, and they better be good ones too."

"You're leaving? We can still hang out, you know."

I stopped by the doorway and turned with a smile. "I know your sneaky little ways, Marcus. Don't try and cheat either. It won't work." I blew him a kiss and went on my merry way. *This should be very interesting.*

Skipping down the steps heading toward the first floor, I couldn't stop a huge grin from spreading across my face. I had been miserable the previous morning, and less than twenty-four hours later, I was the happiest I'd been in a while.

Marcus DeLuca could have that effect on a girl.

The second I reached the front door, a familiar voice stopped me in my tracks. "Mia, is that you?" Turning on the heels of my feet, I saw Theresa DeLuca leaving the kitchen and heading toward me.

I hadn't seen or spoken to Marcus's mother in almost a month. The problem was I had thought that everyone in his family knew about our breakup, but Marcus had been secretive as usual. Theresa reached out to me with a relieved expression on her face as she pulled me into a tight embrace. "Oh my God, I've missed you so much. How are you, honey?"

"I'm good, thank you. I've missed you too. How are you?"

Stepping back to inspect me at arm's length, her eyes glistened. My heart ached. From the moment I'd met Theresa, she was filled with so much joy, and her presence radiated nothing but positive vibes. Even if you were in the gloomiest mood, the clouds hanging overhead disappeared when she walked in the room. Though, from the look of Theresa standing in front of me now, I could tell there was definitely something wrong. I could feel it.

"Are you okay?"

She sniffed back tears and forced a smile, showing just the slightest dimple. "Yes, I'm just so happy to see you. I've missed our weekly catch-up lunches."

How could I have been so selfish? I leaned back in for a hug and held her tightly as tears sprung from my eyes. Theresa loved me as much as I loved her and the entire DeLuca family. I had allowed my issues with Marcus to affect my relationship with all of them. "I'm so sorry, Theresa. I just couldn't . . ."

"No, no need to explain. I know."

I brought my stare back at her. "You knew? About . . ."

Nodding, she responded, "I know my boys. I figured it out. I never mentioned it to Marcus, but he wasn't the same the past few weeks, well, not the same as he was when he was with you. He went back to the way he used to be, before you." Waving her hand dismissively, she added, "I'm just happy you're here."

Ashamed, I looked down. I didn't know how to respond. I felt I had to make up for lost time, so I blurted, "Lunch on Wednesday? I would love to catch up, Theresa."

Nodding, she sniffed and reached to tuck a strand of hair behind my ear. "I would love that honey. Our usual spot?"

I nodded, gave her one last tight hug, and left.

***

After parking my car, I strolled along the wet cobblestone pavement toward my apartment building. The afternoon breeze was slightly chilly, but, nonetheless, it was a beautiful day. Breathing in the cool air, I admired how quiet and beautiful my neighborhood in Cambridge was. Trees lined the sidewalk along the park. Vehicles parked on the side of the street, in front of the brick townhomes. I was lucky and grateful to have had the opportunity to invest in a building in this neighborhood.

Spotting both Megan's and Jeremy's vehicles, I felt a slight burst of excitement rush through me. I couldn't wait to tell them that Marcus and I were giving it another try. I walked through the front door and saw Ms. Connor standing in the hallway with her evil pug, Gypsy. "Good evening." I nodded as I passed her and headed up the stairs.

"Oh, Ms. Sullivan." She exclaimed in a high-pitched annoying tone. I needed to take a few calming breaths before turning to face her.

"Yes, Ms. Connor?" I managed a slight smile.

"These past four nights, a gentleman was sleeping in front of your door." She waited for me to respond, and when she realized that I wasn't going to say anything, she continued. "I thought you should know, and I felt very uncomfortable with the entire situation."

I gently nodded, "Not to worry, Ms. Connor, it won't happen again. Is that all?"

With a smug look, she lifted Gypsy into her arms then turned to exit the building after saying, "I suppose that is all." God! She managed to crawl under my skin every time.

I dropped my keys on the side table by the door after entering my apartment. It was completely dark except for the TV screen casting light from the movie being shown. I approached the couch and saw both Jeremy and Megan cuddled up together, with a bowl of popcorn between their laps. Jeremy's aqua blue eyes shot back at me as he smiled. "Hey, Mia, just in time, we were getting ready to watch *Dirty Dancing*." His tone was tinged with sarcasm as he rolled "dancing" off his tongue and he waved his hand in the air mockingly.

Biting back a laugh, I made my way around and sank on the couch beside him. "Yeah, Mia, you should so watch it with us." Megan said excitedly.

"Since when do you watch romance movies?" I questioned Jeremy. Also, taking notice of the time, I added, "And what happened with your date last night? You're usually sunk between a pair of legs around this time. Aww, did she send you home early?"

He cringed before answering. "Ugh, did you have to go there? Worst date ever. And Missy over here," he nudged his head toward Megan, "forced me to watch it. She swears my day will get better."

Flinging my shoes and jacket off, I made myself comfortable beside him and grabbed a handful of popcorn. I leaned back against the armrest, "That bad, huh?"

"Mia, it was worse than bad; it was excruciating."

"What happened?"

Megan rolled her eyes, clearly not wanting to hear the story again. Reaching for the remote, she paused the movie. Adjusting in his seat to fully face me, he began his story. "First off, let me start by saying that I went out of my way to take her out to dinner." He raised an eyebrow, waiting for me to respond. Shoving popcorn into my mouth, I nodded.

"Okay, it was a pizza joint, but that's the not the point. Everything was going great. I picked her up and gave her my best Jeremy charm." He flashed a grin. "She was going for it. Then we got to the restaurant. Wasn't the best place, whatever, we're seated in a booth, but she wanted to sit *next* to me?" He spread his arms and widened both of his eyes as if the act were illegal.

Confused, I raised a brow, and with a mouth full of popcorn, I asked, "And . . . what's wrong with that exactly?"

He tilted his head and stared at me as if it was obvious. "Mia. No elbow room."

I shot him a puzzled expression. "What?"

"You know *elbow room.*" Jeremy waved his bent arms. "Dude, she hovered over my shoulder, breathing heavily on my neck, while I tried to look at the menu. Then she snuggled close while I was trying to eat." Sighing, he shook his head in disbelief. "You know how much I love my food."

"You can't be serious?" I asked.

He was serious. I looked over at Megan for a better explanation, but she simply shook her head and raised her hands in defeat.

"I took her straight home afterwards." He reached for more popcorn and straightened into the chair.

"You're a dick." I shot out.

"Yeah, well, I get that a lot."

"I feel sorry for the woman that marries you. Seriously, it'll be like marrying a thirty-year-old toddler with no manners whatsoever."

He cocked a brow with a curt nod. "You, know I get that too."

"Shut up!" I nudged his shoulder.

"Can we please watch *Dirty Dancing* now?" Megan spat out.

Jeremy tilted his head to the side. "Yes, please, let's watch Patrick Swayze save Baby from the corner." Megan rolled her eyes, grabbed the remote, and hit play. Within the next few hours, we watched several old movies, ordered in pizza, and laughed at Jeremy's goofy ways. At first, I wanted to mention that Marcus and I got back together, but instead, I decided to save it. That evening, I was going to enjoy a night with my friends.

The evening passed by quickly, and before I knew it, Jeremy stood and stretched. "I'm going to hit the bed. Megan, you joining me?"

She widened her eyes and looked at me as her cheeks turned a light shade of red in embarrassment. "Jeremy."

"What? Mia's fine. She won't think anything of it." Megan shook her head and slumped back in the seat. Jeremy reached down, grabbed her wrist, and lifted her to her feet. He wrapped his arm around her shoulder and pulled her into his side. "Megan, don't be shy around Mia. You slept in my bed last night."

Megan glared at me and quickly added, "Not in the way that you think, Mia."

I raised my hands. "Hey, no judgment here." I could tell she was completely horrified by Jeremy's public display of affection.

Before she could respond, my phone rang. I glanced at the screen, and my entire face lit up when I saw it was Marcus. "Hello." I answered with a huge grin.

"Hey, just wanted to call and check up on you."

"Oh really?"

"Yes, and to also ask what your plans are for tomorrow." I pressed my lips together to hold back the slight squeal that was trying to escape. I excused myself from Jeremy and Megan and ran into my bedroom.

As I flopped back on my bed and stared at the ceiling, I listened to his steady breathing on the other end of the phone. "I'm not sure yet, why?"

"Well, if you're not busy, I would love to take you out on a date."

My stomach fluttered with nerves. I wasn't sure why it did, although it felt nice. "What kind of date?"

I could hear him shifting as he chuckled in a low raspy tone. "That's for me to know and for you to find out."

"So we're playing that game?"

His vibrant laugh forced an even wider grin across my face. I wasn't sure that was even possible. "No, baby, you're playing that game. I'm just simply here as an unwilling participant."

"Hey play nice, remember?"

"Right . . . so tomorrow?"

"Yes, I'm free."

"Good, be ready by noon."

"By noon? That's early."

"You're lucky I didn't say early morning, but I'm playing nice."

I laughed and caved in. "Okay . . . what are you doing now?"

Hesitating, he took a deep breath. "I'm in the car waiting for Jimmie. We were called in for a meeting."

I took a quick glance at the time. It was almost ten. "Oh." I whispered. It wasn't a surprise to me that he was out at a meeting that late. Although I had I accepted him with all of his flaws, this was one I wanted so desperately to take away. I hated his lifestyle, but I loved him.

CHAPTER THREE

MARCUS

Mia's tone was filled with disappointment. I wanted to shake off the silence between us through the phone. Not wanting to end our call on a bad note, I blurted, "Hey, the next two weeks will be fun, taking my girl out on the best dates she's ever had."

"Ha! I'll be the judge of that." She giggled, and even though I couldn't see her, I knew she was smiling on the other end of the phone. Jimmie stepped into the car and eyed me suspiciously. He wasn't used to me smiling like a fucking kid.

"Babe, I have to go. I'll call you later?"

"Sure, well, maybe tomorrow. I'm pretty tired and might call it a night. Is that okay?"

"Yeah, that's fine. I love you, Mia."

There was a slight sigh before she replied, "I love you too . . . and Marcus?"

"Yeah."

"Please be careful." After I told her I would, we ended our call.

As I drove off, I let Jimmie in on everything that was going on between Mia and me, even told him about the bet I lost. He burst out laughing and thought Mia was pretty damned clever. He laughed harder when I punched his bicep for thinking it was funny to begin with. Jimmie seemed happy that Mia and I were working it out. In the beginning, when Jimmie found out that Mia was related to Michael Sullivan, he wanted me to end things immediately. He felt it would backfire, not just on me, but on everything we had been working so hard for so long to do—bring down Lou Sorrento.

I was fucking hardheaded and couldn't simply walk away. Deep down, I knew she deserved better. You could call me a selfish man, I guess. I couldn't see her with anyone else. She was meant for me in so many ways. Since she came into my life, everything had changed; I learned to laugh again, to smile, to break down, and be the person I was before my father's death. I didn't think that was even possible. I learned to live again, and I could not walk away from that.

I had this feeling deep down that I couldn't live without her. When you finally find a person who makes you feel alive, how could you possibly breathe if she were gone? I knew I couldn't.

Jimmie shifted in his seat, and my attention was brought back to him. He cleared his throat before speaking. "I need to find a new babysitter fast."

"What happened to that Melissa chick?"

"She starts college in a couple of weeks. It's hard to find anyone you can actually trust." He bounced his right knee and began chewing on his thumbnail, as he usually did he was stressed or worried about things that involved Elle.

"Don't worry, man, we'll find someone. And you have me and Mom until then. You'll be fine."

He nodded and changed the subject. "So what do you think this meeting's about?"

Thoughts of my earlier encounter with Lou brought forth several conclusions. "He's pissed about the last warehouse that was raided by the FBI. He knows there's a rat in the group and demanded that I find out who it is within the next week, and that if I don't, he'll do it his fuckin' self." At a red light, I took a glance at Jimmie who was staring straight ahead, lost in thought.

After a few seconds, he tightened his jaw and nodded. "Fuck. I can't think of who the fuckin' rat could be. Everyone in the group is just too fuckin' loyal to Lou, you know?" He took in a deep breath and then scratched his head. "Michael wasn't working with the FBI. It was just the three of us trying to build a case before we brought the evidence to any agents."

"Well, maybe before he died, he gave some info to an agent that he trusted."

Jimmie shook his head. "Maybe, but Michael and I met up the night before his death. He told me that there were no updates. He said that we were getting close and that he might have some leads, but didn't say anything about any FBI agents. It just doesn't make any fuckin' sense."

Jimmie was right. None of that shit made any fucking sense, so I began to go through the list of Lou's people in my head. "Well, hands down, I know Vinnie and Larry are not involved. What about Buddy?"

"Buddy's a douchebag, but a rat? Nah, he's beyond loyal to Lou. If Lou told him to suck his cock, he'd ask for how long."

I let out a deep, frustrated breath. Yeah, that was definitely true. Buddy had worked for Lou since he was a kid. He had nothing but the utmost respect for Lou and looked up to him like a father. Trying to find out who was the rat was going to be more difficult than I'd anticipated. Fuck. Lou was not going to let it go.

For the rest of the ride, Jimmie and I drove quietly. I was sure Jimmie was trying to figure shit out in his head just as much as I was.

As I pulled into the back of Club21's private parking lot, I slowed down when I saw a crowd that had formed a circle in the middle of the lot. Jimmie and I quickly exchanged confused glances. I parked the car as we both hopped out and jogged towards the commotion.

Men chanted and yelled, raising beer glasses in the air, hooting and hollering from the top of their lungs, "Get 'em. Beat his ass. That's right—blood—I want to see fuckin' blood!" Hurriedly, I snaked my way through the crowd and was finally in the center of it all. One guy I didn't recognize was covered in blood with a swollen eye and busted lip. His shirt was torn, and he wobbled from side-to-side sluggishly. He brought his fist up to his face in an attempt to block oncoming punches.

Larry, one of our men in charge of the club when I'm not around, was standing in the center of the circle. He seemed to be sober, bouncing back and forth on his toes, fist secured at eye level, positioned and ready for another swing. Larry knew fucking better than to start a riot. Anger building within me forced my legs toward them. When I got deeper into the center, I could hear that all of the shouting and yelling had died down. Once I was behind him, I yanked Larry by the shoulder and pulled him away from the other guy. Larry's eyes flamed when he saw that I got in the middle of it all. "What the fuck, Marky? He deserves it!" He pointed at the drunken man, who was mumbling something unintelligible.

"Not here, Larry!" I pointed a finger toward the back of the club. Hovering over him, I pointed that same finger into his chest. "You fuckin' know better! Not at my club. Get your ass inside and clean up." I heard the sound of shoes scattering along the concrete surface as employees and customers rushed away and back into the club. Looking around, I spotted Vinnie, my number one main man. Nodding at him, I yelled, "Take care of this loser." I nudged over at the drunken man and made my way into the club.

The hallway was clear by the time I entered. Everyone must've rushed back in. Instead of going toward the dance floor, I walked through a private door in the back hallway that led up a staircase toward the second level. Once I entered the second level hallway, I rushed and pushed through the crowds of people wandering around. Finally, I made my way into our VIP room at the end of the hall. When I entered, all eyes were on me: Jimmie was seated at the end of the white sectional, Buddy was leaning against the glass wall that overlooked the dance floor, and Larry hovered over the sink washing his bloody hands.

Snapping the door shut, I shoved off my jacket and threw it over a chair. "What the fuck was all that about, Lar?"

Wrapping a towel around his hands, he shook his head and took a seat by the table. "I got a page from the blond bartender about a drunk acting rowdy. I went to check it out, and the guy was giving me a problem, so I roughed him up a little bit and kicked him the fuck out. When I did, he took a swing at me, so . . . you know how I get." He shrugged.

"No, you know fuckin' better. I don't want police around here. You should have taken him out, closed the fuckin' door, and left it at that. Not only were employees out there but so were customers! I want this to be a fuckin' clean club, Larry. You got that?"

Cocking his lips aside, he nodded, "Yeah, I got that."

"Good."

It was going to be a long fucking night.

***

We all hung around in the VIP room, waiting for Lou to arrive. No one had said a word for the past forty minutes as we all sat there silently wondering why the meeting was called. Lou never asked to meet with all of us at once, unless it was something of the utmost importance. I grabbed myself a second drink and realized that the ice machine was broken. After making a phone call to one of the maintenance men, I downed the warmth of the smooth whisky in one shot. I knew that I should have stopped drinking, but it too was difficult. Liquor was my solace, my time away from all the bullshit, my only escape until I met Mia, but Mia wasn't there at that moment, and I needed something to ease my mind from the hell-hole issue I called Lou.

Jimmie glanced my way and raised a brow. I knew he hated it when I drank, but the waiting game was beginning to bore me, and, even though I shouldn't have done it, I poured myself another drink. That's when Lou walked in with his nephew, Giovanni Sorrento. I hadn't seen Gio in years. Last I'd heard of him, he was involved in a bad deal and skipped town. Now he was suddenly back from out of the blue . . . which only meant Lou was up to no good.

Lou made his rounds of acknowledgments, while Gio made his way towards me. He looked exactly the same, a younger version of Lou: dark hair, olive skin, and the same cockiness about his persona. Since Lou never had children of his own, he always took care of his nephew like a son. Anyone that fucked with Gio was taken care of, no questions asked.

He reached his hand out to me with a grin. "Marky, hey how you been?" I took his hand, and he pulled me in for a quick hug.

"I'm good. How 'bout you? You back for good or just visiting?"

"Oh, you know, visiting, but it may be permanent." He laughed. "So I hear you're settling down now. When will I be able to meet this woman of yours?"

Buddy walked up beside us and shook Gio's hand. Then he faced me with a wiseass grin. "He keeps her hidden. I haven't met her yet, and it's more like pussy whipped than settled down."

Arching a brow at Buddy, I stepped into him. "Shut the fuck up, Buddy! And you'll never get to meet her, anyways."

Buddy's expression grew cocky. "What's wrong, Marky? Are you afraid the minute she sets her eyes on me she'll want to suck my cock instead of yours?" He winked.

Every fucking thing around me turned red. The sound of others chatting went dead. My chest stilled as my fist clenched. My face burned as I held my breath, afraid that once I blew out air I would attack. It didn't work. One minute, I was standing in front of Buddy. The next minute, I had gripped him by the neck and had begun pounding his face against the wooden table. I felt someone trying to pull me away, but I continued to smash his face along the surface, grunting with each impact as blood splattered.

Finally, I was pulled back and pinned down by Jimmie and Vinnie. "Let me the fuck go, now!" I yelled, wrestling to be free.

Buddy lifted his head from the table as blood gushed out of his nose. He cupped his face with his hands. "What the fuck, Marky! I was joking around with you."

"Yeah? Well that'll fuckin' teach you that I don't take jokes very fuckin' lightly."

Everyone immediately turned their heads in the direction of the door that just opened. The maintenance man stood by the doorway with seven angry guys glaring at him. "Ah, um, I got a call that something's broken?" His voice was shaky.

"Yeah, his fuckin' nose!" I huffed out, pointing my head at Buddy.

Gio shook his head and stared me up and down laughing. "Well, I can see your temper hasn't changed." His laughter went louder when Buddy glared at him. "Well, Buddy, Marky may be pussy-whipped, but he ain't no pussy. Lesson learned." Gio patted Buddy's shoulder.

"Fuck off." Angrily, Buddy shoved away and stormed out of the room.

Still pinned to the floor, my body jerked. "Let me go!" After a moment, both Jimmie and Vinnie hesitantly loosened their grip. Jumping up, I straightened my shirt. "What?" I asked, responding to Jimmie's dubious expression.

Raising his hands, he shook his head. "Nothing little bro, it's your show."

"Fuck off, Jimmie."

"Marky, go clean your fuckin' face. You have blood all over it, and let's get this fuckin' meeting over with, eh?" Lou's raspy tone pierced through my growing anger. I stared at Lou for a few harsh seconds before sniffing and heading toward the sink.

After a few minutes, we surrounded the sectional area. I stood and leaned against the glass wall as everyone sat. "Okay, as you all can see, I brought my nephew Gio back for a reason. He's going to be working on figuring out who the rat is. Marky, don't worry about it. Just keep doing what you do for me, and Gio will take care of the rat." I nodded at Lou in response. "As far as the pigs sniffing the warehouses, we have to move to a different location. Marky, we're doing it here."

"No." I blurted. "We're not doing exchanges here. I refuse. You should know better than to ask that."

"Did I fuckin' ask?" Lou spat with a tightened jaw. Gio put his hand on Lou's shoulder.

"We don't have a choice, Marky." Gio chimed in. "Unless you have a better suggestion?"

"Pick another fuckin' warehouse, somewhere out of the city, or even a storage unit."

"A storage unit don't sound like a bad idea, boss." Vinnie mentioned.

Lou shook his head. "No, too many people go in and out of storage units, and if a deal goes wrong, they'll hear gunshots. It's too risky."

"We do exchanges at three sometimes two in the morning; storage units are packed during the day. There's no way we'll bump into anyone." Vinnie argued.

"I fuckin' said 'no' and that's that. Anybody got a problem with that?" He looked around the room, and when no one responded, he went on, "Your job, Marky, is to come up with a new location for our exchanges by next week. Vinnie, you can help him with that, but no storage units. *If* you can find a warehouse outside of Boston that's been secluded for years, I'm in. Other than that, it *will* be here."

"You do understand this is a club, full of people six nights a week?" I clarified.

Cocking his head, his stare hardened. "Exactly, six nights a week, Marky. Our exchange dates can easily be changed to Sundays." With that said, he and Gio were gone.

***

After the meeting with Lou and the men, I took care of a few issues regarding inventory at the Club and then headed home. By the time I got into bed, it was close to three in the morning. What a fucking night! Tossing and turning, I couldn't get comfortable and had trouble falling asleep. My mind drifted back and forth between the night before when Mia and I were standing in the pouring rain as I begged her to take me back, and a few hours before when I found

out about all the shit I was going to have to deal with in trying to
locate a new spot for Lou's exchanges.

I felt physically drained with all of the fucking stress between
Mia and me, as well as the whole fucking Lou situation. I wished
Mia was lying next to me so I could feel her warm soft skin, kiss her
lips, and lose myself in those eyes. She made everything go away,
even if it was for a few hours or just a couple of minutes. If it
weren't so early in the morning, I would have called her just to hear
her voice. Not able to control myself, I sent her a quick text telling
her that I loved her, and to my surprise, she responded immediately.

Mia (2:58 a.m.): I love u too. Why r u still up?

Me (2:58 a.m.): Can't stop thinking of u. The real question is
why r u still up?

Mia (2:59 a.m.): Can't stop thinking of u.

My phone rang, and it was her on the other line. "So I guess
we're having the same issue, huh?" I asked.

"I guess so. Want to talk until we fall asleep? It's probably our
best bet."

"Or, I could just go over there, and we can fall asleep together."
I was hoping she'd say yes, because I'd jump in my car within
seconds.

"Mmmh, as tempting as that sounds, I know you, Marcus, and
your charming ways, so for now, as we live through our bet, no
sleeping in the same room."

"Damn it, for a second there, I thought you would cave in."

She giggled. Yes, I could fall asleep to that sound! "You should
know me better than that, Marcus. I never back down from a bet."

"Well, you should know me better too, because I will try
everything in my power to force you to back down from your bet."

"We shall see. We'll see each other tomorrow, oh well, a few
hours actually. We're still on for our date at noon?"

"Of course, we are. I promised my girl a good time."

As we talked through the early morning, I didn't remember
falling asleep with the phone pressed between the pillow and my ear.
As stressful and as long as my day had been, it didn't matter. None

of it mattered because I was able to hear the sound of her voice, the sound of her breathing, and everything else at that moment just faded away.

CHAPTER FOUR

MIA

Beep. Beep. Beep.

Reaching for my phone, I shut the alarm off. My head felt as if I was recovering from a hangover, but it was from lack of sleep. Yawning, I stretched a little longer than usual, tossed the covers off, and prepared for the day ahead.

Coffee. I needed coffee. Marcus was going to be there in a few hours, and I wanted to be well energized for the day he had planned for us. As curious as I was about what those plans were, I shoved the thoughts aside and settled on being surprised. After I entered the kitchen, I made a cup of Joe, grabbed a magazine, and nestled into a stool by the island. As I inhaled the freshly brewed coffee, my mind drifted through scenes from the last four months.

Marcus and I had been through a lot in our relationship. We'd been through more ups and downs than most couples. Despite everything, it all boiled down to the fact that, no matter what happened, I still loved him. Looking back, I realized that we could only grow from our experiences, which would hopefully make us stronger.

Taking another sip of my coffee, I glanced over the mug and saw Megan walking out of Jeremy's room. I knew she'd slept in his room the night before, but it was her appearance that had me in shock. Her long, light brown hair was tousled with the I-just-got-fucked-look and the t-shirt she wore wasn't hers. Megan stood frozen when she took note of me. The both of us stared with puzzled expressions on our faces. Slowly I placed the mug on top of the granite counter, raised a brow, and cleared my throat. "Why are you wearing Jeremy's shirt?"

Megan's lips curved into a mischievous grin as she placed a hand on her hip. "Well, if you must know, we started by making out.

Then . . ." She ran her hands up the side of her curves with a slight shimmy to her shoulders.

She stopped her show at the wave of my hand. "No, please spare me the details. I don't want specifics. I want to know what's going on between the two of you. Are you guys dating?"

Megan laughed, shook her head, and opened the fridge to pull out a carton of orange juice. "Don't be ridiculous. We're just fuckin'." She stated nonchalantly while pouring herself a drink.

"Ah, just fuckin', yeah, that clears it up. How long has this been happening? Last night you didn't seem to be interested. Meg, you know Jeremy has never been in a committed relationship. I don't want you to get attached and then—"

"Please, Mia, we're just having fun; that's all it is. Last night I didn't want you get the wrong impression. I wanted to tell you first, instead of you finding out like this. I know what Jeremy is about. I'm a big girl. I can handle it."

"Okay, but you're my cousin. He's my best friend and roommate. The last thing I want is to be stuck between two hurt people that I care for dearly."

"Don't worry. You won't." She snatched the magazine, sat on a stool across from me, and began flipping through pages. "So, want do some shopping today?" She asked, still looking at this week's fashion section. Her quick change of the subject told me that the topic of her and Jeremy was off limits. "I need to find an outfit for this weekend. Ooh, these shoes are cute!" She pointed at a pair of royal blue peep-toe heels.

"I can't." Standing, I padded toward the sink and dumped out the rest of my coffee. "I have a date."

"With?"

Turning, I leaned against the sink and crossed my arms with a smile. "Marcus. He'll be picking me up soon."

She flashed a huge grin. "Good. I'm glad you're working things out. Honestly if it were me, I would've forgiven him the first night he slept in the hallway. Poor guy—you made him sleep four nights out there." She shook her head while continuing to flip through the magazine.

"Megan, I had valid reasons for not giving in too soon." Thinking back on it, my stomach turned when the image of Marcus and Boston Barbie at Club21 played through my head. Then I thought of all the females he may have slept with during our separation.

"So where are you guys going?" Megan's voice broke my thoughts.

Smiling, I uncrossed my arms and made my way toward the bedroom. "Don't know. It's a surprise. Want to help me pick out an outfit?"

With that, Megan jumped off the stool and followed me down the hall. She loved going through my closet.

For the next couple of hours, I tried on a few outfits as we talked. She filled me in on how she and Jeremy began sleeping with each other. It started a couple of weeks ago with innocent flirting, which led to full-blown crazy sex, as she described. She lit up every time she mentioned his name, which had worried me. Even though she said there was nothing more, I was afraid Megan would get attached and Jeremy would end up hurting her. I'd kill him if he did.

Standing in front of the mirror, I twirled around to examine my outfit. Since it was chilly out, I settled on a cream cashmere sweater dress, a pair of caramel colored knee-length wedge boots, and a matching thin belt. "You look hot! You are so getting laid tonight." I laughed once and let Megan in on the entire bet issue. "No you didn't!" She squealed.

I nodded as I began to apply my makeup. "Yes, I know it's going to be hard." Marcus was so hard to resist, and, God, the way he touched me and the way his lips felt on mine, I just knew it was going to be difficult to push him away.

"You're so going to break this bet. Come on, Marcus is hot! And not to mention you guys haven't slept with each other in what, a month?"

"It was three weeks, until last night." I turned and stared at her wide-eyed expression. I bit my bottom lip and blocked the pillow she tossed at me.

"See! You are not going to be able to resist him. Heck, I wouldn't." I arched a brow at her. Shrugging, she continued, "I mean can you blame a girl? But, of course, he's off limits for me."

"For anyone, he's off limits." I was never the jealous type, but with Marcus, I was horrible. The thought of his hands touching someone else, or his lips kissing another woman—I shuddered at the image. Shaking the nasty thoughts out my mind, I twirled around. "So what do you think?"

Waving her fingers, she purred, "Fab, darling, just fab."

***

After I swung the door open, I studied the gorgeous man standing in front of me. Marcus, with a crooked grin, showed off the adorable dimple I loved so much. His dark hair still damp from a fresh shower and his powerful, luxurious scent weakened my knees. Yeah, it was going to be hard not to jump his bones. I continued to admire him, until I took note of his wardrobe. He was dressed down in jeans, a black t-shirt, boots, and a jacket. "Should I change?" I felt overdressed beside him.

Marcus' smile widened. "No, you look perfect, beautiful as always." He reached in and kissed my forehead.

"Are you sure, Marcus? I would only be a minute to change into jeans and a top."

Grabbing my arm, he tugged me out the door. "No, come on. We have a long day ahead of us."

After fastening my seatbelt, I turned to face him in the driver's seat. "Where are we going?"

"I told you it's a surprise."

"I know. I'm just excited about the whole dating thing. It's kind of sexy."

Marcus let out a low raspy laugh, leaning in to me. His stare traced from my eyes toward my lips. "Is it now? Will it be sexy enough for you to—"

"Don't count on it, DeLuca." He burst into a full belly laugh. I missed that sound. He quickly kissed my lips and then pulled out of the parking spot. Sighing with contentment, I slumped back onto the headrest and studied his features as he drove.

"Are you hungry?" He asked.

"Actually, I am."

"Okay, we'll have lunch first, and then we'll have fun." He winked at me and then focused on the road. My stomach fluttered. I felt like a teenage girl on her first date with the most popular boy in school. I knew it was a cliché thought, but it was my cliché moment. I thought every female was entitled to at least one.

After thirty minutes, we pulled into a parking lot in the north end of downtown. It was also the neighborhood where Marcus lived: Back Bay on Commonwealth Avenue. His home was absolutely beautiful with the entire original historic structure and a few modern touches.

We exited the vehicle and strolled down the strip hand in hand, passing by a few restaurants and bars. We settled for a laid-back bar and grill. Marcus ordered a beer, and I ordered a martini as we waited for our meals.

"I'm sure it's too early for me to drink."

"By all means, Mia, please drink as much as you like. Besides, you get horny when you're drunk." He winked.

With a dramatic gasp, I slapped my hand against my chest. "Are you saying that you would take advantage of me while drunk?"

"Yes, I most definitely would." Letting out a laugh, he shook his head. "Nah, I'm kidding."

"No, you're not."

"Alright, maybe a little." We both burst out laughing.

After we ate our lunch, we decided to go for a long walk before he took me to the surprise spot. It was a little chilly out, but still a beautiful afternoon. We continued to joke around, flirt, and laugh. It was fun and nice to have that innocent moment for a change. No thoughts of all the issues we needed to work on crossed my mind. I wanted that moment to last forever. I loved seeing Marcus like that. It was the side of him that made me fall in love with him in the first place.

Marcus came to a complete halt, causing me to jerk in his arm. I studied him suspiciously. "Are you okay?" I asked.

"We're here." His lips spread into a boyish grin.

Bunching my brows together, I looked around us. We were in front of Lucky Strikes. "Your big surprise is a bowling alley?"

He nodded.

"Um . . . thanks?" I didn't know what else to say. My handsome, top notch lawyer/mobster boyfriend took me bowling as a surprise date. I was at a loss for words, and not in a good way.

"Trust me. You'll love it." Grabbing my elbow, he dragged me into the building.

After we rented our lane and grabbed our bowling shoes and some alcoholic beverages, we made our way toward lane number eight. I couldn't believe we were going to bowl. Still in shock by it all, I tossed off my boots and laced up the bowling shoes. I was in a freaking dress for Christ's sake! I was sure I looked ridiculous. I stood and stared down as I rocked in the blue-and-red bowling shoes. My eyes darted to Marcus at the sound of him chuckling. "What?" I asked.

"You look adorable."

Suspiciously, I flashed him another glare and grabbed my martini. I sipped on my drink as he entered our names onto the screen. The last time I went bowling was probably a few years ago with some college friends in undergrad. No, it was with an ex-boyfriend, the one who'd cheated on me with my roommate. Good times!

Marcus was up first. He searched for a bowling ball. Once he found the perfect one, he turned and winked at me. "Babe, don't be discouraged if you don't win. It's a learning process; you'll get better with each try." I cocked a brow at him. He laughed at my expression and then turned around, slowly walking toward the edge of the lane. Straightening his position, he took a deep breath. He took the game seriously, I could see. Marcus gently stretched his arm back with the bowling ball in hand and then tossed it down the lane. It gently rolled down the smoothly waxed wooden surface. His aim was a little too far to the right, so by the time the ball hit the pins, only three went down. He tried again and missed completely as the ball rolled into the left side gutter.

"My fingers were stuck."

"Yeah, sure they were." After downing my drink, I went and searched for the perfect bowling ball. I settled for a nine-pound orange one. Walking toward the edge of the lane, I straightened my position and scooted lightly toward the right. Staring down the lane, I focused on the first pin. Keeping steady, I swung my arm back and tossed the ball down the lane with no hesitation. All I could hear was the sound of the ball rolling along the wooden surface at a rapid speed until it collided with the middle pin. My eyes and mouth spread wide open when all ten pins were knocked down. Strike! Turning, I ran toward Marcus, who was just as shocked as I was, and jumped into his arms. "Oh my God, I got a strike on my first try!" I squealed.

"That's awesome." He laughed.

The next few rounds, I continued with my strikes. I was on a high, beating Marcus. He was failing miserably. I found it hilarious that he came up with a ludicrous excuse every time he missed the pins or didn't bowl a strike. The more I drank my martinis, the looser I got and the better my aim was getting.

It was beginning to get crowded in the bowling alley. Groups of people chatted and sang along to the loud music playing. The lights were dimmed as colorful strobe lights flicked through the space. I was actually having a really great time.

It was Marcus's turn again, so I decided to help him out. I walked up behind him, and he must have sensed I was near, because he looked over his shoulder. "Here, let me help you." Placing my hand behind his, I straightened the ball in his hand. "You want to have a straight angle."

"Mia?" He arched a brow.

"Shh, listen, don't be discouraged if you don't win. It's a learning process. You'll get better with each try." I threw his words back at him then innocently batted my lashes.

Laughing, he shook his head. "I'm not sure if I should kiss you or kill you."

Looking aside, I raised a finger toward my chin. "Mmmh. Decisions, decisions. I would prefer the kissing." I nodded and looked back at him.

His eyes brightened as his smile widened. Tossing the ball in his hand down the lane, without bothering to see if it hit any of the pins, he turned to face me. He picked me up in his arms. My legs wrapped around his waist as he kissed me eagerly. He bit on my lip playfully, forcing me to laugh.

He slightly pulled away from our kiss, allowing me to rest my forehead against his. The humor in his eyes was gone. "What would I do without you, Mia?"

Tightening my arms around his neck, I pulled him in closer to me, our lips mere inches away. "You'll never have to find out because I'll always be here, Marcus. I'll always be yours."

With that, he gripped the back of my neck, pulled me in, and kissed me hard and passionately.

After our date, Marcus drove me home and parked in front of my building. We continued to talk, laugh, and make out like two teenage kids for what seemed like hours. I wanted to take him in the car or even ask him to come up, but I was not giving in too easily. With my insides throbbing and aching for him, I pulled away, kissed him one last time, and wished him a good night. I spent the rest of the night staring at the ceiling and smiling about how wonderful it felt to spend time with Marcus. A night of pure fun was just what we needed after all the heavy drama we'd been through. Sighing, I shut my eyes and hoped that things stayed this way.

CHAPTER FIVE

MARCUS

It had been almost a week since Mia and I had rekindled our relationship, and everything was going smoothly. We met up for dinner or drinks three days out of the week. It was hard for us to meet up with our schedules, between her attending school and my working at the firm or meeting up with the guys, but somehow we made it work.

It was a Thursday late night, and I was in Lou's office. Lou called in all of his men, but he wasn't there yet. I stood by the far right wall of his office as I heard the door open. Jimmie walked in with Vinnie. He nodded when he spotted me and greeted the other guys before making his way towards me.

Once he shook my hand, he stood beside me and crossed his arms. "What's going on?" Jimmie whispered as he leaned in.

"I have no fuckin' clue."

"Vinnie was about to drop me off at home after a job when we got the call to meet here." He ran a hand over his face and breathed out a heavy sigh exhaustedly.

"Who was the job with? I just had one with the Quincy boys."

He nodded, knowing who I was talking about. "It was with the men in little Italy, James's men."

"Yeah, I know who that fucker is."

"Yeah, he wasn't too keen on you either. He said you were a wiseass if he remembered correctly."

"I was fuckin' seventeen, and it was my first deal."

Jimmie chuckled at that.

For the next forty minutes, we stood there in the office observing everyone. Buddy was leaning against the wall, humming a tune as he tapped his foot against the marble floor. Gio sat on top of a desk, scrolling through his phone. Vinnie and Al stood by the door, discussing the previous night's boxing match. Lou had more men who worked for him, but we six were his main guys that were given specific, important, top jobs or assignments.

Before we arrived at Lou's office, some of us were on a job with the Irish cartel. Carrick Boyle a.k.a. Rick was in charge of his family crime organization in Quincy. Rick and his men were known as the Quincy boys. Rick had done business with Lou for many years, gaining a respectable and trustworthy relationship. Everything worked out smoothly with the transaction, so I couldn't pinpoint what could have caused this meeting.

Our heads swung toward the door the moment Lou stormed in. He stopped midway into his office and glared at his nephew. "Are you fuckin' dumb or something, Gio?"

Gio's brows molded together in confusion. "Huh?"

Lou waved his hand toward the antique mahogany desk. "Get the fuck up! That desk is a fuckin' original, imported from Sicily." He snapped his fingers eagerly.

Gio jumped off the desk, inching toward the far left with both his hands raised in surrender. "Sorry, Uncle Lou. I had no idea."

Lou shook his head, walked behind the desk, and hung his suit jacket onto a coat rack. "Yeah, well, I guess that education I paid for was a fuckin' waste." Gio shrugged and then placed his phone into his back pocket.

The six of us moved closer toward Lou, forming a U surrounding his desk. Lou placed his wallet and revolver on top of a stack of papers and then eased down into his chair. Once he was situated, he took a long hard look at each and every one of us, not saying a word—just taking his time, scrutinizing the six men before him. I straightened my shoulders as I shoved my hands into my front pockets. Jimmie, to my right, had his arms crossed and was intently focusing on Lou, while the others waited patiently.

Lou leaned back in his chair, laying an elbow on the armrest, as his index finger and thumb framed his face. Crossing his legs, he let out a roguish laugh. "I call bullshit." Each of us gave the others questioning glares and then turned our attention back on Lou. His smile widened. "I call bullshit because it's come to my attention that someone in this very room has been lying to me."

My breathing remained steady, but I felt a rush of heat course through my veins. Jimmie shifted uncomfortably beside me. As I quickly glanced over at him, I could see his forehead becoming damp. It was warm in the space we occupied, but I knew my brother. He was fucking nervous. No one seemed to notice the change in his demeanor but me.

Come on, Jimmie, don't fuck this up.

"For years, I truly thought my men were loyal." Lou sucked his teeth three times as he slowly shook his head. "Tsk, tsk, tsk. Shame on me for believing there were still devoted men in this world." After one hard look at each of us, he uncrossed his legs and leaned into the desk. His elbows were placed on top of the wooden surface. He pointed an index finger and brought it toward his lips as his thumb rested beneath his chin. He sat in deep thought for a short period of time.

"What to do?" Lou questioned in a low voice. Then, as if something lit up in his head, he spread his arms wide with a cocky grin. "Ah, that's right. If I need something done, I must do it myself!" He stood from his chair, straightened his shoulders, and cracked his neck. Reaching for his revolver, he tightened his grip around the handle, twirling and examining the black metal piece in his hand. Everyone straightened, adjusting their positions.

Lou walked around the desk until he was in the center of us. He slowly walked back and forth with his left hand behind his back. He gestured with his right hand, tightly holding the gun, as he spoke, "See what I don't understand is, while thinking back on it all, I truly thought I took very good care of my men." Stopping to face me, he angled his head and asked, "Do you think I do, Marky? Take good care of my men, that is?" I gave a curt nod in response. With a crooked grin, he tapped the cold metal gun in his hand along the side of my face, turned, and made his way back to the center. All traces of humor washed away from his features as he stood tall and eyed every one of his men before him. "If I take good care of my men, then tell me why the FUCK am I having this fuckin' conversation!" His arms spread wide as he glanced around the room like a lunatic.

"Tell me!" Lou's face was slowly turning red as his anger built. It was dead silent. The drop of a pin could be heard a mile away. Landing his glare on Vinnie, he pointed his gun. "Vinnie, you got something to say?"

Vinnie shook his head. "No, boss."

"Hmm." Then Lou's arm shifted over to Buddy. "Buddy, what about you?" Lou asked.

Buddy raised a brow. "I'm the most loyal to you, Lou."

Amused by that statement, Lou smiled mockingly as he approached Buddy. "Is that so?"

Buddy stood his ground and nodded. "Yes, it is." With both hands folded behind his back, Lou leaned into him, their faces mere inches away from one another as Lou drilled his eyes into Buddy's for an awkwardly long time.

As if another idea just popped into his head, Lou swirled around and made his way back toward the center. Raising his gun, he aimed it at Buddy. "Eeny." Lou smirked and then began pointing at each and every one of us, as he continued. "Meeny. Miny. Moe. Catch a Rat." The gun landed on Jimmie. I stiffened. My body dampened with sweat as my heart thrashed against my chest. All sound went faint, except for my breathing, which grew hasty. Everything around me felt as if it was going in slow motion. I showed no sign of uneasiness as I exhaled when Lou took the aim off of Jimmie and began to go down the row of men again. "By his toe. If he squeals." Mischievously, his smile grew lopsided. "Then let the fucker go." Without a second thought, Lou pulled the trigger.

A loud ringing noise echoed in the room after the gun went off. My eyes traced from the blood splattered on Lou's shirt to Al dead on the ground. He lay flat on his belly, his head landing on Lou's leather shoes. Kicking the head aside, Lou spit on the lifeless body and then made his way behind the desk. The other men, including Jimmie and myself, looked at each other, confused.

"Uncle Lou, Al was the rat?" Gio asked in astonishment.

Lou grabbed a cloth from the inside of his jacket. Removing his shoe, he began wiping off the blood. "From the sound of it, Gio, it seems as if you don't believe my source was accurate. Is that so?" He asked. After wiping off his shoes and putting them back on, he then unbuttoned his shirt, replacing it with a fresh one that was removed from the desk drawer.

"No, not at all, it's just when you mentioned a rat, my first guess was Buddy. You know what I mean?"

"Fuck you!" Buddy coughed back and spit at Gio. The saliva fell on top of Gio's shoes.

"Fuck you. You fuckin' cocksucker!" Gio began making his way toward Buddy. The two of them had been going at it for days; it was some unfinished business from years ago before Gio had skipped town. If you asked me, it was really just a competition for Lou's affection. They both were like sons to him.

"Enough!" Lou slammed his hand on the desk and began barking orders. "Vinnie and Buddy, take care of the body. Gio, go fetch the car and bring it out back. I'll meet you down there in five minutes. Marky, you got my money?"

Gio walked out the door. On his way out, he and Buddy exchanged pissed-off glares. Buddy and Vinnie picked up the body from the floor and carried it down the stairs. Jimmie reached for the duffle bag that was beside him and handed it over to me. I placed the bag on top of Lou's desk and unzipped it. "It's all accounted for."

Lou reached for his jacket, slipped his arms through the well-tailored dark blue sleeves, and smiled. "Good, how was the exchange?"

"Same as always with the Boyle's: smooth. He placed another order for this time next month."

Nodding, Lou reached in the bag, took two large stacks of money, and handed them to me. "You did good, Marky. Keep it up." After grabbing the bag, he left the room.

Once the door was shut, I turned and looked at Jimmie, gesturing my head toward the door. Without a word, we both left Lou's office and made our way toward my car. When we entered, I twisted in my seat to fully look at him. "What the fuck was that?"

"What?" He asked.

"Don't play dumb with me, Jimmie. I know you. You were shitting bricks in there. Care to explain?"

"What do you think, Marcus? When he said someone was hiding something, I instantly thought about Michael. He's going to find out sooner or later."

"No, he won't."

Jimmie tossed his hands in the air and rolled his eyes. "Come on, Marcus! You can't be that naïve? If he doesn't know already, Lou is going to figure out that Mia is Michael Sullivan's sister, and when he does, Lou will begin to piece together the fuckin' puzzle. It's only a matter of time. Al wasn't the rat. Lou was trying to send a message." Huffing out a deep breath, he sank his head back onto the headrest. "The one person that crossed my mind while we were in there was my little girl. I can't be a failure to her. And I know you love Mia. I truly understand, but now you have to think about her too. We need to dig deeper and get more info. There had to be someone Michael was working with besides us. He was too smart to have done it any other way."

With one last glance at him, I turned in my seat, started the car, and pulled off.

What the fuck was I supposed to do now?

***

That night I lay in bed, staring blankly at the white ceiling. My mind was sprinting with all of the chaos. I wasn't being naïve as Jimmie insinuated. I knew that eventually Lou would figure it all out. I guess I had been in denial, keeping that thought tucked away in the back of my mind, hoping it would all go away. My main focus for so long had been Mia, but I couldn't stop Jimmie's words as they trampled through my head.

I fought back the urge to grab a drink. There was always something soothing about having liquor course through my bloodstream. It made everything seem to vanish in that moment. It was another weakness of mine along with Mia.

I was becoming weak, and that was the one thing that I couldn't become while managing that lifestyle. Weakness was a sign of failure. I'd come too far to fail. Mia was my greatest weakness and I knew that. I had to find a way to juggle it all, because if I kept going about everything the way I had been, she'd be the death of me.

CHAPTER SIX

MIA

"What's wrong, Mia?" Megan chirped from the other end of the clothing rack.

I hadn't realized that I was dozing off. Yawning, I forced a smile. "I'm just tired. I stayed up all night studying for an exam."

"Sorry, I promise I won't keep you long. This is the first date Jeremy is taking me on, like an actual date." She smiled as her eyes glistened. "I'm nervous."

"It's normal to be nervous. Do you know where he's taking you?"

"Yeah, the restaurant is called La Matrix d sover?"

I bit back a laugh. "*La Maître de saveur*?"

Megan's eyes widened. "Yeah, that place."

Not able to help it the second time around, I burst into a laugh. "It's French for 'The Master of Flavor.' It's a *very* nice restaurant." I was beyond impressed with Jeremy. He never took a date to an elaborate place. That was a definite sign that he appreciated and respected Megan.

Megan clapped her hands excitedly and jumped in place as her long light brown waves bounced along with her. "Oh, I'm so excited. So you know what's appropriate to wear for this restaurant?"

"Oh yeah, come on, we are off to search for the perfect cocktail dress." I winked.

***

Several hours later, we found the perfect dress for Megan's date. We went our separate ways as I went home and she went to her place, well, the place that she shared with my mother. Sara had come a long way since the day she waltzed back into my life. Our mother-daughter relationship wasn't perfect, but we were working on it. We had made it a priority to meet up once a week, despite our busy schedules. Tomorrow, we had plans for dinner.

In the meantime, Marcus was coming over that night, so I had to prepare for our evening. It was our fourth date night. An entire week had passed since we made up. As much as I would have loved to have spent every single day with him, our hectic schedules just didn't allow it, unless we had been living together, and that wasn't going to happen anytime soon. After a long, exhausting week for the both of us, we decided to stay in and watch movies.

I had set up the living room so that we could have an indoor picnic, with an oversized blanket and pillows spread across the floor, along with all the junk food known to man. As I stared down at my grand attempt to romanticize a regular night at home, a hint of disappointment ran through me. I hadn't exercised in weeks, and all the junk food and late night take-outs were beginning to show—on my ass and hips. *Tomorrow*, I thought to myself. *Tomorrow I'll begin working out again.*

"So, what do you think?"

I swirled around, and my earlier concerns about my rapidly increasing weight vanished. Jeremy looked positively handsome in a black suit, light grey shirt, and matching silk tie. His curly blond hair was well kept and blue sparkly eyes glistened.

"I take it by the huge smile on your face that you like what you see?" He raised a brow.

"Jeremy, you look amazing!" I stared at him in awe for a few seconds before padding my way toward him. Resting my hands along his chest, I ran them across his suit jacket. For some reason, I wanted to make sure every single crease or wrinkle was smoothed perfectly. I felt like a proud mom, which was an odd thought. I loved that he and Megan were becoming closer, though I hadn't had the chance to discuss their relationship with him. "Jeremy?"

"Yes?" He whispered.

As I adjusted his tie, I quickly glimpsed up at him. He was staring down at me with a slight grin. His aqua blue eyes sparkled with humor. Nerves pricked through me, and I began to fiddle with the tie. I brought my focus back down to my fingers. Wetting my lips, I cleared my throat. "So, you and I really haven't had time to talk."

He shrugged. "Talk about what?"

Letting out a soft sigh, I pressed my hands along his shoulders. "Well . . . about you and Megan." I looked up. His expression grew serious. "We don't have to talk now. . ." I quickly added.

"What do you want to know?"

"How are you feeling? What are your intentions? Are you taking this seriously?" I blurted all out at once. His lips twitched aside. "Look. You're my best friend, Jeremy. Hell, I see you as more of a brother than a friend. Megan's my cousin. I just want to make sure that neither one of you gets hurt. I've never interfered with your relationships unless I was asked, but I feel as if I need to know what's going on between the two of you, for my sanity." I laughed once.

Jeremy slightly bent his head back and exhaled deeply. "It's hard to explain what I'm feeling." He looked back at me and pressed his lips as his brows kneaded together in confusion. "When I'm around Megan, I'm happy and nervous, both at the same time. Does that make sense?"

Nodding with a knowing smile, I said, "Perfect sense."

"Yeah?" He shook his head with a rugged moan. "It's confusing. I feel like I have to be around her all the time, and when I'm not, I think about her constantly. In the beginning, I tried to go on dates with other girls, to take away the thoughts I had of Megan. Though, every time I was on a date, I began nitpicking every little detail in my head of why that particular girl wasn't right for me."

"Like no elbow room?"

"Exactly, and because of you and how close we are, I didn't want to ruin our relationship if I turned into my usual dickhead self. These feelings are new to me, Mia. I just don't want to let her or you down."

"Jeremy, you could never let Megan or me down. Just be your usual dickhead self, minus the prowling, and you'll be just fine."

His laugh echoed the room, causing me to burst into a hard laugh right along with him. "Alright, enough of this mushy, girly shit." He pushed back, spreading his arms wide, with brows molded together. "You sure I look alright?"

"You look awesome. If I know Megan well enough, I would say she'll probably skip dinner and go straight for the car sex." I winked.

He laughed again, kissed my forehead, and left without another word. Sighing in contentment, I turned on my heels and headed toward my bedroom.

***

An hour after Jeremy left, I showered, brushed my teeth, and combed my hair into a ponytail. There was no need to doll up, so I threw on a pair of black leggings and my favorite University sweatshirt. Since Marcus was bringing the movies, I placed an order for pizza and wings. As I poured a glass of wine, the doorbell rang.

Perfect timing.

After swinging the door open, my smile faded as I saw the troubled expression on Marcus's face. He shrugged his shoulders slightly, mouthed "sorry" as he tilted his head, directing my eyes downward. Elle was standing in front of him with a backpack in her hand.

"Hi, Mia!" Elle chirped.

With a smile, I bent my knees so that we were at eye level and pulled her in for a hug. "Elle, I'm so happy you're here."

Her lips curled into a huge grin, and then she ran into the apartment. Marcus followed in behind her. Leaning in, he landed a kiss on my forehead. "I'm sorry, babe." He whispered. "Jimmie had a date and I—"

"Whoa, Jimmie's on a date?"

"Yeah, he met someone at Elle's school. Her son and Elle are in the same class. They've been spending quite a bit of time together. Elle doesn't know. Jimmie doesn't want her to know just yet."

"Oh my God, that's amazing that he's dating. I'm happy for him."

Elle ran up to us and pulled on Marcus's jacket. "Uncle Marc, show Mia the movies we got."

With a light groan, Marcus's eyes widened. "Ah, yes, the movies." The three of us walked to the living room and sank down onto the quilt. He pulled each one out of the bag. "You have a choice of three: *The Little Mermaid*, *The Lion King*, and *Beauty and the Beast.*" Marcus raised his brows mockingly as he held all three in both hands.

Elle glanced at me with an expression as if it were a very difficult decision to make. "So which one would you like to see, Mia?"

I pursed my lips to try and hold back my laughter as I looked over the selections in Marcus's hand. "Well, I love all three, but if I have to choose only one, my favorite is *Beauty and the Beast*."

Elle nodded. "Good choice, that's my favorite too." Tilting her head, she faced Marcus. "Well, Uncle Marc, *Beauty and the Beast* it is."

Marcus deeply sighed as he stood and headed toward the flat screen. He placed the movie into the Blue-ray player and pressed play. The previews began. "Marcus, would you like anything to drink?" I asked.

"You have anything strong?"

Laughing, I stood. "I have wine." He nodded his head and then looked over at Elle. "Elle, would you like something to drink?"

"What do you have?" she asked, looking at me.

"Grape juice?"

"Sure!"

Smiling at her, I added, "Anything else?"

Her eyes scanned over the junk food. "Do you have any fruits or veggies?" Where was this little girl from? Planet thirteen going on thirty?

Marcus cocked a brow, "Elle, you know better than—"

"No, it's fine, seriously. I do have fruits and veggies. I'll bring them right over, Elle." She smiled at me widely and then turned her head back toward the flat screen.

I made my way toward the kitchen and into the fridge. Marcus followed behind me. He grabbed a glass and filled it with wine. I smirked at him as I began to chop up and prepare some produce for Elle.

Leaning back against the counter, he studied me. "You find all of this amusing, don't you?"

"You have to agree it's hilarious." I winked.

Marcus took a gulp of wine and then made his way to me. Nestling behind me, he wrapped his arms around my waist, resting his chin on my shoulder. "I've missed you," he whispered in my ear, following with feather-like kisses along the nape of my neck.

"I've missed you too."

He remained in that position as he gently swayed our hips from side to side, humming to a soft beat. I continued to chop an apple, smiling and laughing under his embrace. "I'm sorry about tonight, Mia. I know it was supposed to be just the two of us. I'll make it up to you."

Baffled, I stopped what I was doing and turned in his arms to face him. Wrapping my arms around his neck, I ran my fingertips through the back of his hair. "Marcus, don't ever feel sorry about bringing Elle. I love and enjoy being around her."

Marcus leaned down and placed a kiss on the tip of my nose. "That's one of the reasons why I love you so much."

"Because I accept your family? Of course I do."

"That, and because I know one day you're going to make an amazing mother." He reached down and planted a kiss on my lips. Those words caught me off guard. An amazing mother? Marcus and I hadn't discussed the loss of our baby since that day in the parking lot—the day I told him about the miscarriage. Hearing him say I would make an amazing mother hit me hard. "Are you okay?"

Blinking, I focused on him again. "Huh? Oh, yeah, I'm fine." I turned and continued prepping Elle's healthy tray, and then we made our way back into the living room.

***

"Marcus, Elle fell asleep. Maybe you should lay her down in my bedroom. We can sleep out here." Marcus nodded, grabbed Elle, and carried her off into my room.

We had watched two of the three movies, much to Marcus's displeasure. As the screen played, my mind drifted off into another direction during the movie. I was there physically, sitting beside Marcus as his arm was draped around my shoulder. I even nodded a few times when Elle made a comment about a character and laughed when she did. Still, mentally my mind was engaged with thoughts that Marcus had brought back to life.

Of course, I hadn't forgotten about the miscarriage. It was a subject that I had learned to tuck away in the back of my mind and no longer think about it: an out-of-sight, out-of-mind type of ordeal. When it had been brought back to surface, it felt as if I had been smacked head first into a concrete wall—a throbbing pain that was so brutal I couldn't recover from it.

The miscarriage was not the only memory that flashed through my mind throughout the night. I thought about everything that had happened prior to and following the miscarriage, about the way my life had evolved within a few short months of knowing Marcus, and how a brief random meeting at Club21 started it all. If I had met him at his office instead, would we have still fallen in love? Would we have followed the same exact path that led us to where we are now? Would we have suffered with the constant arguments, the lies, the betrayal, and the heart-aching memories of losing one another? Would it all have been the same?

My mind ran back through how it had all played out: finding the file in his office with the information about my brother, the miscarriage, and the pain and confusion I dealt with for weeks from loving someone who I hated at the same time. I hated that I fell madly in love with him so quickly and when I wanted to be angry with him I couldn't because he had a power over me that no one ever had.

You can't help who you fall in love with. Yet I had fallen in love with a man that most women would run away from. Even after finding out about it all—his lifestyle, his involvement with the mafia, his knowledge of my brother's death, and the constant lies—I fell in love with this man who had turned my world upside down in such a short period of time. No matter how hard I tried, I couldn't stay away, and I would never walk away again.

"Mia, come here." Slightly turning my head, I stared at Marcus sitting on the sofa. I hadn't heard him walk back into the room. Absentmindedly I stood, making my way toward him as the vision of him became a blur. The tears building up in my eyes forced me back to reality. I desperately tried to fight them from running down my face. I strained, held my breath, hell, I even focused on the collar of Marcus's shirt, but it all failed. By the time I reached him, the tears wouldn't stop.

Marcus pulled me in to sit on his lap. I positioned myself so that I was straddling him. With my head lowered, I fidgeted with my fingers. Tilting his head aside, he ducked under so that he could get a better look at me. I chanced a quick glance his way. Marcus had a worried look in his eyes, "Baby, what's wrong?" he whispered.

"Nothing." My throat was low and hoarse.

With the tip of his fingers, he lifted my chin to fully look at him. "Mia, why are you crying? Simba didn't kill his father. It was his evil Uncle Scar who did."

Laughing once, I nudged his shoulder and sniffed a few times. "I'm not crying about the movie."

"So if you're not crying about the movie, it has to be about something else. Tell me. What's wrong?"

Letting out a shaky breath, I pressed my lips together before responding, "I was thinking about the last four months." Shaking my head, I looked at him. "All of it, Marcus: my brother, our baby, and us. I thought I could lock it away in my head and not think of it again, but it's easier said than done."

"What are you saying exactly? Are you having doubts about us?" His eyes searched my face, trying to find meaning behind it all.

"No, I'm not at all. What you said in the kitchen about me making an amazing mother hit me hard. It brought me right back to the miscarriage, and all the pain resurfaced again. Then I began thinking about everything else, and my mind just . . ." I waved my hands in circular motions, trying to find the right words.

He grabbed my face, and with an unreadable expression, he stared at me for quite some time. "You will make an amazing mother one day. You will have a beautiful baby boy or girl that will love you and look at you as if you're the most perfect person in the world. I know that losing our baby left a scar that you feel may never be healed, but it will, Mia. Trust me. One day you will have a child, and I hope and pray that you have that child with me."

Swallowing the large lump in my throat, I sniffed, "You still want to have children in the future?"

Shock registered in his expression. "You're my life, and I wouldn't dream of a life without you being my wife and having my kids."

"I love you, Marcus. I really do, but I don't think . . ."

"Mia, I get it." He caressed his thumbs along my cheeks. "You deserve better than me. I put you through so much."

"Marcus, you're perfect for me in every way imaginable."

Breathing out a smile with no sign of humor, he said, "That's crazy talk."

Shaken by his response, I reached for his face to get his full attention. "No, it's not." Leaning my forehead against his, I whispered, "Before you, my life was filled with loneliness. I struggled each day to get by. I wasn't happy. So as crazy as this may sound to you," I lightly shrugged, "it's not to me. I'm completely in love with you, Marcus. Ever since I met you, I've found a purpose in my life that makes each day worth living."

There was a whirlpool of emotions clouding his eyes: love, lust, pain, and desire. Gripping the back of my head, he pulled me in, crushing his lips against mine. There was so much passion behind that kiss. All of the love we had for each other poured into one magical kiss that left us breathing heavily. Our tongues twirled in soft circular motions as his hands gripped my face to pull me in closer. My arms wrapped around his neck as my fingers gripped his hair. That was the first night that we ever showed our affection for one another without the urgency of sex. He kissed and held me, allowing me to pour out all my love for him in one simple kiss.

That was the night I remembered why I fell in love with Marcus in the first place.

CHAPTER SEVEN

MARCUS

As I walked into the office, I was greeted by Stacy, the receptionist at the firm. After handing me messages from this morning, she tilted her blond head and examined me. I flipped through the messages and felt her continued heated stare. Raising a brow, I asked, "Anything else?"

"No." Tilting her head to the opposite side, she added, "You just look different."

"It's probably my haircut."

"Yes, that might be it. It looks good."

"Thanks." I made a move for my office until I remembered something. "Is Ms. Grant in this week?"

"I'm afraid not. She's still not feeling well after her surgery. There was a voice message from her over the weekend that she'll need another week."

Shit. I had a major trial the next week. Ms. Grant had been working closely with me on this case. There was so much to wrap-up before the jury selection began on Monday. The only co-worker other than Ms. Grant that had worked closely with me on that case was Stephanie.

Fuck. I had transferred Stephanie to another department after she texted an inappropriate photo to my phone that Mia had found a couple of months back.

"Is Stephanie in today?" I had no idea what I was doing, but I was desperate. Still, with the research for relevant case law and the legal memorandum that was due tomorrow, I was at a loss. I needed someone to work on the trial binders, as well as contact all of the witnesses and schedule them to be prepped before trial. Stephanie was the only person I could rely on to resolve this mess.

I had to call Mia and give her a heads-up. I didn't want her to feel uncomfortable. I was also trying to do the honesty and trust thing. It meant a lot to her and the success of our relationship.

"She is in. Would you like me to send her to your office?" Stacy stabbed through my thoughts.

"Yes, please."

As I entered my office, I felt awkwardly nervous at the thought of Mia being angry over the situation. We'd been doing very well, especially over the past weekend. It was as if everything was going perfectly. I knew Mia loved me, but the feelings she expressed a couple of nights ago sealed it for me. So being the fucking wimp I was when it came to my girlfriend, I sank in my chair behind my desk and dialed her number.

"Hello." Mia answered in a sleepy tone after the third ring.

"Good morning, beautiful, did I wake you?"

"Yes, you did." She laughed. "But I have to get up anyway. I have to study for an exam that's scheduled for tomorrow and meet your mother for lunch at noon. After lunch, I'm meeting my mother and Megan for some shopping."

"Sounds like a productive day."

"Yes, it is. What are you up to?"

Unbuttoning my suit jacket, I leaned back into the chair. "I'm at the office. It's going to be a busy week with the Di Angele trial coming up next week."

"I thought that trial was scheduled for last summer?"

"Yes, it was, but it got continued as most trials do."

"Right, I remember now hearing that on the news. Well, I know you'll be brilliant."

I laughed once while my eyes glanced toward the door. Stephanie popped her head in. Whispering, she said, "Stacy said you needed me?"

I covered the phone with my hand and responded to her, "Yes, can you give me a minute on the phone?"

"Sure." She shut the door, making her way back into the hallway.

"Marcus?" Mia's voice pricked through the phone.

"Sorry, babe. I need to tell you something." Fuck, I had no idea why I was fucking sweating and nervous.

The squeak from the bed led me to believe that she shifted—probably sitting up. "Okay, what is it?" She sounded concerned.

Letting out a deep breath, I pressed my lips together. Here goes nothing. "Do you remember when I mentioned that Ms. Grant had surgery a week ago?"

"Yes, is she okay? Did something happen?"

"Oh no, well, she needs another week or two. She's not ready to come back to work." Hesitating for a few seconds, I continued, "With her being out, I need an assistant. With witness preparation, trial binders, case law research, and so much more, there's no way I can do it all on my own. There is only one person that's familiar with the case and . . ." I trailed off knowing that I was rambling, but couldn't find the fucking nerves to just flat out and say it.

"You need Stephanie to help." She completed for me.

"Yes. I wanted to let you know first, Mia. I don't want to make you feel uncomfortable or keep it from you. I promise it's nothing more than a professional relationship."

"Marcus, that's fine. I trust you, and I appreciate that you're being honest. That means a lot to me. Seriously, you have a firm that you need to successfully run and a trial to prep. If she's the only person who can help, then you have no other choice." Hesitating, she sighed and then added, "But if she touches you or tries any crap, I will go right down to your office and cause some mayhem. Make sure you let her know that."

I laughed at her attempts to sound intimidating, and my breathing became steady. "I'll be sure to tell her, but I'm positive I can handle myself."

"I'm sure you can, but it would make me happier to handle it instead." The sound of her hopping off the bed and landing on the wood floors came through. I could hear her padding around her room. "Well, I'm going to shower. Are we meeting up tonight? I missed you last night."

"I missed you too, but I can't. I have something to do tonight. I wish I were there to shower with you."

"Yeah? Well as you sit for the next few hours with Stephanie, I want you to picture me standing in a hot steamy shower with my hands slowly lathering every inch of me. The entire time my thoughts will be of you, Marcus: the way you touch me, the way your hands feel against my skin, my breasts, and every single inch of my body. Oh, and Marcus?"

"Yeah?" Sucking in a sharp breath, images of her naked body glistening with soap suds were running through my mind.

"Only four days until you can have me any way you want."

"You do know you're a tease, right?" My pants felt uncomfortable with the fucking hard on I had. She had been teasing me for fucking days, counting each day down. I swore when I got my hands on her I'd make sure she'd have no choice but to break this stupid fucking bet early.

"I love you, baby," she whispered then blew me a kiss and ended the call.

I waited five minutes to calm down before I opened the door and let Stephanie in.

***

For the next couple of hours, Stephanie and I worked together on the case. At first it was awkward. Neither one of us mentioned the incident that had occurred. Instead, we dived right into the work that needed to be done. With piles of files and documents scattered everywhere, we continued to work persistently. I sat behind my desk, keeping my distance as she lounged on a chair by the coffee table with a laptop on her lap.

I could tell at first that she was nervous. Every time I was close by to hand her documents, she would fidget with her fingers, shift uneasily, and be sure not to make direct eye contact. I felt bad that my presence was uncomfortable for her. When it was dead silent in the room and all you could hear was the sound of papers shifting or the sound of our fingers typing along the keyboards, I had the urge to start a conversation, but I managed to stop myself. I didn't want to mislead her in any way, shape, or form.

I was in the midst of deep concentration on the legal memo I was preparing, when the sound of my office door opening forced me out of it. I turned my head to see who it was and was both shocked and pleased to see Mia walking through the doorway. Her trench coat hung over her arm as her perfect hips swayed with her confident stride. She was wearing the tightest and shortest black long sleeved dress with fuck-me knee boots. I could also tell she took her time to make sure her hair and makeup was at its best. My smile broadened as her lips twitched into a slightly playful smirk. I also wanted to burst out laughing because I knew *exactly* why she was here and I found it beyond amusing.

"Hi, baby," she chirped, leaning in as she planted a long kiss on my lips. She jerked back to a straight posture, and her eyes turned toward Stephanie. Mia's lips slightly trembled in place and then formed a huge smile. "Oh, hi, Stephanie, how are you?"

Not taking my eyes off of Mia, I could hear that Stephanie had shifted and made her way across the room. "Hi, Mia, wow you look great. Better than great, you look awesome."

Mia's face slightly slanted as she studied Stephanie. Mia waited a few seconds before responding as if she were biting her tongue. "So do you, Steph."

"Thank you. Marcus, it's only eleven. Would you like me to come back after lunch hour? Say one o'clock?"

"That sounds great. Thanks, Stephanie."

"No problem. It was nice seeing you again, Mia."

"Same here, Steph. Take care."

I waited until I could hear the sound of the door close behind Stephanie before fully giving Mia my attention. I angled my head and studied her. She laid her jacket down as her fingers trailed along my desk. She hummed to a tune, attempting to avoid eye contact. My eyes trailed down the V-neck of her dress that enhanced her cleavage. The scent of her perfume heightened my senses. My mind drifted to the thought of forcing her across my desk and fucking her senseless. The thought of being inside of her caused my pants to tighten against my hard on.

This two-weeks-without-sex bullshit was killing me.

My eyes continued to trace the flawless curves of her body. My stare-down froze at the end of her dress, which landed at mid-thigh. Wetting my lips, I leaned forward in my chair and ran my hand up her inner thigh. "This is a nice dress. It's kind of short, though. You usually wear dresses like this when you meet my mother for lunch?"

"Actually, I do. I dress like this all the time, minus my low-down days. I'm surprised you're just noticing." She said sarcastically. Turning her head, she looked down at me, and then her eyes lightened upon realizing something. "You got a haircut."

"Yes I did. You don't like?" I continued to trace small circles on her inner thigh.

Her lips curled into a smile as she reached for my hair and ran her finger tips through it. "I love it. It's short but still long enough for me to play with."

That small gesture of her fingers caressing my hair caused a burning sensation that shot through me. I dragged my hand higher and cupped her sex as I ran my finger along the seam of the panties. Looking up, I caught that she took in a sharp breath. Standing from my chair, I firmly pressed my body against hers. Out of balance, she sank down on top of the desk. Her breathing became heavier as my palm rubbed against her clit and two of my fingers slipped between her sleek walls. I could feel that she desperately wanted me. She was ready for me in every way: the unsteadiness of her breathing, the quickening of her heartbeat, and fuck, most importantly, how *fucking* wet she was for me as I worked my fingers in and out of her.

Desire poured into her eyes as she stared into mine. "Marcus, what are you doing?"

"Why did you come here?" I demanded in a low tone.

Her brows kneaded together as her face washed over with frustration. Lifting her hands, she tried to push me away, "Can I not visit my boyfriend at his place of work? Or was I interrupting you?"

"Stop it!" I grunted as I shoved both of my fingers deeper inside her. Her lips slightly parted as she panted heavily. "Why did you come here?" I asked again, this time my tone harsher. Without answering, she wet her lips and gave me the you-should-know look.

Leaning in, I brought my face toward the side of hers, my lips brushing her soft cheek along the way. The fresh scent of her hair drove me insane. She let out a slight cry as I removed my fingers from inside of her and ran my hand up the side of her body to cup her breast. She arched into me as she sucked in air between her clenched teeth. With my other hand, I very gently wrapped it around her throat. Her breathing hitched. I felt her heartbeat quicken as my arm lay against her chest. "You came here for a reason, Mia. Tell me. What do you want?" I blew out in a harsh whisper as I caught her earlobe between my teeth and ran my tongue along her flesh.

"I came here for you." Her voice was a low whimper.

"You came to tease me again?"

Slightly spreading her legs wider, she leaned back on the desk. Her lashes fluttered. "No." She gripped my hand and brought it back down between her legs. I wanted her to ache and suffer as I had. I gripped her thigh and yanked my hand from her grasp as I brought it up to lie on her waist.

Frustrated, she huffed out, "Now who's the tease?"

Laughing once, I brought my face around to hers so that we were a mere inch away from one another. "What do you want from me?" I caught her bottom lip between my teeth and sucked against her flesh. The cherry scented lip gloss she wore tasted just as good as it smelled. "What do you want me to do?"

With the sweet warmth of her breath against my face, I couldn't take it anymore. Gripping her ass, I shoved her against me. I wanted her to feel the effect she had on me, the desperate need to relieve the sexual tension. Lifting a hand, I balled a fist full of her hair and tugged her head back, forcing her to stare at me. I could see it deep within her eyes: the fuck-me look. She didn't give two fucks about that bet anymore. She wanted me right then and there.

"You know what I want, Marcus." She whimpered.

Tightening the grip in her hair, I brought my lips against hers as I said, "Do you want me to fuck you hard, Mia, or make love to you?"

Her mouth opened with anticipation as her breathing became evidently needy. "I want you to fuck me hard then make long sweet love to me."

I flashed a crooked smile and whispered, "That's my girl."

She melted in my arms the moment my lips crushed against hers: deep, passionate, hungry kisses that were fucking amazing. God, I wanted her more than anything. I longed to touch her, to feel her, to enjoy the way she felt in my arms as her body quivered after her orgasm, the panting and screams as I slammed my cock inside of her. I wanted that feeling right then and right there.

It was the perfect time, until there was a knock at the door that ruined the whole fucking moment. Mia jerked back as her hand came up to a halt. Cursing a storm, I backed away from her and watched my beautiful, hot-as-hell girlfriend jump off my desk and adjust herself.

Fuck.

Fuck.

Fuck.

I wanted to kill whoever was behind that door. Cold-blooded fucking murder.

My head whipped toward the entry the moment it opened. As soon as I saw it was Jimmie, I flipped him the fucking bird. "My bad, Bro, should I come back?" He asked with a mockingly raised brow.

"No, no, no." Mia blurted. "I was just leaving." Catching her breath, she grabbed her jacket and turned to face me. "Sorry," she mouthed. When she leaned in to kiss me good-bye, I grabbed her arm and whispered in her ear, "You have got to be fuckin' kidding, Mia?"

"I'm sorry, Marcus. It's only four days. A bet is a bet."

I pulled her into me again and harshly blurted, "You weren't fuckin' saying that a minute ago."

"Please don't be mad, okay?" she whispered back.

Fuck, I didn't want to be mad, but my dick was on the verge of exploding. That's how horny I was. Her eyes pleaded with mine, and I couldn't be pissed anymore. I let out a deep breath and nodded. "Fine, have a good time at lunch." I planted a kiss on her lips.

She gave me one last slight smile, turned, and made her way toward the door. Jimmie gawked at her. "Whoa, you have a hot date, Mia?"

She smiled at him and leaned in to kiss his cheek. "Yes, with your mother."

Nodding, Jimmie smiled, "Ah, well the two of you will be the hottest chicks in the place that's for sure. Have fun."

"Thank you, Jimmie. Catch you guys later!" And just like that, she was out of my sight. My body heated with the adrenaline.

Jimmie turned his head my way pointed at me and burst out laughing.

"Fuck you, Jimmie, you fuckin' cock-blocker."

CHAPTER EIGHT

MIA

With wobbly legs, I exited Marcus' office and treaded toward the elevators. I needed to get out of there fast. Once the elevator doors opened, I entered, pressed a button, and sank against the cool metal barrier. Breathing heavily, I stared at my reflection along the silver-plated wall opposite me. Emerald eyes narrowed back at me with the I-want-to-fuck-and-fuck-now look. The red smeared lipstick was not pleasing. I reached in my purse to grab a tissue and my lipstick. Wiping my lips clean, I gave myself a fresh coat of red. Giving myself one last look, I straightened my dress, teased my hair with my fingertips, and walked out of the elevators and into the lobby to meet up with Theresa.

If Jimmie had never entered Marcus' office, there would have been no stopping me. Marcus would've had me, right then and there. I was angry with myself, not for letting myself cave in but rather for thinking that I was being childish with the stupid bet. I just wanted something different for us. Before our separation, we never talked. Everything was resolved with sex. Now Marcus confided in me. He trusted me enough to pour out his feelings and secrets. I didn't want to lose that. However, deep down, I knew I had to please my man, because I felt that if I didn't I might lose him to someone else who was more than willing.

Someone like Stephanie.

That brought me to the reason why I showed up at his office unexpectedly, overly dressed, with my best pair of four-inch boots, along with my hair and makeup done as if I were scheduled for a photo shoot.

What was wrong with me?

Hearing her name over the phone left an unsettled burning deep within my stomach, and as much as I wanted to brush it off, I couldn't. I did trust him with every inch of my being, but what woman would have just let it slide? Again, was I being childish, or it could just have been *me* reminding *him* what he had.

No, I guess it was juvenile. I was frustrated that I allowed myself to stoop so low. There was no turning back now. What was done was done, and I couldn't change anything about it. Though, I had to admit seeing the look on his face when I entered his office unannounced was priceless. The way he gawked at my appearance forced me to laugh at the memory.

I spotted Theresa the moment I entered the Japanese restaurant. Waving her hand, she stood at my approach. "Hello, Theresa." I leaned in hugging her.

"Whoa, Mia, you look amazing." She pulled away from our embrace and settled back in her seat.

"Thank you. So do you." She surely did. Theresa was in her early fifties but could easily pass as Marcus and Jimmie's older sister. With smooth, long, brown hair and bright green eyes that brightened with her smile, she stood at four feet eleven inches. Even with heels, she was tiny. Theresa was also fashionable as she dressed in a classy but sexy way with her cream fitted dress, royal blue peep-toe pumps, and gold accessories. I aspired to be just as chic at her age.

A waiter approached our table. "Hello, can I start you off with anything to drink?"

"Yes, I'll have a glass of merlot. Mia, would you like one as well?" I nodded with a smile. She ordered two glasses and the waiter left us. "So how's my favorite lady?" She asked with bright smile.

"I'm good. I've been stressing over this exam that's scheduled for tomorrow, but after taking a day break from studying, I think I'll be fine." The waiter brought us our glasses, and then we ordered a variety of sushi. "How are you?" I asked when it was just us again.

Sipping on her glass, she slightly nodded. "I've been okay, just a little down lately, but that's to be expected this time of year."

Theresa was never one to be upset or at least from what I'd witnessed, which worried me. "This time of year?"

"Yes, it's the anniversary of my husband's death. It'll be fifteen years next Saturday."

A chill ran through me as I leaned in and folded my arms on the table. "I didn't realize he passed a week after Marcus's birthday?"

Theresa ran a freshly manicured hand through her hair as she slightly nodded. "Oh yes, Marcus didn't want to celebrate his birthday for years after James' death." Laughing once, she continued. "Can you blame him? I think it wasn't until his twenty-first birthday that he allowed me to plan a party for him; even at that age, he was hesitant." She took a few more sips of her wine.

"So is he going to be okay with the surprise this week?"

"We'll find out then." Laughing at my wary expression, she added, "I was kidding by the way. I think Marcus will be just fine, especially because you'll be there." She leaned in and grabbed my hand, reassuring me.

Nodding, I shifted the focus back to her. "It must be hard to deal with the loss of your husband. Even after fifteen years, how did you find the strength to move on after losing the only man you've ever loved?"

Theresa looked as if she had just been punched in the gut. Removing her grasp from my hand, she leaned back in her chair and blankly stared at me. I felt beyond terrible. I didn't realize my words would be too painful for her to handle.

"Theresa, I'm sorry I didn't mean to . . . ."

She waved me off with a sway of her hand and shook her head. "No. That's the thing, Mia." She rested a fist under her chin as her eyes focused on mine. "That's why it was never easy to let go. The guilt . . . I just . . ." Her eyes began to water. She reached for a napkin and gently dabbed the cloth along her lids. I was confused by her reaction. There was definitely more behind the loss and mourning of her husband. It was as if she were carrying a burden that weighed heavily against her shoulders.

Looking back at me with wet eyelids, she pressed her lips together and studied me for a few seconds. "Can I confide something in you?"

Stunned by her instant change in demeanor, I simply nodded.

She wasn't convinced, "Mia, you have to promise me that you will never tell anyone. Okay?" Reaching for my hand, she gripped it tightly. "No one, Mia. Not even Marcus. Please promise me this."

Anxiety ran through me as I stared at the woman who was more damaged than I had assumed. So many scenarios sprinted through my mind as she begged me with her eyes to keep quiet. I wanted desperately for her to trust me and to be able to disclose anything.

But why was I so nervous? One side of my mind was yelling, "Please don't tell me!" The other side was saying, "Just tell me. I can handle it."

With that, I nodded, allowing her to spill her deepest and darkest secret.

***

As I entered the shopping center with both my mother and Megan, I nodded at their comments and suggestions. I was there physically—laughing, talking, and even trying on shoes—but my mind kept drifting back to Theresa and our discussion at lunch. I felt every bit of the pain and guilt from the load she had been carrying for so many years. I cried along with her as she confessed and spilled everything. How I could keep it from Marcus was beyond me, but it wasn't my secret to tell.

"Mia, are you okay, sweetie?" Sara, my mother, reached her hand out and tucked a strand of hair behind my ear.

Smiling at the gesture, I glanced at her, "Yes, I just have a lot on my mind."

"Ah, Marcus and you are doing fine?"

"Yes, we're doing better than fine. Thank you for asking."

"Good." She smiled and adjusted the few pieces of clothing that hung from her arm. "Are you going to try those on?" She pointed at the few blouses I held.

"No, I'm just going to grab them."

"Okay, I'm going to go to try these on. I have no idea where Megan ran off to, but I'll meet you at the register?"

"Sounds good." Slightly nodding, she turned and headed toward the dressing room.

With thoughts of Theresa and Marcus constantly running through my mind, I continued to rummage through racks of fabrics in the boutique. I had to try to forget the information Theresa had just confided in me. It was the only way I could stop feeling guilty for keeping it from Marcus. As my guilty feelings continued to pour out, I decided to send Marcus a text to apologize for my earlier encounter and to tell him that I loved him.

"Hey, Mia, look at this bad boy!" Looking up, I saw that Megan held a tiny piece of lingerie pressed against her.

"It's an oversize stocking, Megan."

Laughing, she stroked the fabric as if it were a fur pet. "What, you don't think I'll look hot in this? Jeremy will die! Well, after he bangs the hell out of me." She winked.

Shaking my head, I yanked the thin fabric out of her hands. It was a netted full body suit, with only a hole at the crotch area. "Yeah, he'll have a field day with this." I handed it back to her.

"Come on, you never dressed up for Marcus before?"

Yes, I had. I looked pretty damn hot too, but I also remembered waiting for over six hours for him and the night had taken a bad turn. I didn't want to go into that story with Megan. I nodded and headed toward the shoes in the store. She was following quickly behind me. "Have you ever stripteased for him?"

Frozen in place, I slowly turned. "No. Wait, have you?"

"Not with Jeremy, but with my ex back in Philly. You should so do it, Mia!" Her smile spread with her eyes wide open.

"I would be too embarrassed." Still, when Marcus stared at me naked, he never made me feel uncomfortable with my body. Instead, he made me feel sexy. He stared at me in awe, as if he had never seen a naked woman before, and I knew that wasn't true. Though standing in front of him, dancing, having him watch my every move—I could never do it.

"Oh come on, Mia. Take a few shots to loosen up. I'm telling you he'll love it! You can do it on the night of his birthday—a little birthday striptease and sex." She wiggled her perfectly arched brows. Then her face turned serious. "Besides, you still have that stupid bet going. You have a lot of making up to do."

Damn you, Megan. Damn you. I couldn't believe I was actually considering it. Megan could convince me sell my organs on the spot, and that comment about of a lot of making up to do hit me hard with guilt. "I wouldn't even know what to do, how to set it up, or what to wear?"

Crossing her arms, she dropped a hip and flashed a crooked smile. "Oh yeah, now I can finally teach you something. Come on. Let's go into the lingerie section. We have lots to do."

***

For the next few days, nothing major had occurred. Marcus and I saw each other when we could. On Wednesday, we went on a nice date on to the same Italian restaurant he took me on our first night together. It was nice to catch up with Mr. Giuseppe again; that old man had such a humble soul. We truly enjoyed his company. Marcus eventually got over the entire office teasing incident. He hadn't brought it up since, but I knew he was looking forward to getting together tonight. It marked two weeks since we had made our bet.

I should have jumped his bones the moment he picked me up, but I decided to let it drag a little longer because he was going to have me that night. He was dressed down in jeans and a white t-shirt, looking yummier than ever. How that was possible, I wasn't sure. He didn't mention the bet all week after the incident in his office, and he didn't mention it the entire ride to the movie theater either.

We talked about the exam that I had just passed. We discussed his birthday plans—he did not know that a surprise party was being planned by all of his family and friends. We even talked about the case he was preparing that that was supposed to have started on Monday. We talked about everything else except the bet. Had he forgotten?

We pulled into theater parking lot. Marcus walked around and opened the door for me. "Why thank you, Mr. DeLuca." Reaching for my hand, he smiled, shut the door behind me, and hit the alarm for his car.

"So what did you want to do after the theater?" He asked nonchalantly as we strolled side by side into the building.

Here it goes. He was going to bring it up. I was sure of it. Smiling, I leaned into him as I wrapped my arm around his waist. "Well, I was thinking we could go back to your house and hang out." I looked up at him with a broad smile. "I was thinking I could sleep over?"

"Sounds good to me. Which movie did you want to see?" He nodded toward the listings. I couldn't help sulking slightly as I stared at the selections. I was sure that his mood would have changed when I asked to sleep over. He acted as if it didn't faze him, which kind of upset me, so I chose the most non-manly, non-grim, non-action movie possible.

After grabbing our snacks and popcorn, we entered an empty theater. Marcus arched a brow at me. Okay, so I forced him to watch a chick flick. "Popular movie, huh?"

"It's been out for a while now. I heard it was good." He shook his head with a slight grin, as I followed him toward the back of the theater. We sat in the middle of the back row. After adjusting in my seat, I turned to face him. "I'm sorry for making you watch a chick flick. If you want, we can see something else. I can come back and watch this with Megan some other time."

He brought his hand up and cupped my face. "Babe, seriously, it's fine. Besides, we're the only ones here. We could practically get away with anything." He wiggled his brow.

I tossed some popcorn at him. "Play nice." I teased. He laughed and leaned back in his chair. I did, in fact, feel bad for forcing him to watch a romance movie.

We talked for a few minutes before the lights dimmed and the previews started.

Marcus wasted no time as he lifted the arm of the chair between us and scooted over. I followed his movement with my eyes.

His hand slowly rose up my skirt. He stopped midway as his fingers gently traced circles on my inner thigh. My insides tightened. I knew I was going to stop him, but as I nibbled on my bottom lip, I didn't. I wanted to test how far he would go. He stayed there gently stroking my inner thigh, teasing me with his touch. It was as if he were clueless to what he was doing, as if he didn't know the effect that small movement had on me.

I sucked in a ragged breath, and his lips curled into a slight smile. He focused on the screen as I watched him the entire time. His fingers moved again; this time he went further up. I swallowed hard as his fingertips played with the rim of my lace panties. My heart picked up its pace.

Pushing my panties aside, he rubbed his fingertips along my clit. Leaning back on the chair, he turned his head and focused on me. Humor washed from his face, and his eyes filled with desire, with want. I shut my eyes and tossed my head back on the chair as he slid two fingers inside of me. My insides were throbbing and yearning for him. I should have stopped him, but as I caught his wrist, I found myself guiding him in and out of me.

His skillful fingers continued working me, his thumb rubbing over my clit, as he leaned down and ran his tongue along my neck, towards my earlobe, sucking it in. I turned my chin, catching his mouth, and his tongue twirled, sucking along mine. My breathing became heavier as I became aroused. It was as if he knew my body better than I did. His finger thrust and pounced faster and harder into me. A moan escaped me as I gripped his shirt, digging my nails into him, and bit on his bottom lip to keep from screaming as I released all of the aching tension.

Sucking in air, my eyes flashed opened, and I stared at him. I wanted him in so many ways. The past two weeks had been haunting. I needed him inside me more than ever.

Unzipping his pants, with his hand coated in my wetness, he began stroking himself. Breathing heavily, I looked around. We were still alone. I had this instant adrenaline rush. I was turned on and nervous about the possibility of getting caught.

His eyes were dark and I knew he was ready. Reaching over, he pulled me in and on top of him. With my back pressed against his chest, I faced the large screen. Gripping my hips, he slid himself into me. I gasped.

Oh my God. My entire body shuddered at how good he felt. A burning and aching sensation shot through my core, and I wanted him deeper inside me. I wanted to feel all of him.

My head fell back onto his shoulder. Slowly, he rotated his hips as his fingers gripped onto my thighs. Matching him, I jerked my hips deep into him. I tightened my walls around his thickness as I raised my hips and slammed back down into him. "Fuck, Mia." He groaned in my ear. My body was sweaty and coursing with desire. I was on a high, and I didn't want to come down. He felt so good inside me. I felt him thick and hard with every movement of our hips. One of his hands was gripping my breast, while the other rubbed along my sensitive skin.

The sound of laughter caused me to stop. My eyes flashed open, and I noticed two women walking in and taking a seat at the bottom row far from us. My heart pounded against my chest. My eyes were still a blur from the high I was on. Catching my breath, I tried to move away, but Marcus gripped my thighs, digging his fingers into my flesh, and slammed me onto him again. The painful pleasure of it caused me to cry out slightly, but Marcus wrapped his hand around my mouth and pulled my head aside his.

"No." He growled in my ear. Pulling my hips away slowly with his free hand, he slammed me down against him again, that time harder. I began to pant. "I'm going to take you here." My head sank back into his shoulder in defeat. "I don't care who's around. I'm going to finish this. Do you understand?"

I nodded as he removed his hand from my mouth and cupped it around my throat. I wet my lips and shut my eyes. At that moment, I didn't care if we were caught. I moved my hips into his harder, grunting with each thrust. He sucked in air between his teeth, which caused me to be turned on even more. Again, I jerked my hips into his. Our breathing became heavier, our sweaty bodies molded against one another, and my nipples were hardened with desire.

The pleasure of it all, being with him, the thought of getting caught, and the last two weeks of the teasing built again deep within me. My body jerked against his as I convulsed for the second time around him. Tilting my head, I placed my forehead on the nape of his neck. He gripped my chin and shoved his tongue into my mouth, kissing me hard. Thrusting his hips, he bit down on my lip and groaned as he released himself deep inside me.

After a few minutes and with him still inside of me, we caught our breath as he gently patted soft kisses along my lips. Once our heartbeats came to a normal pace, Marcus gripped my chin and lifted it so that he could look at me. "We are never fuckin' going that long again. You understand?" Nodding, I let out a sigh in contentment. I one-hundred percent agreed. "Good, let's go home, so we can do that again." He winked.

CHAPTER NINE

MARCUS

I couldn't help but smile as she giggled beneath me. "Marcus, what are you doing?" Mia's eyelids flashed opened. I playfully flexed my hips into hers, and she let out another soft laugh. As she lay beneath me unclothed, with the warmth of her skin pressed against mine and the way her hair was tangled and tossed along the pillow, she was the most beautiful person I had ever seen. Even first thing in the morning.

Mia reached up and ran her fingers through my hair, as she placed her other hand on the side of my face. I brought her hand toward my lips, trailing soft kisses on her palm and down to her inner wrist. Mia's lips curled into a huge grin. Smiling along with her, I continued to stare into her eyes. I was intoxicated by her beauty, her scent, and, most of all, the love in those eyes for me. Right there was where I wanted to be always. I'd never felt so much peace in my life than when I was with her.

I lowered my head toward hers and traced my lips along the softness along her jawline. Making my way toward her ear, I could feel the goose bumps that formed along her skin. I kissed her in that sensitive spot underneath her earlobe then slowly down the side of her neck until I reached the middle of her collarbone. "Mmmh, I can never have enough of you." I purred along her skin. Her lips parted into a smile as she stretched beneath me.

"Well, I guess I should make you wait two weeks more often."

I shook my head and groaned at the thought. "No more ridiculous bets. You're mine, completely. I'll have you whenever and wherever I want."

Shaking her head, she giggled again and then changed the subject. "So what are we doing today?"

With my brows pressed together, I leaned in closer to her. "We're not going anywhere. I have plenty of things in mind that I have in store for you, but they all involve you, me, and the bed all day."

"So you're keeping me hostage here? What if I get hungry?" She asked as she batted her eyes innocently.

I gave her a crooked smile, "Well, if you get hungry, I have something to fill that appetite." I flexed my hips into her again.

"You. Are. Such. A. Guy!" She laughed.

"You know it, baby. Now come here."

***

"Bro, is your dick swollen?"

"Fuck off, Jimmie." I bit back as I opened the fridge door.

Bursting into a hard laugh, he put down the paper he was reading. "I'm just saying you haven't left your room all day. Fuck, I know Mia kept you hanging for a while, but did you have to seriously nail her the entire day? Poor girl." He shook his head. "She probably won't walk for the rest of the week."

Annoyed by his remark, I shut the fridge door, turned around to face him, and leaned against the counter as I snapped open a can of soda. Taking a few sips, I pointed at him. "You're jealous."

Snorting, Jimmie shook his head as he folded the paper. "Trust me. I'm not jealous."

"When was the last time you got laid, Bro?"

He raised a brow and stood from his chair. "That's none of your fuckin' business."

Laughing once, I nodded. "Yeah, just as I suspected, you're jealous."

"Whatever, man, are you able to still watch Elle tonight?"

Fuck. I'd forgotten about that. "Yeah man, what happened to that Melissa chick. You know her actual sitter?"

Jimmie rubbed his palm over his face. "She started college, remember?" Oh that's right. He did mention that. "I've been looking for a new sitter, but it's fuckin' hard to trust anyone nowadays." He pressed his hands down and leaned into the granite counter. "Look, if it's too much to ask, I can cancel my date with Jessica."

Mockingly, I smiled. "Ah, Jessica's her name, huh?"

"What's that supposed to mean?"

After I gulped down the rest of the soda, I tossed the can into the trash. "Nothing man, I just don't see you as a 'Jessica' type."

He raised a brow as he straightened his shoulders. I was starting to get under his skin, and as a younger brother, I couldn't help but find it amusing. "And what *type* do you see me with?"

I shrugged. "Fuck if I know."

"Whatever, man, are you able to watch Elle or not?"

"Yeah, that's cool. Will someone be getting laid tonight?" I wiggled my brows.

Before he could answer, Mia walked in. "Who's getting laid tonight?" She asked as she made her way toward us. She was wearing a pair of my pajama bottoms and t-shirt. Although it was loose on her, she managed to make it look completely sexy.

Jimmie shifted uncomfortably. I laughed at how awkward he felt about the discussion around Mia, and I decided to fuck with him some more. "Jimmie's going on another date tonight *with Jessica.*"

Mia's smile brightened. She scooted onto one of the stools at the end of the island, facing the both of us. "Ooh, *Jessica*, huh?"

I snorted. Jimmie glared at me, and I burst into a full-blown belly-aching laugh. Jimmie tossed his arms in the air. "What's wrong with the name Jessica?"

Mia's eyes switched from my laughing to Jimmie's concerned expression. "Nothing, it's a cute name. I knew a Jessica once. She was really sweet." She shrugged, trying to lighten the mood. "We should all go on a double date."

My laughing stopped and I straightened. Jimmie whipped his head in Mia's direction. "We've never been on a double date." I answered.

Jimmie nodded in agreement. "Yeah, that's awkward. I live with the dick. I rather not hang out with him too."

"Fuck you." I spat out.

Laughing, Mia ran a hand through her untamed hair and yawned. "Well, maybe a triple date with Megan and Jeremy also. We can go to Club21 to break the ice. Loud music and drinking?"

Jimmie looked as if he was actually considering the offer, and then he shrugged. "I'll ask her. Thanks, Mia." He turned and faced me. Lifting his hand, he flipped the bird. "Take care of my daughter, dickhead." He sent me a pointed glare, and without another word, he was gone.

After I shook my head, I went over to Mia. She turned on the stool, wrapped her arms around my waist, and pressed her head against my chest. I ran my fingers through her hair and began massaging her scalp.

"Mmh, that feels good."

Smiling, I continued to massage her, tracing my fingers in circular motions. "Are you hungry?"

"I'm starving." She mumbled.

Laughing, I made my way down toward her shoulders and began working my magic there. She tossed her head back. Her eyelids fluttered. "Ugh, that feels good. I'm so sore."

"I wonder why." I flashed a grin.

She shook her head and smiled. "You're too much."

"Well, I've heard that too much is a good thing."

Mia snorted and arched a brow mockingly. "Well, whoever said that was clearly mistaken."

Before I could reply, the doorbell rang. Mia, with a confused expression, tilted her head toward the door. "Were you expecting anyone?"

"No. I'll be back. Stay here." I made my way toward the front door. Of course, Mia couldn't wait in the kitchen, and she treaded along behind me.

Without saying a word, I opened the door to find Gio standing on the other end of it. "What are you doing here?" I asked as Mia gripped my bicep and pushed up on her toes to have a better look.

"We need to talk." His eyes traced over my shoulder and landed on Mia. Gio's brows rose with a full-blown smile. "Are you *the* Mia I've heard so much about?"

Rolling my eyes, I stepped aside so he could enter. Closing the door behind him, I took a quick glance at Mia. "Mia, this is . . . my friend, Gio."

Mia roughly ran a hand through her hair then tugged at the t-shirt she wore. "Sorry for my appearance." Smiling, she reached her hand out to shake his. "Nice to meet you, Gio. I've never met any of Marcus's friends."

Smiling, he continued to ogle her. "I see nothing wrong with your appearance." Mia's face flushed. What the fuck was that about? At that moment, I felt a surge of jealously rush through me.

"Gio, you can go into my office right through there while I grab a shirt." I pointed toward the door. He nodded, waved at Mia again, and then headed toward my office.

"Mia, come with me." I gripped her wrist and dragged her toward the stairs. I was angry, even though it wasn't her fault, but the way he was looking at her and the look she gave back to him filled me with a possessive rage. I had just gotten her back, and I was not going to lose her to anything or anyone. Call me an overbearing, over-protective and over-possessive boyfriend. I don't give a fuck.

The thing that bothered me most about the relationship I had with Mia was the jealousy I felt when someone looked at her. I knew men could stare, but the possibility of Mia taking action on it made my every nerve burn with anger.

Mia trampled behind me and pulled on the grip I held. "Marcus, can you loosen your hold?" I shook away the thoughts and let go of her wrist. Once I entered my room, I pulled open the drawer, removing a shirt. Tossing it on, I turned and Mia was standing a few feet away with a serious expression.

"Who is he really?" Mia blurted with a demanding tone. Crossing her arms, she dropped a hip. "If he were a friend, you wouldn't be acting the way you are."

"And how is that?"

She waved a hand up and down the length of me. "Your entire demeanor changed, Marcus. The moment he walked through the door. You seem angry or agitated with something . . . with me even." Her brows pressed together. "We were fine a few minutes ago. Hell, we've been fine for a couple of weeks now. I don't know." Mia shook her head and then let out a deep breath. "Maybe I'm overthinking it."

Great. I'm a fucking asshole. Bending my head back, I let out a heavy sigh and rubbed the palm of my hands over my face. Mia had her arms wrapped around my waist and her head pressed against my chest before I could register that she had moved from where she was. "Marcus, sometimes I have no clue what goes on in that head of yours. It can be frustrating in so many ways. Either way, I still love you."

My arms tugged around her as I pressed my lips on top of her head. "I love you too, Mia." Fuck, I did. I loved that woman more than she'd ever know. "There's no need to worry about Gio. He's an old friend. That's all." I kept the fact that Gio was Lou's nephew hidden because I knew how she felt about Lou, and I truly didn't want to spark another issue. "Can you go see what Elle wants to eat for dinner, and I'll take care of Gio?" Mia nodded, squeezed me tightly one last time, and then made her way toward Elle's room.

Gio stood by the oversized mirror toward the right side of my office. His head was tilted as he continued to admire it. He turned and faced me at the sound of the door shutting behind me. "This is an interesting object you have here, Marky. The carving in the frame is quite unique. The mirror stands alone as an art piece."

"It's an original. I had it designed." I pointed toward the side bar. "Would you like a drink?"

With a wave of his hand, he gave the mirror one last quick glance and then sat on a chair by my desk. "Nah, I'm good. I've cut back on drinking. You should try it. You'll see a huge difference in your mood swings."

I sat behind my desk as I bit down on my tongue before responding, "I don't have fuckin' mood swings." I grew agitated as he laughed at himself. "What did you need to talk about?"

Gio smiled and leaned into the desk. "The club, we need it."

"No. Was that all?"

Raising a brow, his expression grew serious. "I wasn't asking, Marky. You haven't found a suitable place for exchanges, and the shitty ones we've been going to are starting to look bad for business." He leaned back in the chair. "We have an important exchange next month, Marky. We need the space."

I folded my hands, leaned into the desk, and stared at him, with all of the possible other places running through my head. Gio was right. None of them were suitable. "I have people in and out of my club all of the time. What if a deal goes wrong? And where do you expect to do these exchanges?"

"I've visited your club a few times now. There's a separate entrance to the basement. It's fuckin' huge too. There's nothing down there but a few pieces of unused furniture. The entrance is on the left side of the building away from the front entry and the back parking lot. It's perfect."

"Gio, it's too fuckin' public. Lou has always wanted to keep his exchanges low-key. Why is he suddenly pushing the issue of doing them at my club?

Standing, he adjusted his jacket. "I never know why my uncle chooses half the shit he does, but he's Lou. He can fuckin' do anything he damn well pleases. With that said, we're using the club."

It was the worst fucking idea Lou had thought of yet. Nothing good would come of it.

CHAPTER TEN

MIA

"Mia, would you come here, sweetheart? I'd like to introduce you to someone." Theresa shouted from across the room. I raised a finger at her to give me a second and then turned my attention back to the chef.

"So we're all clear for the menu tonight?" I asked him.

The chef nodded, "Yes, ma'am, I have it all under control. I began prepping the hors d'oeuvres for the cocktail hour. I have here. . ." He looked down at the clipboard he held in his hand. "No mushrooms due to allergies. Correct?"

"Yes, please, no mushrooms. My boyfriend's niece is highly allergic."

"Okay, I'm all set. Hors d'oeuvres are to be served at six this evening and dinner will begin at eight."

"Perfect. Thank you so much." I patted his shoulder then began making my way down the room.

It was the weekend of Marcus's thirtieth birthday party, and it also marked three weeks since we'd been back together. It felt as if we'd never left each other's side. We'd become closer in a way that was much more than just sexual or even a romantic relationship—we had built a friendship as well. He had confided in me and discussed memories or issues he had been struggling with ever since his father's death. The fact that we had both tragically lost beloved family members had bonded us and allowed us to express feelings that others would not understand.

"Miss Sullivan," a voice poked through my thoughts. "Where would you like the equipment set up?" One of the band members asked.

"There's a tent set up on the patio. You can put your equipment down in the far right corner." He nodded and then brushed past as he held an amp in his arms.

After a few more interruptions, I finally caught up with Theresa. "Mia, this is Leo, the party planner."

"Hi, Leo." I shook his hand. I was happy he had made it and was able to take over from here. We discussed all the plans over the phone the past week, but he was running late today and couldn't make it until the afternoon. Marcus's home had been a hellhole the entire day.

"I'm here now, Mia. You and Theresa can run off and get ready. By the time you're back, it will be spectacular."

"Thank God!" I let out a heavy sigh.

"Where's the birthday boy and what time is he expected?"

I pulled out my phone from my back pocket and checked the time. "Well, he's out with his brother. Jimmie took him away for a brotherly bonding day. Jimmie will bring him back around six-thirty. That will give plenty of time for people to arrive."

"Wonderful. Three hours is plenty of time for me to have it all set up. Everything and everyone is accounted for, so I will take this out of your hands." He took the clipboard from Theresa.

Theresa and I eyed each other. It was a relief that we were no longer handling it, but it was also somewhat nerve-wracking handing over all the hard work to someone else. Theresa shrugged and passed the clipboard over.

"Want a drink? We deserve it." Theresa said as she wrapped her arm around my shoulder.

Shrugging, I looked at her and smiled. "Sure, why not?" We both laughed as we headed toward the bar.

A few martinis later, I was relaxed. Guests would be arriving in a couple of hours, so I began getting ready.

I showered, put my makeup on, and pinned my hair into a low curled-up bun with tendrils falling from the back. After dressing, I stood in front of the mirror inside of Marcus's walk-in closet. My black dress was very straightforward with a simple neck line that lay along my collarbone, although the silk fabric hugged my curves and landed mid-thigh. I twirled around to check out the back of the dress, which was the best feature—the dress draped, exposing my skin as the fabric landed on my lower back. The dark grey platform pumps I wore had a bit of sparkle on them, allowing the dress to pop.

After I finished getting dressed, I made sure Marcus's room was set up perfectly as well. I had a surprise for him and wanted that night to be special. Last time I had tried to surprise him, everything went wrong, but there was no way I was allowing his birthday to be ruined. Jimmie promised to have him back thirty minutes after the party guests were scheduled to arrive.

After I was finished, I made my way downstairs.

I was in complete shock from how quickly Leo had gotten everything set up in the party area. It was beautiful and simple like Marcus. Candles burned on top of the linen-covered tables as twinkling lights sparkled throughout the outdoor tent. Vases of all sorts of shapes and sizes surrounded the inside, full of large flower arrangements. Laughter sounded in the room as guests began to enter. I hadn't recognized anyone yet. I assumed they were friends of Theresa, rather than family and friends of Marcus. I looked around until I spotted Theresa, who was speaking to an older gentleman. She was dressed in an emerald sleeveless cocktail dress. Her hair dropped down her back in flawless waves. She was absolutely stunning.

"Mia?" A familiar tone trickled through my mind. Spinning around, I couldn't help the slight squeal that escaped me when I saw Romeo standing a few feet away, looking more handsome than ever. With a smile, I pulled him into a hug.

"Romeo, how are you?" I squeezed my arms tightly around him. The last time I saw him was in this very house as he sat in the kitchen with a bruised and bloody face. We pulled away from our embrace. His eyes danced with humor.

"I'm doing well, Mia. Well, school's a bitch." He laughed. "But I've been okay. How 'bout you?"

Grabbing his face, I studied his features. There was a slight scar over his brow where the cut that I had once nursed for him used to be. A slight frown formed on my lips. "I'm doing well." I brushed a finger over the scar. His eyes averted as his grin fell. I didn't want to bring down the moment, so in an upbeat tone, I said, "Well, have you stolen any girl's heart yet?"

He burst into a loud laugh. "Nah, no one wants me."

"Are you kidding? You're gorgeous!" Playfully, I lightly nudged his arm. "I'm sure you have tons of girls after you." He was gorgeous. He was the younger version of Marcus with his dark brown hair, chocolate sparkling eyes, and million-dollar smile. He was surely a heartbreaker.

"Yeah, okay, whatever you say, Mia." Changing the topic, he looked around the room. "So is this still supposed to be a surprise or has Marcus figured it out?"

"As far as I know, it's still a surprise, unless Jimmie spilled the beans while they were out."

Romeo raised a brow. "Jimmie and Marcus are hanging out together?"

"Yeah, I sent them off to have some brotherly bonding. They're drinking and hanging out."

Sucking his teeth, he smiled mockingly. "Yeah, good luck with that. I'm sure by now they've gotten into a fist fight and Jimmie ruined the entire surprise." My expression fell. "Just kidding, Mia. I'm sure it'll be fine." He laughed. Shaking my head, I gave him one last hug and then went off to find Theresa.

For the next hour, I was introduced to a decent amount of people. There were a total of fifty guests by the time six-thirty rolled around. The nerves trembled in my stomach as I anticipated Marcus's arrival. The martinis I'd consumed in the short period of time to calm my nerves were beginning to take effect. Grabbing another drink, I made my way toward the living room and leaned against a wall, observing my surroundings. Several groups were engaged in conversations: one in particular was laughing to a few jokes told by Uncle Marty, another group seemed to be in a serious discussion, while a few of the women sipped on glasses of wine and talked about the latest gossip.

"Mia?" A deep male's tone sounded beside me.

Tilting my head, I stared up at a five-foot-eleven, nicely built man. His gentle light brown eyes met mine. "Hello, I'm sorry. Do I know you?" I felt rude for not knowing who he was, but it was clear that he knew me.

"I'm Vinnie, a friend of Marky's."

Vinnie? The name sounded familiar and then it dawned on me from my recent conversations with Marcus. "Oh yes! He's mentioned you lots of times. He refers to you as his 'right hand man.'" I laughed.

Vinnie nodded with a wide smile. "Yeah, that's what he tells me. It's nice to finally meet you." He reached out his hand, and I took it.

"Nice to finally meet you too. I don't meet many of Marcus's friends, but he talks fondly of you."

"Ha, that's good to know. So next time he's grilling me about a job, I'll make sure to mention that."

"Don't tell him you heard it from me!" I stabbed a finger at his arm.

"I won't, although, it'll probably save my ass." We both laughed.

Vinnie and I continued to talk as we waited until the lights went off in the room, getting our attention. "Okay, everyone, Marcus will be here in five minutes. Please gather around." Theresa's voice pierced through the room. My heart crushed heavily against my chest as I straightened my posture but remained against the wall. I could hear footsteps scattering around the hardwood surface as people attempted to reach the entrance. After a few minutes, the whispers had died down when tires screeched along the driveway.

My lips curled into a smile after I heard the car door shut following the sound of Marcus and Jimmie's voices. The sound of their boots crunching against the gravel surface came closer as their laughter erupted. After the jingling sound of the keys, the door opened, and then the lights flicked on.

"Surprise!" Everyone yelled.

Stretching my neck, I tried to look over the crowd that had formed around Marcus. I had yet to see him and had totally missed his reaction. I knew he was in the center of the crowd because I could hear family and friends yelling and wishing him a happy birthday. There was no way I was going to be able to push through that crowd, so I stayed in place until I felt I could get to him. "Happy birthday, Baby!" Theresa squealed. My eyes moved toward the right, where I saw that Theresa had thrown her arms tightly around Marcus. My entire body relaxed at the sight of him. He seemed thrilled by everyone's presence. When he finally looked up, his eyes locked with mine. After thanking his mother, he made his way toward me.

With a bright smile, I moved forward toward him until we met in the middle. "Happy birthday," I mouthed. Without a single word, he pulled me into him, wrapping my arms around his neck. I looked up. "Have you been drinking?" I asked, the answer written all over his eyes and the smell of beer lingering on him.

With a lazy smile, he pulled me in tighter, "Yeah, Jimmie and I were playing a drinking game." He shrugged. Laughing, I shook my head and reached up for a kiss. "Marky!" Uncle Marty shouted from behind. Marcus pulled away from the kiss and rolled his eyes before he turned around. Uncle Marty held two shot glasses in his hand and gave one to Marcus. The both of them clinked glasses and downed the shot. More family members approached him with drinks.

"Sorry, Mia." Jimmie said from beside me.

Crossing my arms, I looked up at him and smiled. "No, it's fine. As long as he has good time, that's all that matters." Sighing, I looked over at Marcus, who was surrounded by a few more men with shot glasses. "As long as he behaves too." I knew how Marcus could sometimes turn into a sloppy drunk as I recalled our unpleasant encounter at Club21 with Boston Barbie.

Jimmie placed his hand on my shoulder. "I'm usually the first person that's against Marcus drinking, but trust me. He's been doing well with it." He shrugged and averted his stare toward Marcus as well. "And we really had fun hanging out." I simply nodded with a bright smile. It was nice to hear that they enjoyed themselves together. After a few minutes, I went toward the bar that was set up for the night and grabbed another martini.

Within the next hour, I was approached by a few family members and friends of the DeLucas. The party was going well, and I couldn't have been happier with the outcome. Marcus and I barely had time to look at each other, but I expected that when his house was flooded with over eighty guests. Feeling more at ease, I settled onto a bar stool and continued to sip my drink. That was when I saw Jeremy approaching me. His lips curled into a small grin, but I could tell from the look in his eyes that there was something troubling him.

"Hey," he said, reaching in and tapping a kiss on my cheek.

With both brows pinned together, I studied him, "Hey. Everything okay?" I searched behind his shoulder. "Where's Megan?"

Jeremy averted his eyes as he sank into the stool beside me. "I'm not sure. She'll probably show up though." Raising a finger at the bartender, he ordered himself a shot and a bottle of beer.

"What happened, Jeremy?" He didn't answer me, but instead waited patiently for his drinks. After the bartender placed his drinks on the table, Jeremy downed his shot and chugged the beer. "Jeremy?"

He ordered another beer and then turned to face me, annoyed by my continued badgering.

"She found out about us."

Taken aback, it took me a few seconds to collect my thoughts. "What do you mean *us*?"

He grabbed the new beer and took a long pull but kept his eyes remained on me. "She knows that we slept together . . . several times."

"What?" My heart began to race. *This could not be happening.* "How did it come up?"

He shook his head. "I don't even know. First, she asked about my past relationships, and then she asked playfully if you and I had ever hooked up, and it just slipped. I wasn't sure if you had told her, and I wanted to be honest."

I tried to think of words to comfort him. I knew Jeremy was beginning to develop strong feelings for my cousin, and that information could ruin them as a couple. As I placed my hand on his shoulder, I caught sight of Megan. She was stunning in a red mini cocktail dress. The light brown waves of her hair framed her face beautifully. Her eyes were usually hazel with a hint of yellow in them, but her golden and brown eye shadow caused her eyes to have more of a green sparkle. She stood tall with her shoulders straight as she waved her hand awkwardly at me. A tiny smile formed on her lips.

Taking in a deep breath, I leaned into Jeremy. "Megan is here. I'm going to have a talk with her. Everything will be okay."

He couldn't help himself as he twirled around in the stool and stared at her. His brows kneaded together as his eyes stared at her with so much passion. His body slightly jerked as he stopped himself from moving toward her. Megan looked away, ran a shaky hand through her hair, and let out a breath. I patted Jeremy's shoulder one last time to assure that I would take care of it, and moved my way toward Megan. Every step I took, I began to come up with several scenarios of how it might play out.

I wrapped my arms around her when I reached her and pulled her into a tight hug. "You look so beautiful, Megan."

Her arms returned the gesture as she hugged me even tighter. "You do too, as always." Her voice cracked a bit.

"Let's go out back where it's quieter so we can talk. Okay?" I asked. We broke from our embrace after she nodded and walked toward the back yard side by side with our arms interlocked with one another.

As we stepped out onto the cobblestone patio, the cool breeze whipped through us, giving me a slight chill. There were a few guests in the tent where the band and tables were set up. Others were lurking around the patio, drinking or smoking cigars as they laughed and enjoyed the party.

Spotting an empty corner, I nodded my head towards a seating area. Megan led the way and then sat down on one of the wicker chairs. I took a seat across from her, crossed my legs, and leaned in, placing my elbow on my knee.

Megan leaned back into the chair as she crossed her arms, and turned her head to study a group of men that were laughing on the other end of the patio. "I guess he told you." She had finally spoken in a low tone.

"Not much, but he did, in fact, say that he told you about him and me."

A mocking laugh escaped her lips. "More like it slipped." She paused, shook her head, and then turned her chin to fully look at me. "You know, Mia, the fact that the two of you slept together doesn't bother me. Well, it does a little, but I know it happened before I came along. I think what bothers me the most is that, despite all of the women he's been with, the last person I thought I ever had to compete with was you."

It was shocking to hear her say that. I leaned in closer. "There's no competition, Megan. None. Jeremy and my relationship can be a bit difficult for others to understand. When we slept together, it was after Michael's death, during a time that I felt so much sadness and loneliness." I forced a smile. "Jeremy even said he kicks himself in the ass for allowing it to go as far as it did, because I was so vulnerable. Don't get me wrong. He did not take advantage of me, but I just wanted to forget about the pain, and at the time, I thought that was the only way to go about it." Closing my eyes, I took in a deep breath, and after exhaling, I opened my lids. "Now, thinking back on it, it was dumb, wasn't it?"

"No, it's not dumb. I understand. I also see how close you two are. He opens up to you more than he does to me. I wonder if he'll ever be like that way with me."

Scooting toward the edge of my seat, I reached and placed my hand on her knee in a way to comfort her. "Don't you see how special you are to him? I've never seen him react towards any woman the way he has with you. He truly cares about you, Megan. He's frightened. That's all. Jeremy has issues with commitment. I think it might have to do with dealing with his parents' divorce at a young age. He's afraid if he lets all of his feelings out that they might get ripped away from him."

Megan sat there in silence for a moment, considering what I'd said. Leaning toward me, her eyes glistened as she held back tears. She placed her hand on top of mine, "Do you really think he cares for me as much as I do for him?"

A smile of assurance touched my lips. "Yes, I truly believe he does. I know Jeremy, and he is completely strung out." She laughed out loud and quickly wiped away two tear drops that escaped. "Go talk to him, Megan." She pressed her lips together and nodded. Before standing to leave she pulled me into a tight hug.

"Thank you so much, Mia. I love you."

"I love you too. Now go get your man." We laughed together, gave one last squeeze, and then she left in search of Jeremy. Feeling a bit better and dazed from the alcohol, I sank into the chair, tossed my head back, and stared into the night sky.

Dinner hadn't been announced yet, and I was already exhausted. *What a long day it had been.* I was looking forward to snuggling in bed beside Marcus. I could hear his laughter coming from somewhere in the house. It wasn't hard to miss. It'd made me smile, knowing he was enjoying himself, and the exhaustion I was feeling was well worth it. When I thought of making my way back in, I heard a familiar voice come out of the darkness. "My night has just gotten better. Well, if it isn't the one and only Mia Sullivan."

My. Entire. Body. Froze.

Every sound around me went faint. All I could hear was the sound of my heart thrashing against the cage of my chest. It burned as I tried to gasp air through the tightness of my throat. My mouth went dry, the palms of my hands beaded with sweat, and the hair on the back of my neck stood on end. Every thought about the man behind that voice sped through my mind. I wanted that moment to pass, for him to go away. I sat with my eyes shut tightly, dreadfully hoping and wishing that that moment was a nightmare. But it wasn't. The sound of his shoes treading against the cobblestones came to a halt. Fear had crept into my veins as I felt his presence directly beside me.

Then rage.

A wrath of emotion erupted deep within me. I was fuming with anger, my shaky breathing became heavier, and my skin seared with heat. I fought against my will and my eyes flashed open. His frame slightly hovered over me as he stared down at me smiling with a grin that I wanted desperately to smack off his face. Removing the cigar from between his teeth, he let out a quick puff and gave a curt nod. "Don't you remember me, sweetheart?" Oh, I remembered him alright. I remembered him with every fiber of my being. Anyone who was ever so unfortunate to meet him could never forget.

Lou Sorrento.

At that moment, I stood to face him. He tilted his head aside, and his lips curled into a full-toothed grin. He looked exactly as I remembered: his salt and pepper hair was his only age indicator. Although he wasn't taller than Marcus, he still stood as a powerful man—a man with a power that came from years of barking off orders. A man that could put a gun to someone's head and pull the trigger with a smile splashed across his face. A man without a care in the world except for himself, not even my brother.

Angrily, I bit down on my lip as I stared at him with nothing but hate. Although I stood calm, my mind was screaming and racing with so much rage. I visualized myself shoving him to the ground and pounding my fists into him until I saw blood. That bothered me. I was never a violent woman or wished harm against anyone, but being in the presence of Lou possessed me to be one. Who gave Lou Sorrento the right to walk this earth? He deserved to be six feet underground, not my brother. Michael deserved to be alive, not Lou.

Who gave him the right!

I slightly shook my head as I tried and fought back the tears. I would not give him that. I would not show one ounce of fear or the effect he had on me. Lou Sorrento, did not value any of my emotions: good or bad. He deserved one thing and one thing only: death.

I wished him a long and painful death.

His eyes slightly squinted as he took another puff of his cigar. "You're bleeding, sweetheart." He glanced at my lips.

His remark distanced me from my trance. Confused, I wiped my hand along my chin. Blood was dripping from my lip. I'd bitten down so hard that I'd punctured through the flesh. The metallic taste of the blood was potent as I sucked my bottom lip in, squeezing as much as I could. "Excuse me." I mumbled as I made my way past him. I rushed away from Lou, as fast and far as I could.

I rushed through the crowded room in search of anyone familiar. I finally spotted Megan and Jeremy by the bar, laughing and flirting, in a much better state than earlier. I headed toward them. As I got closer, Marcus came into view. He was beside Jeremy, ordering more shots. "There's my girl." He said with a huge smile. "Where you been? I missed you."

After a few deep breaths, I forced a smile and leaned into his open arms. "I've been around. Are you having fun?" I tried to steady my voice.

"I'm having a blast. Thank you for everything. I love you." He leaned in and planted wet kiss on my cheek.

I wanted nothing but to join in his happiness at that moment, but after the encounter with Lou, I couldn't push him away from my thoughts. Clinging to Marcus, I tightened my eyes and desperately tried to rid myself of the memory of the man I hated more than anyone or anything.

"Hey." Marcus placed two fingers under my chin and lifted my face so that he could look at me. "Are you okay?" Although he wasn't slurring, I could tell how much alcohol he had consumed by the bloodshot look in his eyes. That was exactly where I wanted to be, in the same drunken state of mind as him.

"I don't think I'm drunk enough." I mumbled.

A smile formed along his lips. "Well, let me take care of that for you." He reached over to the counter where there were a few filled shot glasses and grabbed two. Handing me one, we clinked glasses, smiled, and downed the shots. The warmth and burning sensation that the shot of whisky caused was a better reaction than I'd anticipated. Nodding, I glanced at Marcus and asked for another one.

That night, I would get rid of the pain, the bad memories, and allow alcohol and Marcus to take it all away.

CHAPTER ELEVEN

MARCUS

"Dinner is ready. Sorry for the delay." My mother announced.

By that time, there were so many guests in my home, and all I wanted was the night to end. I looked around as all the guests followed my mother's directions toward the back where dinner would be served.

Mia stumbled into my chest. I wrapped my arms around her to stay balanced. I'd been drinking since this afternoon with Jimmie, and I still wasn't as intoxicated as she was at that moment. Leaning into the side of her face, I brushed a few tendrils of hair behind her ear as I whispered, "Let's go upstairs."

Her eyes flashed up toward me. "No, your mother will be angry if we miss dinner." She hiccupped.

Smiling, I ran the back of my fingers along her soft cheek. "She'll be fine, Mia. Let's go upstairs." I wrapped my arm around her shoulder and maneuvered her toward the stairway.

Mia came to a stop, causing both of us to slightly jerk. She turned to face me. "But, Marcus, it's your birthday. We can't end it early." She swallowed and stared at me with beady, gleaming eyes. "We haven't even sung happy birthday yet."

Megan came up beside us. "Do you need help, Marcus?" I quickly glanced around and saw that Jeremy had remained seated by the bar.

"Yes, please. Can you take Mia up to my room? It's the last door at the end of the hall." Nodding, Megan tossed Mia's arm around her shoulder. "I'll be up in a few, Mia." She caved in with a simple nod and allowed Megan to guide her up the stairs.

I ran a hand over my face as I let out a deep sigh. I was beyond drunk. But I was able to handle my liquor better than Mia, obviously.

"Marky! You're a hard man to get a hold of." I felt a hand clasp my shoulder and turned to see who it was.

"Lou, I didn't think you would make it. Did you just arrive?" Thankfully, Mia was upstairs and had just missed him. I relaxed my shoulders.

"And miss my nephew's thirtieth? Ah, that hurts." He placed his hand over his chest, pretending that he was wounded. "Nope, I've been here for about an hour now. I was catching up with a few old friends." He looked around me. "So where's that gorgeous girl of yours? We ran into each other earlier. She seemed upset and left. I hope I didn't scare her off." Lou's eyes squinted, and he focused on my reaction to that comment.

Fuck. That was the reason why Mia wanted to drink. It wasn't like her to lose control unless something was bothering her. Why didn't I realize that earlier?

Shrugging, I patted his shoulder, "She's been like that for a few days. Personal issues she's dealing with. Don't take it personally. Thank you for coming." I played it off. He nodded, and I gave his shoulder a tight squeeze when I caught sight of my mother. Curious, I excused myself from Lou and made my way toward her.

"Mom, are you okay?" I asked as I reached her.

She blinked a few times, let out a deep breath, and then glanced up at me. "Oh yes, baby, I'm fine. You seem drunk." She smiled lightly as she reached out her hand and cupped my face. "I'm guessing you're having a good time?"

"Yes, thank you. It was great, but I'm going to call it a night."

Her brows bunched together, "Oh? It's still so early, Marcus."

"I know. I'm sorry. Mia is upstairs. She drank a little more than usual and so have I."

She smiled with understanding and then nodded. I leaned down, squeezed my fragile mother in a tight hug, and thanked her one last time before heading up the stairs.

While I was walking down the second floor hallway, Megan had exited my bedroom with her head lowered as she laughed to herself. When she looked up, she burst out laughing again at my questioning stare. "Oh my God, Marcus, she's so drunk." She patted my arm when we met in the middle.

"How drunk?" I asked, concerned she may have been sick.

"Let's just say that she had something planned for you and she insisted she wanted to still go through with it. I had to help her get ready."

With a raised brow, I quickly glanced at the closed bedroom door and back at her. "Thanks, Megan."

She laughed again, shook her head, and headed back down the hall toward the stairs.

I closed the door behind me as I entered my room. The lights were dim, candles burned all around, and soft music played in the background. My lips curled into a smile as my eyes scanned the room, but I couldn't find her. I was slowly making my way further into the dark room when she stumbled out of the bathroom. My heart raced at the sight of how beautiful she was: her hair down in waves tossed over her shoulders and a short thigh-revealing red silk robe wrapped around the curves of her body. She stood in black heels that caused her to seem taller.

Mia let out a barely noticeable smile as she slowly and seductively made her way toward me. In the few steps it took for her to reach me, my heart pounded with each one. I couldn't get enough of her. Every single aspect of her drove me insane with want, desire, love, and so much more.

She slightly tripped into me and let out a light snicker as she tried to straighten herself. She didn't say a word as she ran her hands under my shirt, taking it with her as she went up. I lifted my arms as she pulled it over my head. She held the fabric of my shirt on a finger, allowing it to dangle there for a few seconds before she tossed it over her shoulder. Mia kept her eyes locked with mine as she ran her finger across my bare skin, and then she leaned in and pressed her lips along my chest.

The warm touch of her lips shot an electrifying current through me. Mia pulled back and continued to stare at me as her finger slowly made its way down, past my abs, down my torso, plunging toward the rim of my jeans. She teased and twirled her finger along my lower abdomen, causing a tingling sensation in my groin. She smiled as she took notice of the goose bumps that formed along my skin.

Impatient, I leaned down to kiss her, but she shook her head as she waved a well-manicured finger in my face. I couldn't help the smile that crept along my lips from amusement. Mia glanced up through her long lashes. Her eyes were the most beautiful I'd ever seen: big emerald green eyes, with long curled brown lashes. "Not yet." She whispered through luscious red lips.

She began to unbuckle my belt and jeans. "I want to make love to you, Marcus." She lowered herself, bending and bringing my pants down with her. I slid out of my boots and removed my jeans completely. As she stood straight again before me, she wrapped her hands around my neck. "Will you make love to me?" She asked her eyes back on mine, though they seemed to sadden for a mere second. Confused, I framed her face with my hands.

"What's wrong?" I asked, and then it dawned on me. "I saw Lou downstairs. I know you ran into him. Do you want to talk?"

Her eyes snapped up. "No, I don't want to talk about him." Her face softened. "I want to forget about it." She brought her hands down and pressed them along my chest and began moving me forward. I took a few steps back with every step she took. She stumbled a few times, so I placed my hands on her elbows to keep her balanced, until the back of my legs touched the bench in front of my bed. I took a seat on top of it. Mia ran her fingers through my hair. With her eyes closed, she stumbled out of her heels. I gripped her waist as she slightly swayed.

"I'm supposed to give you a striptease." She slightly pouted.

I bit back a laugh. "Says who?"

She shrugged. "That was the plan for tonight." She stated as she leaned into my lap and straddled me. Wrapping her arms around my neck, she pressed her forehead down to mine. "But all I want is for you to pull me in close to you, kiss me, love me, and hold me." She brought a hand around and grabbed my face, lifting my chin, our lips mere inches away. "It's just you and I, always. When you touch me, there's no one else in this world. No one. It's just us." I knew that she was drunk, but Mia's declaration tugged at my chest. I loved that woman more than anything, and to hear that she felt the same way about me triggered an emotion stronger than I'd ever felt for her, if that was even possible.

Her eyes flashed toward my mouth. She puckered her lips and lightly kissed me. "Make love to me, Marcus. Make me forget where we are." She whispered against my lips. I groaned at her request and opened my mouth, allowing her access as she drove her tongue right in. I savored every bit of her taste as she thrust her tongue deeper with a slight moan. I couldn't help the growl that escaped at the scent of her perfume, the feel of the tug as she gripped into my hair, and the way her body molded into mine—as if we were meant for one another in every way possible.

Breathless, she pulled away from the kiss. I tried to catch my breath as she stood in front of me and slowly pulled on the strings of her robe, allowing the thin fabric to fall on the floor, revealing the most perfect naked body. I stood to face her and looked down at what was mine. She was mine. Mia wasn't afraid to let go. She wanted to be taken, to be possessed, to lose all control, and I did that for her.

Mia shut her eyes as I ran my fingers up her arm, twirled them around her shoulder, and made my way toward her collarbone. Wrapping my hand around the back of her neck, I pulled her in and crushed my lips against hers. She weakened in my arms. Still kissing, we slowly made our way toward the edge of the bed; I guided her as she stepped back. Once we reached the bed, she tossed herself on top of the mattress.

Admiring her once again, I slightly hovered over her as she leaned up, bringing her lips back to mine. Our tongues twirled and twisted into another passionate and scorching kiss. Then something came over her: Mia pushed me aside, forcing me to lie on my back. There was a burning desire in her eyes as she traced her tongue down my torso and toward my groin. She pulled my briefs off, and my lips slightly parted as she grabbed me and slowly jerked her hand up and down my length.

Wetting her lips, she dragged her teeth along her bottom lip, and then she glanced up at me one last time. She then traced her tongue around the tip of my cock. Fuck. I tossed my head back as soon as she sucked and took me in her mouth. In consistent strokes, she continued to work her way up and down, topping it off with a flick of her tongue, and then sucked me in again. The pleasure was uncontrollable. "Fuck, Mia." I gripped the back of her head and forced myself deeper in her mouth. She moaned and began jerking her head at a faster pace.

"Mia, I'm 'bout to fuckin' explode." She ignored me and continued with her strokes. I felt it coming, so I gripped her head with both hands and forced her down on me again and again. I throbbed inside her mouth, and she let out loud moans that forced the pressure to build in me. With each glide up and down my cock, she tightened her grip around me again and again until I couldn't take it anymore.

Slamming my head back into the mattress, I groaned as I released the building pressure. After a few seconds, Mia lifted her head and climbed her way on of top me. I tried to turn over so that I could exchange the favor, but she stopped me. "No, I want this to be for you." Puzzled, I rose on my elbows but sank back down the moment she slid me into her. She caught my wrist and brought my hands to her breasts. I traced my fingers along her hardened nipples. Mia tossed her head back and began rotating her hips in slow motions.

I'd never seen her like that. It was as if she wanted to get lost in herself, in us. It was also a fucking turn on. Leaning up, I took her breast in my mouth and sucked on her nipple. Mia gasped as she picked up pace, wrapped her arms around my shoulders, and lifted herself, tightening her walls around my cock and slamming back down. Fuck. She continued doing it over and over again, until her eyes rolled with pleasure. She slammed her mouth into mine and sucked on my tongue.

Not able to take it anymore, I needed to be in control. I rolled us over so that I was on top and pounded my hips into hers. "Oh, God." She cried out and continued to whimper as I kept pounding into her. Her mouth opened in anticipation as she began to pant heavily. "Marcus." She called out my name as she dug her nails into my shoulders. Her nipples peaked with desire, and I sucked one into my mouth again, twirling my tongue around, tugging with my teeth. Her body arched into mine. She cried my name out again and it made me insane. I drove my hips into hers profusely, until neither of us could take it. Before I knew it, her body convulsed beneath me. I tightened my grip on her hips and jerked my hips into hers a few more times until I released hard and long for the second time.

Breathless, I sank on top of her as I left kisses along her lips. With worn-out eyes, Mia smiled and rolled her head side to side in pleasure. I adjusted us so that she was lying beside me under my arm. We lay in silence as our breathing and heartbeats steadied. I traced my fingers up and down Mia's arm, and before I knew it, she was sound asleep.

***

I abruptly awoke from a dream. Sitting up, I tried to collect my thoughts. I couldn't remember the damn dream, yet I woke with my heart racing and my skin beaded in sweat. Frustrated, I stood from my bed and headed toward the bathroom. I rinsed my face with cold water and took a quick glance in the mirror. I couldn't help the uneasiness I felt from the mysterious forgotten dream. I shook it from my head and decided to grab a water bottle from the fridge.

As I entered the kitchen, I froze when I saw my mother at the table, her head slouched as she sniffed and whispered into the phone. "I told you no. You can't do this to me. You need to leave it *alone*. If either of my boys find out . . ." She shook her head as she sniffed a few more times. I stepped in closer and she looked up. Her eyes widened. She didn't say another word. Instead, she ended the call, hanging up on whoever was on the other line.

"What was that about?" I asked sternly.

Swallowing a lump from her throat, she rose from the chair. "Marcus, what are you doing up?"

Ignoring her, I continued to question her. "Who was that on the phone?"

"No one. Are you hungry? I can make you something to eat."

"Are you going to pretend I didn't just walk in on your conversation?" She pressed her lips together and then headed toward the fridge.

"I can warm you up some leftovers or make you a sandwich. Which do you prefer?" She pulled out containers from the fridge. "I hope you don't mind if I sleep over. The guests left a couple of hours ago, and I was straightening things up so you wouldn't wake up to a mess."

"God damn it, Mom." I spat out frustrated.

She twirled around and gave me a cold stare. "You watch your mouth, Marcus. I'm still your mother." She continued to stare at me until her expression softened. Letting out a heavy sigh, she leaned against the door of the fridge. "That conversation has nothing to do with you. I would appreciate it if you can respect my privacy."

"Interesting you say it has nothing to do with me, but whatever that conversation was about, it was about something you didn't want either Jimmie or me to find out. Why is that?"

Angry, her breathing became heavier. "Drop it, Marcus. End of discussion."

I gave a curt nod and turned to leave, not remembering the reason I entered the kitchen in the first place. Before exiting the door, I turned around and said, "I'll drop it for now, but I will find out what that conversation was about."

Her nostrils flared as she breathed out. I turned to head back upstairs.

CHAPTER TWELVE

MIA

As I sat in class, my mind drifted. It'd been a few days since Marcus's surprise party, and since then, he'd been distant. I couldn't put my finger on it. I thought we had shared a special moment. The next morning after the party, I woke to a note that said he had to run off. That was three days ago, and since then, we hadn't seen each other. He'd sent me a quick reply to my text or was short over the phone. I couldn't help but think I was responsible for whatever was troubling him. Although it kept pricking my mind, I pushed it aside and focused on the professor's lecture in my Ethics class.

As the class ended, I packed my laptop and textbook. I took a quick glance at my phone, but there was still nothing from Marcus. Sighing, I dialed my mother's number and put the phone to my ear as I exited the room. "Hello." She answered on the second ring.

"Hi, Sara. Are we still meeting up for coffee?" I exited the building and walked down the cobblestone pavement.

"Yes, I should be at the cafe shop in about ten minutes."

"See you soon."

As I entered the shop, I spotted an empty table by the far right corner. I made my way there and settled in by placing my laptop bag and textbook aside. Marcus tugged at my thoughts again, and I couldn't help but reach for my phone. Screw the waiting around; if he didn't call me, I'd call him. I needed to hear his voice, so I dialed his number.

"Marcus DeLuca. Leave a message." The greeting for his voicemail answered after the second ring. He ignored the call. My heart sank a little at that. What could have been so important that he cut my call short? Not wanting to think the worst, I assumed he must've been on a job and left it at that.

A beep after his greeting sounded, and I left a message, "Hi, baby, I was just calling to check up on you. I hope you're doing okay. I'm having coffee with my mother in a bit." Sighing, I finished off saying, "I miss and love you. Call me tonight. Bye." I tucked my phone in my pocket at the same moment my mother approached.

"Hello, honey." She reached in for a hug. With my arms wrapped around her, I felt a sense of comfort. I always did when she was near. Sara untangled herself from our embrace and sat in the chair across from me, smiling. "Let's grab our lattes and then catch up." I nodded and we both stood and headed toward the counter.

After we ordered, we sat back in our chairs. "So how was Marcus's surprise party? I'm sorry I couldn't make it. I was needed at the office." She shook her head, annoyed, as she took a bite of a blueberry muffin.

"It was fine. I'm sorry you weren't there, but I understand. It was fun. He enjoyed himself and he was surprised. It was a good night."

"Oh, I'm happy to hear that." Brushing a strand of hair behind her ear, she leaned back in her chair as her expression softened. "What's bothering you?" I looked up from my cup of latte with wide eyes. "Come on, Mia. Spill the beans. I think I know you well enough by now to realize when something is on your mind."

Damn it. Was I always that predictable? She was right. I had something on my mind and I couldn't concentrate. I let out a deep breath and caved in, telling her everything that I was feeling. I told her about how strange Marcus had been acting the past few days and about the message I had just left him. "I don't know what's going on with him. It's frustrating."

Her expression filled with compassion, and I was grateful she didn't think I was an over-possessive girlfriend. "Isn't this week the anniversary of his father's death?" I nodded in response. "Well, maybe this is his way of coping with it."

"Maybe. I just wish he let me in on things like that. I want to be there for him."

"And you will. He'll come to you when he's ready, honey. Men don't like to be pressured into anything, especially when it comes to dealing with their feelings. He'll come to you when he's ready."

She was right. I decided I should leave it alone. "You're right, thank you."

"No problem, honey." She reached for my hand and rubbed it as a way to comfort me. "It'll be fine. Hey, I'm going this weekend to visit my parents in Philly. You should come. Megan and Jeremy are tagging along. And your grandparents are dying to see you."

Philadelphia? My grandparents? Was I really ready for that?

"I'm not sure. Can I get back to you on that?"

"Of course, we're driving there. It was Megan's idea. She thought a five-hour road trip would be fun. Oh, that girl . . ." She rolled her eyes. "I'm not sure what to do with her sometimes." I laughed at that comment. Megan could be a bit over the top.

We finished our lattes, leaned in for a hug, and said our good-byes. She insisted on driving me home, but I wanted to walk to clear my head a bit.

During the entire walk, of course, my mind drifted toward Marcus and the upcoming anniversary of his father's death. Even after fifteen years, I was sure it wasn't easier. I knew how Marcus must feel. I lost my father when I was only fourteen years old. I missed him every day. He had made such a huge impact in my life. I wondered at times, if my father were alive, what his opinion would've been of Marcus. My thoughts were intruded upon by the sound my phone ringing. Thinking it may have been him, I quickly picked it up without looking at the screen. "Hello?"

"Hey Mia, Megan and I are ordering Chinese tonight for dinner, is that cool with you?"

Disappointed that it was Jeremy, I answered, "Yes, that's fine. Thank you."

"I'm ordering our usual and Megan wants to add some fried dumplings. You cool with that?"

"Yeah, that's good." After I agreed, we ended the call.

What the hell. I needed to listen to my mother's advice and wait for when Marcus was ready to talk, but if he wasn't ready before the week was over, I was definitely going to reach out to him. I could only take so much of the growing distance between us.

When I arrived at the apartment, Jeremy and Megan were on the couch, cuddling and watching TV. They had already ordered the Chinese food. I told them I was going to get settled in before coming back out to eat with them. I went into my room, put all of my things away, and then entered the bathroom. It was just what I needed— a long hot shower to rid myself of the insecurities planted in my head.

After forty minutes, I was dressed in sweats and a t-shirt, and my hair was tossed up in a messy bun. When I left my room, I saw

Megan and Jeremy eating at the bar. I sat on a stool to join them. "How was school?" Megan asked.

I groaned as I reached for a plate. "It was okay. I met with Sara afterwards for coffee. How was your day?" I asked as I filled my plate with steamed chicken and vegetables, white rice, and fried dumplings.

"It was good. Ooh, did she mention Philly this weekend?" I responded with a nod. "Well, are you going? You should bring Marcus. Jeremy is going."

"I'm only going to judge the so-called famous cheesesteaks I'm always hearing about." Megan shot him a dirty look. "Also, to meet Megan's parents and grandparents, of course," he added and then flashed a huge charming smile.

I laughed and shook my head at Jeremy's goofiness. "I'm still thinking about it. I'll let you know by tomorrow."

Megan shrugged and dug into her plate. I played with my food due to the lack of appetite as we continued to talk. "You want to hear something funny?" Megan asked.

"Sure." I answered as I sipped on water.

"Jeremy and I were out to dinner last night, and one of his *exes* approached our table. She asked how his *fiancée* was doing."

I about choked on my water! Bursting into a laugh, I wiped a tear from my eye. "Oh my God. Was it one of the girls I kicked out?"

"Oh, there was more than one? *Interesting*." Megan turned her eyes toward Jeremy.

Jeremy gave me a look before he charmed Megan. "There was. But you're *the* one." He winked at her. She blushed at that, and I couldn't help but roll my eyes.

"You're weak, Megan."

Jeremy tossed a dumpling at me. "Dude, you're supposed to be on my side. Remember? Bros before hos?"

Megan and I burst out laughing even harder. He just shook his head and continued to eat his food. As I tried to calm down from my laugh, my cellphone rang from the bedroom. I hurried off the stool and practically ran toward it. When I reached my room, I was shocked to see Theresa's name on the screen. "Hello?" I answered a bit out of breath.

"Mia?" Theresa's voice cracked over the phone.

"What's wrong, Theresa?"

"It's Marcus." She sniffed. My heart dropped and my knees buckled in weakness. I knew something had to be wrong. Numerous thoughts flashed across my mind.

"What happened? Is he hurt? Where are you? Where can I meet you? Where is he?" I blurted out all the questions in one breath.

"No, no. He's fine. Well, he's not. Mia, he found out about my secret."

Relief rushed through me that he wasn't hurt, but then fear crept in just as quickly. "How did he find out? I promise I didn't say a word, Theresa."

"I know. I know." She took a few calming breaths before continuing. "He overheard a conversation I had the night of his party. He wouldn't let it go. Over the last few days, he dug for information and asked around until he had enough to question me. By that time, I couldn't deny it. We just had the biggest argument. He's extremely angry. I've never seen him so angry before. He stormed out of my house about forty minutes ago. He won't answer my calls. I don't know what to do." She burst into hard sobs. I couldn't take the pain. I wished I was there to comfort her.

My head snapped up at the sound of the doorbell. I hurried toward the entryway of my bedroom. Peeking out, I watched as Megan looked through the peephole. "It's Marcus." She yelled out as she reached to open the door.

"Theresa, he's here. I'll call you later, okay?"

"Okay, and, Mia, he doesn't know that you know. I kept that from him. This is my mess, not yours. I didn't want him angry with you as well." I closed my eyes as another rush of relief ran through me. I quickly told her I would keep her updated and tossed my phone on the bed. By the time I headed toward the entryway of my bedroom, Marcus had stormed in and shut the door behind him.

I watched as he paced back and forth distracted by his own thoughts.

"Marcus?" I approached him cautiously.

Ignoring me, he continued to pace around the room. Finally he froze and turned to face me. "Come away with me."

Puzzled by his instant urge to go away, I studied his unreadable his expression. "Where to?"

His brows rose as he shrugged. "I don't know—anywhere—my vacation home in the Bahamas? Anywhere you want to go. I just have to leave."

My heart broke for him. I knew the information he just found out was hard for him to take, and as much as I wanted to jump in his arms and comfort him, I had to control myself. "When?"

"Now. I'll help you pack." He swiftly passed me and headed toward the closet. I followed him. He reached for a suitcase and started throwing random things in it. His mind was completely distracted. He even grabbed a frame that held an old picture of my brother and me when were kids from on top of the dresser and tossed it into the case.

I caught his wrist and forced him to look at me. I wanted him to stop. "Why are we leaving?" I knew why, but I had to pretend, and that was so hard to do. As I stood in front of him, I wanted to desperately console him. Instead, I had to lie. I felt sick to my stomach for pretending. I had never had to pretend with him before, and I felt disgusted with myself.

"I just need a break. I'm fuckin' stressed, Mia."

I reached up and grazed the side of his face with my fingertips. "What are you stressed about, Marcus?"

He shut his eyes and leaned into the palm of my hand. His face relaxed for a few seconds. Then he shot his eyes open. "With work and the jobs, I just want to go away with you and forget about it all. Just for a few days, I need to clear my mind, before I fuckin' lose it."

My thumb caressed his face as I stared into his worn out chocolate eyes. My stomach tugged with guilt, and I had an urge to break down and tell him everything I knew, but I couldn't. "Okay." I nodded. "Okay. We can go away. Megan, Jeremy, and my mother are leaving Friday for Philadelphia. They invited us to go with them. I know that's two days away, but if you want, we can leave for Philly now and have some time to ourselves before they arrive."

"Yeah, that sounds good. Okay, let's finish getting you packed." I grabbed his arm to stop him again.

"Marcus, how about you take a shower while I finish packing. Okay?"

He stared at me with furrowed brows. "Do I stink?" He lifted the collar of his shirt to his nose and sniffed.

Laughing, I reached up and smoothed the collar. "No, you just seem worn out and a hot shower will soothe you."

"I don't have any clothes to change into."

"I have a few boxer briefs and t-shirts you've left here before. They're clean. Just toss on the same pair of jeans." I went toward my drawer, pulled out his things, turned, and handed them to him.

Marcus looked down at the few things in his hands and then back at me. He nodded and then headed toward the shower. Letting out a long breath, I quickly texted Theresa and told her that we were going away for a few days and that I'd keep her updated. I quickly gathered my suitcase and sat patiently on the bed for Marcus to finish.

After twenty minutes, Marcus came out of the steamy bathroom with his hair damp. I thought the hot shower would relax him, but with his brows creased and his lips kept in a thin line, I knew it didn't work. I wished I knew what was running through his mind at that moment. "You ready?" he asked.

As I stood from the bed, I gave a curt nod and reached for my suitcase. He was faster than me and grabbed it before I could. "Do we need to stop by your house to pack a bag for you as well?"

He grabbed my arm. "No, whatever I need, I'll grab in Philly." I didn't question him on it. I knew him well enough that I was sure he thought his mother was at his home and he wanted to stay away from her.

Before we left, I explained to Jeremy and Megan that we were going to Philly early and that would meet them on Friday. Megan was excited that we were going. I asked her to let my mother know. After our good-byes, Marcus and I hopped in his car and hit the road.

CHAPTER THIRTEEN

MARCUS

We pulled up to a hotel in downtown Philadelphia a little past ten that evening. I had Mia contact them on our drive down and reserve a stay for us in the Presidential suite, which was the best room available. After we exited the car, I removed Mia's suitcase from the backseat, and then I handed the keys and tip over to the valet. He gave us a ticket before we entered the building.

Mia's eyes spread wide open as she gasped when we entered the hotel. I was sure she was admiring the historic structure of the lobby with its oversize marble pillars and the simple touches that were elegant and modern. "It's beautiful." She whispered as she leaned into me.

I smiled at her as we made our way toward the front desk. "Hello, how may I help you?" a brunette asked, with a name tag that read "Sydney" pinned to her vest.

"We called a few hours ago and made reservations under the name Marcus DeLuca."

Sydney tapped her fingers along the keyboard. "Ah, yes." She placed the room key cards in a small brochure and handed it over to me. "Here you go. Your room number is right here. The elevators are just over there." She pointed to my right. "Enjoy your stay." She smiled. I simply nodded.

"Thank you so much." Mia chirped. I grabbed Mia's hand and we headed toward the elevator. I was drained from the long fucking drive. I wasn't sure why we didn't fly in, but I was so pissed off at that moment I couldn't even think of anything else. Mia and I had driven in silence for the last five hours while music filled the space in the car. As much as I needed her, I also needed that time to think on my own.

She hadn't questioned my behavior since we had left her apartment, and I was grateful for that. She was usually pushy when she wanted information. I was glad she had resisted those impulses at that moment. I just wanted a fucking bed, and just in time, the elevator doors opened. We exited and made our way toward our room. Mia entered first, and from her expression, I could tell she was impressed. I was too drained to look around and admire the room or even give a shit. I placed Mia's suitcase on the ground, stripped down to my briefs, and tossed myself in the bed.

I could hear Mia brushing her teeth in the bathroom. After a few minutes, she joined me in bed after she shut off the lamp. I pulled her to me as I pressed my forehead into the crease of her neck. Her sweet scent eased me into a soothing trance. It was all I wanted at that moment: a different place, a bed, and my girl.

***

I was in such a deep sleep that, when I woke the next day, I had forgotten where I was. Until I took note of the hotel room, it didn't dawn on me that we were still in Philly. Mia wasn't in bed, nor could I hear her in the bathroom or the living room area. Looking around, I searched for my phone. When I remembered it was in my jeans, I grudgingly rolled out of bed and grabbed them. As I was about to dial Mia's number, she waltzed through the door. "Good morning, sleepyhead," she sang as she approached me with a few bags in her hands. "I've never heard you snore before. You were pretty out of it, so I decided to grab some clothes for you. I hope you don't mind?"

Still grumpy, I leaned down, kissed her forehead, and then headed toward the bathroom. After I had finished and had returned to the bedroom, I glanced over at Mia. She was on the bed, texting on her phone. Her eyes flashed up at my presence. "I was just texting Megan to let her know that we made it here safely." She shrugged.

I nodded and sank into the space beside her. I had the worst pounding headache. The past few weeks had been a fucking mess. I dropped my face into my hands and leaned over, resting my elbows on my knees. Mia placed her hand on my back and began stroking it. "Are you okay?" She asked in a low voice.

"Yeah, I just have a fuckin' headache." I replied in a grumpy tone. She stood from the bed. I could hear her searching for something and then heard a door open and close. When she sat back down beside me, she tapped my arm. I looked up. She held out two aspirins and a bottle of water in her hand. Without hesitating, I grabbed the pills, tossed them down my throat, and downed them with water. "Thanks." I mumbled.

"So what do you want to do today? We can grab a bite to eat and then explore the city? Or grab a bite to eat and have a laid-back day with a movie? Or anything?"

I shoved a hand through my hair in frustration, not with her, just with everything else. I was in a crappy mood, and I knew I shouldn't take it out on her. "I'd rather stay in. We can do those things tomorrow if you like. I'm not up for exploring. Is that okay with you?"

"Sure." Even though she'd been playing it cool and not questioning me, something seemed off with her.

"Are you sure you're okay with that?"

With a slight smile, she twirled her fingers along the back of my neck. "Of course, Marcus, you wanted to get away to clear your mind. I don't mind staying in. We can order in and rent movies. It'll be fun." She nodded, reassuring me that she was okay.

"Thank you." I leaned in and gave her a quick kiss.

For the next few hours, that was exactly what we did. We lounged around in our pajamas, watched TV, ordered in, and rented a few movies. We were lazy, and it couldn't have been a better day. My mind didn't drift back to all the bullshit. I didn't stop to think about anything that fucking bothered me. I just simply took that day to do nothing but relax with my girl. It was just what I needed. We made long, sweet, gentle love that night, and before we knew it, the late night crept in and we were fast asleep.

***

My eyes flashed open at the sound of a loud banging noise. I jerked forward in my chair. The area I was in was unrecognizable. It seemed as if I was in a vacant room in an old warehouse. I stood up from the rusted chair and continued to search my surroundings. Where the fuck was I? Slowly I circled around and tried to find an exit.

There was none.

How was that fucking possible?

The tarnished eight-by-ten space only held one chair smack-dab in the middle. Beside the leg of the chair on the ground was a black-metal object. I made my way toward it, and as I got closer, I realized it was a gun. I picked it up and checked to see if it was loaded. It was fully loaded with six bullets. Confused, I spun around when I heard the noise again. Where was it coming from? It sounded like a rattling noise against a metal frame, but it didn't come from a particular area. It bounced throughout the room.

For the next hour, I searched in every inch of the corners, walls, and ceiling of the room and came up empty.

Nothing.

Just an empty fucking space.

If there was no way out, how the fuck was there a way in? Frustrated, I sank into the chair and began going through my most recent memories. Images of Mia and I making love burst through my head.

Was she safe? Was she taken too? I gripped my hair as anger surged through me.

Lou. He was fucking responsible. He was responsible for everything!

He was the only one that could've done it. Why? What does he want?

Why can't he just leave my fucking life alone!

Then I stared into fucking space as I looked back on the last fifteen years of my life spiraling out of control.

My father's death.

His gravesite.

Lou taking me in as his own son. The trust I had in him.

Jimmie.

Michael Sullivan. The documents and the news he had of what Lou did to my father.

Michael's death.

Elle.

The drug exchanges. The murders.

Club21.

My mother.

The fucking lies.

Mia. What we shared: the love, the pregnancy, what she found out about her brother, the miscarriage.

FUCK! With the anger burning through me, I shot the gun in the air three times.

Bang!

Bang!

Bang!

Breathing heavily, I continued to blankly stare into nothing.

I wasn't sure how long I sat there, hours or days, but every minute that ticked by my mind began to play tricks on me.

Who was I?

What had I become?

The more I sat there, answering my own questions, the more I hated myself. I was trying to be a better man, but I couldn't change who I really was. I couldn't give more. I wasn't strong enough. I was breaking down piece by piece.

I had tried to bury my memories six feet under.

But there was nowhere to run.

I was tired.

I was drained emotionally and physically.

I was done.

Finished.

I didn't care to beg, to live.

Lifting the gun, I aimed it at my head, and then I pulled the trigger.

***

I gasped for air as I awoke from the dream. Breathing heavily, I jerked up as my head whipped around. My body was damp with sweat, and my heart thundered against my chest. Dazed, I was able to confirm that I was still in the hotel room. My eyes flicked to my side as I heard Mia mumble in her sleep. Sighing, I leaned against the headboard and grudgingly ran a hand down my face. I glanced at the time. It was almost two in the morning.

I hadn't had a dream like that in a long time.

I pressed down on my eyelids until my anxiety calmed. After I was settled, I lay back down in bed and pulled Mia into me again. She mumbled as she nestled her head into my chest. As comforting as it was having her beside me, I couldn't fall back to sleep. I stared at the ceiling for the rest of the morning as I replayed the dream over and over again.

CHAPTER FOURTEEN

MIA

After I spread butter on the toast, I took a crunchy bite. The entire time I kept my focus on Marcus, even as I reached for the cup of coffee. As I took a few sips, I studied him. He seemed distracted all morning as he quietly sipped on his coffee and read the local daily newspaper. The previous day we stayed in at the hotel as he requested, but his mood hadn't changed. I knew what he was bombarded with was hard to accept, but there was no way I could comfort him without him allowing me in. Since we had left Boston the night before, Theresa had texted me non-stop. I had managed to keep my phone away from him then, but it had been a close call a few times. I had deleted all of her messages before Marcus and I went to bed.

"What time are we meeting your mother?" He finally spoke as he kept his eyes on the paper.

"Noon."

Marcus raised his wrist with his watch snugly wrapped around it and checked the time. "It's early. If you want to take a walk around the city, we should go now."

"Okay." There wasn't much for me to say. I hated the distance between us. He was sitting so close to me, but he seemed so far away. Brushing those feelings aside for the time being, I stood up from the table and headed toward the bathroom before we left the hotel.

For the next few hours, Marcus and I strolled through the cool October breeze of Philadelphia's historic area in Center City. It was exactly as I remembered it. Several wonderful memories of my father and brother resurfaced as we passed areas such as the Liberty Bell, shops on Market Street, and Old City—all places we visited when I was just a little girl. When Marcus and I passed certain streets or stores which brought back memories of my father holding my hand or Michael and I racing down the city's pavement, I couldn't help the slight squeal or laugh that escaped me. It was a feeling that brought the memories to life again. Although I always thought of them, being there at that moment made the time we had together to seem real again.

Marcus reached for my hand and gave it a light squeeze. I looked up at him, and there was a slight smile on his face—the first I'd seen since he stormed into my apartment the night before last. His eyes were still lost in his own world, but that tiny smile warmed and tugged at my heart. Without controlling the urge, I leaned up and kissed his lips. "I love you." It was all I could say.

It was true, although I wished there was another word for "love," one that expressed how deep and passionate my love was for him. The word "love" just seemed as if it weren't enough. I had a constant whirlwind of emotions that tugged at every inch of my nerves: I felt lost without his embrace, my heart melted knowing that he was hurt or confused, and my body reacted instantly to the simplest touch from him. The look in his eyes when he gazed into mine with so much passion caused a wonderful and sickening desire that jabbed at my heart: Wonderful, because I could never have enough of him. Sickening, because if I were to ever lose him, there was no way I could recover from the pain. There had to be a word stronger than just "love."

"Love you too." He responded and I knew he did.

We continued to walk around until it was time to head back to the hotel. My mother, Megan, and Jeremy were meeting us at the hotel, so we could all head together to my grandparents' home for a late lunch. As we entered the lobby, I spotted Jeremy instantly. His short blond curls and piercing blue eyes were not hard to miss. He stood as he saw us approaching. Both my mother and Megan were chatting as they sat beside each other.

Marcus shook Jeremy's hand after I leaned in and gave Jeremy a quick hug. "Dude, I'm starving. Where can we get these cheesesteaks?"

Megan stood and reached in to hug me as she rolled her eyes at Jeremy's comment. "He's been talking about the damn cheesesteaks for the entire five-hour drive." She whispered in my ear clearly annoyed.

Laughing, I pulled away and hugged my mother. "How was the ride in?" I asked Sara as we untangled from our embrace.

"It was . . . long." She quickly glanced at Jeremy, who had a puzzled expression.

"What?" he asked. Megan and Sara shook their heads.

"It's nice seeing you again, Sara." Marcus leaned in and hugged my mom to break the tension.

"Same here, Marcus. Happy belated birthday. Mia said you had a wonderful time. I'm sorry I couldn't make it."

"Thank you. It's okay. Yes, Mia and my mother did a wonderful job."

Sara smiled in response and then wrapped her arm around Marcus. As she led the way out the door by his side, she asked, "How is your mother doing?"

There was a slight tug at my chest awaiting his response, but when he did answer, it was in a nonchalant matter. "She's doing well. Thank you for asking."

I quickly padded behind them and out the building as I rolled my eyes at Jeremy and Megan's bantering behind me.

"Can you just behave for an hour?" Megan spat at Jeremy.

"Behave? What am I eight years old?"

Megan took a few settled breaths to calm down before she snarled. "You act as if you are."

"Whatever. I'm hungry."

"Ah, poor baby. Don't worry, honey. Mommy will fill your tummy very soon." I tried to bite back my laugh, but it didn't work.

Well at least she was learning how to handle him.

***

Forty minutes later, we pulled into the driveway of a tiny brick colonial single family home located in the Somerton area of Northeast Philadelphia. It was a corner home on a quiet tree-lined street with a few similar households nestled along it. We exited my mother's SUV rental and walked up the broken pathway toward the front porch. Leaves from the trees were scattered in the front. Some floated in the ceramic fountain that was in the center of the lawn. Sara, Jeremy, and Megan walked up the wooden porch steps as I hesitantly stood at the bottom. Marcus placed his hand on my lower back and firmly squeezed his fingers to comfort me, as if he were telling me that while he was there he wouldn't let anything bad happen to me.

I took a few deep breaths and walked up the creaking stairs, and Marcus followed behind me. "Granny." Megan squealed as she ran into the arms of an elderly woman who had swung the screen door open at our approach. I couldn't quite get a good look at first. Megan squeezed the woman and then pulled back to introduce Jeremy. Sara leaned in and hugged the older woman as well. "Hi, Mom, it's good to see you." Sara pulled away and turned to face me. She waved her hand for me to come closer.

That was when I saw her: my grandmother. She was short and fragile with dark grey hair that was pinned into a twist. Her gentle smile warmed my heart as the blue specks in her wide eyes gleamed. "Mom, this is Mia, your granddaughter."

"Oh, my dear." The older woman blurted as the tears began to stream down her wrinkled cheeks. She pulled me into a tight, warm hold. "You're so beautiful. Oh my. I can't believe how grown up you are. Let me get a look at you." With a sniff, she pulled back to inspect me as her eyes traced my features. "You look just like your mother, but you have your father's smile." That compliment gave me goose bumps and brought tears to my eyes. I couldn't help but pull her into another hug. She swayed back and forth as we hugged and laughed.

Pulling back as I wiped my tears, I slightly turned to introduce her to Marcus. "This is my boyfriend, Marcus." Marcus smiled and reached his hand out to her, but she caught his wrist and pulled him in for a hug. I laughed as Marcus's larger frame overpowered hers.

"Well, come on in. William left to grab some cheesesteaks. Sara said that's what you all are looking forward to eating."

Megan shot an annoyed glance at me when Jeremy clapped his hands and began rubbing them together after yelling out, "Alright! That's what I'm talking about." Then he followed in behind Kathy, my grandmother.

"I might kill him before the weekend is over." Megan leaned into me and whispered.

"If I don't do it first," Sara added.

We all entered the tiny brick home and settled in the living room area. I sat between Marcus and my mother on the plastic-covered sofa. Jeremy and Megan sat on the matching love seat across from us, as my grandmother glided on a rocking chair after she provided us with iced tea. There was an awkward silence before Jeremy chirped in.

"You have a lovely home." He stated with a curt nod.

Lovely? I'd never heard him use that term before.

"Well thank you, dear. I've lived here for over sixty years." She smiled and then turned her gaze to me. "So, Mia, tell me, how've you been? What have you done the past few years?" She asked as I sipped on my drink. I quickly glanced at her and then looked around the room. Everyone was quiet, waiting for me to reply. Setting the cup on the antique claw-leg coffee table, I leaned into Marcus as he wrapped his arm around my shoulder securely.

"Well, I have a bachelor's degree in business, and I'm currently in law school—my second year actually."

"Oh, that's amazing news!" She clapped her hands with excitement. It made me smile. I wasn't used to having someone overly excited about my achievements. It was nice for a change.

She continued to ask me questions about my life, school, where I'd worked, Michael—which was a short conversation because it created a sad vibe—and my relationship with Marcus. She also asked Jeremy a few questions, and his responses helped to lighten any negative energy in the room. We laughed as Megan mentioned past family memories, and I felt a little bit jealous because I had not been there to experience them.

We had been seated for a little over forty minutes when William, my grandfather, barged in with some two-foot-long cheesesteaks and curly fries. I was in awe of his six-foot-tall military frame, perfectly round bald shiny head, grey goatee, and sharp blue eyes. He was intimating, yet his eyes were soft and gentle. When I stood up to greet him, he continued to stare at me as tears formed in his eyes. It was as if no one else were in the room as he continued to ogle me. "Mia." He forced through the lump in his throat.

I simply nodded. In three strides, he reached me, pulled me into a tight bear hug, and lifted me off the ground. With the tight embrace and the whiff of the musky scent of his cologne, there was a warm feeling about him that gave me a sense of comfort. I relaxed in his arms and hugged him back.

He held my chin with his large manly hand. "You look just like your mother." He continued to study my features, amazed at the resemblance. "Are you hungry? Did you eat? Do you want something special? I don't mind going back out and grabbing anything you'd like."

I laughed and then sniffed back my tears. "I'm fine. Thank you."

"Are you sure? I don't mind. I just want you to have anything you like." He paused as if a thought rushed through him, and then remorse filled his eyes. He then he pulled me into another tight hold. As much as I thought I would be angry with these two individuals who forced my mother to choose between her family and them, I wasn't because they showered me with so much love. I could say that I needed it when I was younger, but I didn't. My father and brother gave me all the love I could ever need. So it was the right moment. I needed them more now than I did years ago, and I could no longer be angry.

"Okay, darling, let the poor girl breathe. You don't want her to run off, do you?" Kathy, my grandmother, blurted as she approached us. "Let's all go in to the kitchen to eat."

"Thank God." I heard Jeremy mutter beneath his breath. I laughed after William looked up at him with an arched brow and asked who he was.

Within the next couple of hours, we stayed in the kitchen, which was also the dining room area, and we surrounded an oval-shaped wooden table. We all sat in mix-matched chairs. It wasn't the most elaborate home, but there was a warmth and homey presence to it. Even Marcus laughed and joined in on jokes that William made about Jeremy. The cheesesteaks were beyond amazing and mouthwatering. Jeremy had his fill.

After things died down, Megan sat on William's lap and hugged him tightly as she hummed to a song that he sang to her as a child. Sara and Kathy stood by the sink and washed dishes. Marcus and Jeremy discussed Marcus's recent victorious trial, and I sat back and reflected on how grateful I was. There was nothing that I had ever wanted more than to have a family. When I met the DeLucas, I instantly fell in love with them and the love they had for each other. Now I had my own family. Although it was not as large as Marcus's family, I felt at peace, knowing that I had one.

My phone vibrated in my back pocket, and I excused myself to go outside. As I shut the door behind me, I made my way to a chair swing by the corner of the porch.

"Hello." I answered.

"Hi, Mia, I'm sorry for being a pain, but I just need to know he's okay. I'm going crazy over here. I haven't slept or eaten for the past few days."

With my head leaning back on the chair, I looked out into the evening sky. "He's doing okay. He hasn't mentioned anything about you, but he seems a little better today than he did yesterday."

Theresa let out a slight sigh of relief. "Well that's somewhat good news. I need to talk to him. He hasn't let me explain. He just barged out of here."

A creaking sound along the porch made me jump. As I glanced over, I was relieved to see it was William. I ended my call with Theresa, promising I would call back tomorrow.

I looked up at his gentle smile. He stood a few feet away from me with his hands dug in his front jean pockets. "Everything okay?"

"Yes, just a friend checking in with me." I started to stand, but he raised his hand to stop me.

"No, if you don't mind, I would like to talk with you, privately." He looked down and lightly shrugged. "If that's okay with you?"

"Sure." I scooted over so he could join me. He made his way over and sank down beside me.

The swing lightly swayed in place as we sat there in an awkward silence. After a few minutes, he finally cleared his throat. "It's a nice night."

A tiny smile touched the corner of my lips at his attempt to make small talk. It wasn't easy for me either, so I just leaned back and admired the breeze. "Yes, it is."

There were a few additional minutes of silence before he blurted, "I'm proud of you."

Puzzled by the random statement, I tilted my chin and stared at his profile. He bowed his head and took a deep breath. "You grew up to be a very intelligent, independent, beautiful, and strong woman. I couldn't be happier." He looked up at me then. "I know I can't make up for the last twenty-four years of your life, and it's probably too late to build a relationship, but I can at least try. I want to be a part of your life. The last twenty-four years I've missed, but I don't want to miss any more minutes from here on out."

My heart swelled at his testament. I wiped away the tears that fell, and sniffing, I nodded slightly. "Okay" was all I could say; there was nothing more than that. How could I not give him another chance? Everyone deserved one, and maybe I was optimistic, but for so long I suffered being alone, trying to be strong for myself. There was so much I had faced on my own at such a young age. I didn't want to push anyone away anymore. I had built a high barrier and not allowed anyone in but a simple few. I took a chance with Marcus, and I believed it was the best choice I'd ever made. I wanted to take more risks, to find more chances for happiness, and most of all, to build a family.

The man before me locked his tear-filled eyes with mine as his lip quivered. His body slightly shook as if he was trying to hold it all in, and then he pulled me into a tight hug. "Thank you." His voice cracked. "I promise I won't let you down." He broke into soft sobs. My chest tightened at his promise. I tried to hold back tears and dug my head into his neck. "I know it was stupid, but your mother was so young . . ."

"No." I mumbled into his chest. "Let's leave it in the past." There was no reason to go back to it. I didn't want an explanation, and I didn't care for one. All that mattered was that he was going to make up for it.

After our cries subsided, we pulled away from each other and sat out on the porch for a very long time, talking and laughing about our likes and dislikes—sports, school, and so much more. He was a man who was so comfortable to talk to and so easy to love. He reminded me a bit of my father. It begged the question as to why they didn't get along, but I kept it to myself. All that mattered was at that very moment we created a memory I was able to store away as a keepsake of the time my grandfather and I swayed on a porch swing, laughing and admiring the October late night stars. That was a beautiful night.

"Mia, are you ready to call it a night, sweetie?" Sara popped her head out the door. "It's late, and we have to head back to the hotel." I looked over at my grandfather. I was having such a good time with him, and I didn't want to leave so soon. He gave me a warm smile. "Go ahead, Mia. It's past my bedtime, anyway. I never survive past eight." He let out a raspy laugh. "We're all having dinner tomorrow at a restaurant, so we'll see each other then. Get some rest."

Smiling along with him, I pulled him into a hug, and then we walked into the house so that I could give Kathy a tight hug as well and wish her a good night.

We all drove back to the hotel in silence as I counted the minutes before I could rejoin my grandparents and get to know them even better.

Marcus sensed my brighter mood as we entered the hotel room. He slightly shook his head and smiled as he removed his clothing. "Your grandparents were nice." He flung his boots off.

"They were so cool, especially William." We both stripped down to our undies and climbed into bed. I snuggled into his arms. "I can't believe I actually have a family, Marcus. Is it wrong or cliché to actually have such strong feelings for them, despite everything that's happened?"

He ran his fingers up and down the side of my arm as he pressed his lips on top of my head. "No, baby, it's not. They're your family no matter what. That's what's most important. Even if you feel betrayed for what they'd done in the past, you can only hope for the best in the future."

I squeezed my eyes shut and tightened my arms around him. I knew deep down that what Marcus had just said was more of a realization for him than a speech for me. We lay in bed the rest of the night that way, until we both drifted into a deep sleep.

CHAPTER FIFTEEN

MARCUS

At noon that Saturday, Mia and I had a quiet breakfast at one of the hotel restaurants. Afterwards, we walked around the city before heading back to the hotel. As I waited for her to finish with her shower, I sat on a chair in the living area of our suite. When we first arrived three days ago, I was distraught, and although I felt more at ease by now, I'd almost forgotten that it was the day that marked fifteen years since my father passed.

Fifteen long fucking years.

All the memories I'd had of him were good, not one bad memory. And even though each day since his death I had grown sturdier, I asked myself, "How different would my life have been if he was still alive?" I didn't blame him for how my life had turned out. As he told me once, if I wasn't happy with my life, I alone had to do something to change it. I couldn't wait around and expect it all to work out. But that was a difficult saying for me to put into practice, when I had no fucking clue how to change it.

The person that I wanted my life to be better for had just padded her way out of the bathroom. Just out of the shower, she dropped her towel, revealing the soft skin of her naked body. Bending over to grab a bra from on top of the bed, she slowly tilted her head and looked over at me. A smile formed along her lips as she caught me watching her. She straightened her posture and, with confidence, walked in my direction.

My earlier thoughts vanished as pleasure rushed through me with each stride she took. When Mia reached me, she leaned down and pressed her hands along the armrest of the chair. Mia gently stretched her neck, and with her lips, she grazed my jawline. "You like what you see?" she whispered. The warmth of her breath along my skin aroused me.

"I do." I drew my fingers along the soft skin of her torso.

She brought her head around, and her eyes filled with desire and burned into mine. "Well, what are you going to do about it?" She then grabbed the hem of my t-shirt, pulled it over my head, and tossed it to the ground. "Better yet, the question should be, 'What am I going to do about it?'"

I cocked my head aside and flashed a grin. "Tell me. What are you going to do?"

A playful smile formed along her lips, "Well, for starters, you're too covered up. I need to get these jeans off of you." Her fingers danced along my belt buckle. Unhooking it, she pulled it from the hoops of the jeans, and threw it along the floor beside my shirt.

Mia stood up and crossed her arms under her rounded breasts. I sucked in air, pleased and completely turned on with her playfulness. Her eyes traced down to my jeans. She then raised a hand toward her face and tapped a finger along her chin as if she were thinking. She gently shook her head. "See, that's a problem. What I need is hidden under those jeans." Her eyes flashed back to mine. "They're getting in the way of what I want." I leaned back in the chair as I felt myself grow underneath the denim fabric. Fuck. She managed to do that every time: even a simple word spoken by her gave me a fucking hard on.

Mia reached over and began to remove my jeans and briefs. She tossed my shoes off along the way. Excitement and craving washed through her eyes as she caught sight of my full-blown erection. Without hesitation, she straddled me, both of her legs on the outside of mine, not yet allowing me to fill her. She rested her forearms along my chest as her fingers dug in the back of my hair. "Have you decided what you're going to do?" I asked my voice hoarse.

With a sparkle in her green eyes, her lips curled into a devilish grin. "Oh, I have a few things in mind." She raised her hips and slowly sank down on me. My head settled back into the wingback chair at our joining. There was no greater feeling than when I was with her. She was always ready for me—wet and sleek as she glided up and down my cock. Her lips parted with a gasp, her body trembled, and her nipples hardened as she continued to ride me. She was a beautiful sight.

I gripped her hips and thrust her up and down in a faster motion. Mia's breathing became unsteady. She tightened her walls around my cock, and I groaned at how fucking good it felt. Her nipples peaked in yearning, and I leaned in, sucking on her breast. A moan escaped her, inciting her to move faster. My tongue twirled around, and I tugged on her nipple. Mia began to pant; she gripped my jaw, shoved my head back, and crushed her lips against mine.

Ferociously, she sucked and tangled her tongue with mine. The minty taste of the toothpaste, the scent of her body soap, and the way my cock felt inside of her as she slammed her hips down into mine drove me in-fucking-sane. I gripped the back of her hair and pulled her in, needing and wanting her closer. She moaned as our tongues crushed against one another. My other hand continued to grip her hip, forcing her deeper as she slammed down with each descent. She cried out, and I groaned as she tugged at my hair.

A deeper craving coursed through me: I lifted her from the chair and slammed her back against the carpet floor. Kneeling between her legs, I lifted her hips from the ground and pounded inside of her. She whimpered, as she arched her back, tightened her eyes shut, and gripped my wrists. Digging her nails into my flesh, she cried out my name. Her body jerked beneath me as she released the building pressure. The pleasure in her expression as she came ignited me, causing me to pound into her harder over and over again. Her breasts bounced as I continued to nail her. The sound of our hips slamming against each other, her continued cry of my name, all of it took me over the edge, and I couldn't take it anymore. I fucking exploded deep and hard within her. "Fuck." I groaned beneath my breath.

I collapsed beside her. Both of us tried to catch our breath as we stared at the ceiling. Mia let out an exhausted and pleasurable laugh, causing me to do so as well. After we calmed and our heartbeats settled, she laid her head on top of my chest. I traced my fingers up and down her spine as she sighed in contentment.

With all that had been going on, I knew I had to tell her what happened and the reason I'd been acting the way I was. It wasn't fair to keep her in the dark. Mia didn't push the issue, allowing me to deal with the problem on my own, but I knew she wanted in, to know more. I loved that about her—how she was so passionate about me that she wanted to be a part of my struggles, stress, and pain.

As a guy, it was hard to express my feelings, not because I couldn't, but because it was more of a way to show strength, to show that I could handle it on my own. Sometimes it was difficult to deal with all the bullshit. I would use liquor as a way to escape or cope. I was trying to fight against it, to control it in another way.

Mia was my other way. When she was around, there was nothing else. There was no bullshit, no issues, no lies, *nothing*. In an awkward way, it was as if we were similar; we both needed each other to fill the emptiness we both had. I understood it and she did as well. It was why we meshed so well.

Mia lifted her head to look at me. "What are you thinking?" She asked in a low tone. I reached up and cupped my hand under her chin. My stare dropped from her eyes and followed as I began tracing my thumb along her soft plump lips. "I'm sorry if I've been acting awkward or off lately. It's just that I've been going through some things, and I'm not sure how to—"

"Marcus, I need to tell you something." Mia cleared her throat.

Puzzled by her instant change in demeanor, I tugged at her chin and brought her eyes back to mine. "What is it?" At that moment I was concerned by the look in her eyes. She seemed to be struggling with whatever she wanted to say. "What is it, Mia?" I asked again, that time my tone a bit stern.

Nodding as if she knew she had to say it, she let out a shaky breath and continued, "I know why you've been distant." She paused and stared as my eyebrows kneaded in confusion. "I know about your mother."

I blinked. "W-what?" I untangled from her and jerked up to sit. What the fuck did she mean she knew about my mother? Had she known all along?

"Marcus, hear me out, okay?" Mia stood along with me and followed me into the bedroom. Her eyes followed my every move as I pulled on my briefs and then glanced over at her.

"You knew? For how long, Mia?"

She reached for a t-shirt and tossed it on. Then she sat down on the bed, staring at me, her eyes pleading with me to understand. I couldn't understand at that moment because I was upset. Pissed. Fucking irate. I widened my eyes for her to go on. "A few weeks ago, your mother came to me and confided her secret. She begged me not to say anything." Mia bowed her head and focused on her fidgeting fingers. "I wanted to tell you. Many times I almost did, but it wasn't my secret to tell."

That was un-fucking-believable. My stare hardened as I waited for her to continue, but she didn't. "So, you're telling me that for the past few days you've known what I've been dealing with?"

"Yes," she said in a whisper. "But, you have to believe me. I wanted to say something, but I just couldn't."

I was angry with her, but it wasn't for keeping the secret at the time it was told, it was for something way worse. "You want to know why I'm upset right now, Mia?" I kept my tone low, trying my best not to flip my lid.

She nodded. "Because I didn't tell you."

"No, I can understand why you kept that to yourself. You're right, it's not your secret to tell, but the past fuckin' three days, you waltzed around here," I swung my arm indicating where we were, "as though none of it had occurred. What happened to being honest with each another, huh?" I shook my head as I threw on my jeans and tossed on a shirt. "You knew that it was out of the bag—that I finally knew about it and that was why I've been upset—yet you pretended as if nothing was wrong. Why? Why now? Why did you choose to tell me this very second?"

"I-I don't know—maybe to finally be honest with you. I also couldn't keep it hidden any longer. I was hoping that you would finally confide in me, tell what was wrong with you, but you wouldn't." She stood from the bed, her voice a bit higher. "You want to throw *honesty* out there, Marcus? Tell me. Why weren't you honest with me? I thought our relationship was at a point where you would be able to tell me anything that was on your mind. I didn't want to push the issue, force you into it, hoping that just for once, you'd spill your thoughts and feelings to me."

Anger surged through me. I couldn't believe what she'd said. I may not be fucking perfect and tell her everything, but I was trying. I was fucking trying. With a raised voice, I blurted, "Is that what it was to you? A fuckin' test to see if I would spill my feelings? You don't think I spill my feelings to you, Mia? Do you think it was easy for me to talk to you about my dad? Lou? How Jimmie found our father dead? That was *me* spilling my fuckin' guts to *you*." Frustrated, I raised my arms in the air. "It may not be every damn day or every time something occurs, but I do. Other than Jimmie, you're the only person that has come close to knowing what goes on in my fuckin' head." I finished with a hard stare, my breathing heavy as she stared back at me.

Tears filled her eyes, and I couldn't look at her any more. I tore my gaze away and pressed my hands at my hips. With my head bowed, I looked down at the floor, my heart pounding against my chest. "You're right. You did. Sometimes you're so distant when you have a lot on your mind. I know you go through a lot, Marcus. I can't help it that I want to take away all of your stress and worries and make them mine, to somehow ease your burden." She sniffed a few times. At that statement, I shut my eyes and shook my head. I knew that she worried for me, but I didn't realize how many of my burdens had stressed her as well.

"Mia, I'm . . ."

Before I could finish, the sound of my phone ringing had cut in. I looked up at her wet eyes and had an urge to reach out and grab her, to comfort her, but I looked away and headed toward my phone. "Hello." I answered on the fourth ring, forgetting to check who it was.

"Uncle Marcus, guess what I did today?" Elle's enthusiastic tone chirped through the phone. Even after the entire mess Mia and I had just gone through, I was able to smile at the sound of my niece's voice.

"You got me. What did you do?" I asked as I walked passed Mia. I stopped in front of her and covered the speaker of my cell with my hand. "I'm going in the hallway to talk with Elle. I'll be back soon." I tilted my head, hoping that she would make eye contact with me, but she didn't. Instead she gave me a curt nod, turned on her heels, and entered the bathroom. With a heavy sigh, I closed the door to our hotel room behind me as I walked down the hall and turned my attention back to my niece.

"Daddy took me to my first dance class!"

"That's awesome, Elle. Did you learn anything in your first class?"

"Lots of stretching, but today was ballet, which was okay. Next week is jazz! I'm totally looking forward to it." I chuckled at how damn cute she was. "So when are you coming back home? I want to show you and Mia some moves I learned."

"Soon, sweetheart."

"Oh . . . Okay. Daddy wants to talk to you, Uncle Marc. I love you."

"Love you too, Elle

"Elle go play in the yard. I'll be there in a little while." Jimmie's voice came through the phone. "Hey, little bro," he said after a few seconds in a low tone. I guessed that he wanted to make sure Elle was no longer around.

"What's up, Jimmie." I leaned against the hallway wall and looked down toward our room, hoping I didn't find Mia running off.

"So, Mom stopped by last night . . ." He paused, and with a heavy sigh, he continued, "She told me what was going on."

"She saved me the trouble, huh?"

"Bro, trust me when I say she was not happy with my thoughts when she left, but she's still our mother and a damn good one at that. Her issues with Dad were buried right along with him fifteen years ago."

"You don't think I know that? But she had an affair with that fuckin' bastard, Jimmie. Out of all the men she could have had an affair with, she had it with Lou! It fuckin' disgusts me in more ways than one. You know the fuckin' excuse she had?"

"No, what was it?"

"That Dad was never around. She never felt lonelier in her life. That he was always out on jobs—"

Jimmie blew out a low whistle. "I know, man. I know. I can't imagine what she was thinking when she messed around on Dad." He paused for a second. "Are you afraid that Mia will run off and do the same?"

"What? No." I was shocked by that random question. I hadn't thought of it that way. Well, maybe deep down, there was some part of me that was concerned. My mother had always seemed to be perfect in every way; she always took care of her husband and her children. Then, suddenly, after all these years, I found out that she had been unfaithful to my father. What made me think Mia wouldn't run off and do the same as well? My life now wasn't much different than my father's was back then.

"Look. Trust me when I say that having complete trust in someone is not the easiest part of a relationship. The five years I was married to Cynthia, it wasn't easy. Fuck, we argued all the time, but I loved her, and we made it work. Building a relationship is never easy, Bro. You have to accept and trust Mia and live happily or don't and let her go." He paused, and when he noticed that I wasn't responding, he proceeded. "I know you're upset with Mom because I am too, but your anger is not just directed at her, dude. Your anger is based on your insecurities. You lost Mia once. You're afraid of losing her again. I lost my wife without the chance of ever getting her back. Don't fuck it up."

Fucking asshole. I was pissed that he was fucking right in many ways, and I'd never heard him talk about Cynthia since her passing. "You're right."

He laughed, "What was that? I didn't hear you well. Can you repeat yourself?"

"Fuck off! If you didn't hear me the first time, tough shit."

He burst out laughing. "Fair enough. Don't forget to call Mom. She's freaking the fuck out and driving me insane. I have to take care of an eight-year-old. I don't need to be taking Mom in too."

"Yeah. I'll shoot her a text and tell her that we'll talk when I get back."

"Cool, see you soon."

After we ended the call, I sent my mother a quick text and tossed the phone in my back pocket. I entered the hotel room and immediately walked around in search of Mia. I was probably gone for twenty to thirty minutes. After a quick glance around the living area and bedroom, I made my way to the bathroom. The door was opened and I spotted her by the vanity. She was fully dressed in a chocolate colored skirt, a teal blouse, and brown knee boots, ready for the early dinner with her grandparents that evening. She looked gorgeous. I leaned into the archway of the bathroom door. With my arms and legs crossed, I studied her. Her expression was somber as she applied her makeup. Her back was facing me, but I was able to see her reflection from the mirror in front of her. She hadn't noticed my presence yet.

I knew she was thinking about our argument. Her eyes watered, and she leaned over the sink and took slow steady breaths. After she calmed herself, trying to not cry, she looked back in the mirror and ran a piece of cotton wipe covered with some type of gunk along her cheekbones. She was trying to hide the red blotches that formed when she broke out in tears. I was a fucking asshole. I promised myself that I would never cause hurt or tears for her again, and that's exactly what I had done. There she was crying over me again.

Mia must have finally sensed my presence because she looked up in the mirror and our eyes locked. Her eyes were filled with sadness, and I was the one responsible for it. She tore her eyes away and continued to apply her makeup, as if I wasn't there, as if she didn't want anything to do with me.

And that fucking hurt.

CHAPTER SIXTEEN

MIA

There was no strength left inside of me: I didn't want to argue, cry, or even deal with any of it anymore. I just wanted to get ready and meet up with the others for dinner that evening. Marcus stood by the bathroom door, and I could feel his lingering heated gaze. I wasn't sure how long he was watching me, but the moment our eyes locked in the reflection of the mirror, I wanted nothing more than to reach out to him, touch him, feel him, and somehow comfort him. How could I? I was wrong and I knew it.

I had truly thought our relationship had taken a leap, that we were finally moving forward, but at that moment, I wasn't sure anymore. There would always be doubt and secrets, but how much could a relationship take? I loved him. I truly, with all of my heart and soul, loved him more than any person could love another. Despite that fact, a time may come when even a love that strong might not be enough. Until then, I had no choice but to stick it out and fight for us. Was he willing to do the same? As the doubt crept through my veins, I felt the warmth of fresh tears sting my eyes again. Great, I had tried to steady my tears for the last fifteen minutes, and the fact that he was in the bathroom watching me wasn't helping.

Reaching out for a tissue from the granite vanity, I quickly dabbed it along my lids. *Come on, Mia. Don't cry. Don't cry.* I took a few steady breaths, and that was when I felt him directly behind me. His hand gently clasped my arm. For a moment, he was hesitant as my body immediately stiffened at his touch, but then he twirled me around to face him. My body pressed against the counter top, as my gaze met his.

With troubled eyes, he framed my face with his hands. Gently he caressed my cheeks with his thumbs. We continued to stare at each other at a loss for words, afraid that any simple word spoken could be the wrong one.

"I'm sorry," he finally said. My mouth opened to speak, but he cut me off. "No, listen to me. I'm an asshole. I'm sorry." With pinched brows, he shook his head, as if trying to rid himself of a memory.

"Yes, you are an asshole, sometimes." He raised a brow at that. "But you had every reason to be upset. I should be the one apologizing, not you. I'm sorry."

"Well, I'm trying to grow up." He chuckled beneath his breath, and then expression grew serious again. He then pressed his lips together before tightening his hold along my face. "Mia, I know that my temper sometimes gets the best of me. I'm trying to work on that—on a lot of things actually. Telling you how I feel is a major one, but I'm also trying to do all of this without having to hand over my man card."

I snorted at that last comment. "Is that what this is all about? Maintaining your man card?"

"No, I just wanted to see you smile." He lightly shrugged and flashed an adorable crooked grin. It was difficult to not forgive that smile, but I dropped my amusement to show him that our argument hadn't been forgotten. He must've understood, because he released his hold from my face to grip my hips and lift me on top of the counter. He nestled in between my legs, rested his hands along my thighs, and cleared his throat. "Okay, give it to me." He blurted. Confused, I awkwardly shrugged, unaware of what he wanted me to give. "Tell me what's on your mind, at this very moment." He tapped his fingers against my thighs waiting for me to speak up.

"Well, to be honest?" He nodded once for me to go on. "It's frustrating being your girlfriend." He laughed out loud not expecting that response from me, I was sure.

"Go on."

I let out a heavy sigh. "You have no idea how much I love you one minute and want to strangle you the next."

"Ditto." He nodded once and then laughed at my pointed glare.

"I'm serious, Marcus. I want you to be able to tell me what you're feeling. Granted, not every single thing, because let's face it, I don't tell you every time I'm down, stressed, or in a shitty mood." I raised my hand and pressed it against his jaw line, allowing my fingers to trace along the prickles of his facial hair. "But when something is bothering you deep down, and it's taking a toll on you, on *us,* I expect you to confide me. Believe it or not, I'm not going anywhere, Marcus. I'm not running away from our problems. I want to fix them, even if we have to argue it out at first. That's okay, as long as you know I'm going to be here to talk it out with you at the end of it."

I searched his face and smiled as a soft grin formed along his lips as he said, "I truly don't deserve you, but I'm grateful every single day that you're mine. I know it's frustrating at times, and I appreciate that even through all the bullshit you still stick around. I didn't realize how much my bottled-up problems bothered you. I promise to work harder at it. Just know that I am trying."

My fingers ran down his face. "I know you are, baby. I just need you to try a little harder." He let out a chuckle. "Although, I do have to thank you."

Puzzled, he glanced up, his brown eyes no longer filled with the anger he held earlier. "For what?"

"For coming in here and talking it out, for once not using sex as a way to cope with our issues, for allowing me to spill my feelings, and for just listening."

Marcus still held a confused expression in his eyes as he wrapped his arms around my waist and pulled me in closer to him. "Wait, so no make-up sex?"

Rolling my eyes, I grabbed his face and pulled him in for a quick kiss. "No, we need to finish getting ready and meet up with the others."

"Not even a quickie?" His lips parted into a full-blown grin.

Shaking my head, I slapped his bicep and hopped off the counter. "Get ready, Marcus." I turned around, facing the mirror again to finish applying my makeup, a bit more content than earlier.

He slapped my ass and headed toward the bedroom, yelling behind him. "Fine, but that ass is mine tonight."

Oh my God, what was I going to do with that man?

***

"Mia, you look beautiful." William shouted over the noise in the crowded restaurant as he pulled me into a hug.

"Thank you." I pulled away from our embrace and checked out his attire: khaki pants, a red cashmere sweater, and brown loafers. His grey goatee was neatly trimmed and his musky cologne engulfed the waiting area of the restaurant. "You look very handsome." I smiled up at him as I caught his cheeks flushing.

As my grandfather and Marcus greeted each other, I hugged my grandmother who was dressed in a navy blue skirt and matching blouse, with pearl earrings and necklace. "How are you, darling?" She asked as we untangled.

"Good, where are the others?" I searched over her shoulders to find them but couldn't make out where they were.

With a wave of her hand, she wrinkled her nose. "They're late." Kathy shook her head in disapproval. "That daughter of mine is always late. They'll be here soon."

We waited ten minutes before our table was called. A waitress, who instantly took notice of Marcus, led us to a round table set for seven. After we took our seats, she handed us a wine and drink menu to view while we waited for the rest of our company.

"Marcus, what's your poison? Are you a liquor or beer man?" William spoke as his eyes scanned over the drink menu.

Marcus cleared his throat, and leaned back as he wrapped an arm behind my chair. "I'm more of a liquor man, but I'm always down for a good beer."

"Whisky?" William looked up from the menu with an arched brow toward Marcus.

"Yes, sir."

William's lips curled into a grin. "Atta boy. Ma'am?" He waved the waitress back over and handed over the menu, "Two Johnnie Walkers on the rocks, a glass of merlot for my wife here, and, Mia?" He looked at me.

"A cosmo, please." The waitress nodded before turning on her heels and padding her way toward the bar.

William looked over at Marcus and me. With a huge grin, he leaned his elbows on the table. "So, with all that was going on yesterday, we didn't have much time to discuss the two of you. How long have you been dating?"

I wasn't expecting that, and as I started doing the math, Marcus chimed in, "Six months."

My head snapped in his direction, and with furrowed brows, I questioned it, "Really?"

Smiling, he ran his hand up and down my arm. "Yes, babe. We met in April. Well, to be technical, we met at the end of April, so it'll be six months in a couple of weeks."

"Wow, I didn't realize it was that long. It felt so much shorter."

"That's a good thing, honey," Kathy said with a smile.

"It is?" I questioned.

"Oh, yeah," William chuckled. "Kathy and I have been married for over forty years, and it feels like yesterday when she agreed to marry me." He leaned in and kissed the side of her head.

Adoration filled his eyes as he took a moment to admire his wife. I couldn't help but smile at the two of them. "It wasn't easy. It still isn't easy," Kathy added. "Marriage takes a lot of work, but if you can find someone willing to accept your flaws, it eventually works itself out."

Marcus gently squeezed my arm, and my mind traveled to our earlier conversation in the bathroom. He must have thought about it as well. The discussion about marriage caused my thoughts to wander to our engagement that was put on hold. When Marcus and I rekindled our relationship a month ago, it was something that we both agreed to put aside as we worked on us. Marriage was no longer the priority; building our relationship was.

When the waitress arrived with our drinks, William lifted his glass. "To a long life together." Marcus and Kathy lifted their glasses with a simple nod, and we all took a sip of our drinks.

"You guys started the party without us?" Megan complained as she approached us with my mother and Jeremy trailing behind her.

"Come join us, my dear. Our drinks just arrived," Kathy uttered with a wave of her hand.

All three joined us and took their seats at the table. "Hello, what would you like to drink?" The waitress asked as she took note of the new guests at our table. Megan ordered a martini, Jeremy a beer, and my mother a glass of wine.

After everyone had settled in with their drinks and had placed their dinner order, we began a casual discussion. "So, how are you enjoying Philly, Marcus and Mia?" Sara asked as she sipped on her wine.

Marcus went first. "I like it a lot here. It was nice seeing Mia's face light up at places she'd remembered as a child."

Smiling at his statement, I placed my hand on his leg underneath the table. "It brought back a lot of wonderful memories of Dad and Michael." Sara gently nodded with a soft smile.

"Yeah, I'm really digging this place." Jeremy decided to add, even though nobody had asked for his opinion.

"Oh, Marcus and Mia, I hope you guys don't mind if Jeremy and I ride back to Boston with you. Sara is staying a little longer, and I have work on Monday," Megan stated with a slight shrug and soft playful grin.

"Yeah, that's fine." Marcus replied to her.

Megan's smile widened. "Yay, road trip!"

The rest of the dinner was more fun than I had expected: the discussions, the laughing, the drinking, the jokes—it all was perfect. My grandfather was charming, my grandmother was sweet, Megan was enthusiastic, my mother giggled and talked about the good old days, and Jeremy . . . Well, he was simply *Jeremy*. Now, Marcus on the other hand . . . I was in awe of him by the end of the night. He joined in on specific topics, cracked a few jokes with Jeremy, and laughed along with my grandmother. It was another side to him that I hadn't yet witnessed and an experience that I would never forget.

As the evening came to an end, I said good-bye to my grandparents, squeezed them tightly, and promised to visit again soon. Because I wouldn't see my mother before we left in the morning, I pulled her into a hug and thanked her for inviting me. I assured her that this trip was just what I needed and that I couldn't have been more grateful. We drove back to the hotel with Jeremy and Megan as they sat quietly in the back seat. Marcus held my hand in the front seat. He was talkative and discussed certain subjects that William had brought up at dinner, and I laughed right along with him.

To say that the night ended wonderfully was an understatement.

***

After breakfast that Sunday morning, Marcus, Jeremy, Megan, and I took one last stroll around the City of Brotherly Love before checking out of the hotel. As much as I wasn't ready to leave just yet, I knew I had a life waiting for me in Boston.

Jeremy and Megan hopped into the back seat of Marcus's car as I slid into the front passenger seat right beside Marcus. He reached out and brushed the back of his fingers along my cheek as he flashed an adorable grin and winked before turning on the ignition.

As soon as Marcus turned the car on, the loud pounding music of Taylor Swift's song "We Are Never Getting Back Together" hit the speakers. Marcus shook his head before he reached to change the station, but we both froze as we heard a loud, high-pitched voice singing along with the song. It was an absolute shock to the both of us as we turned our heads and focused our eyes on Jeremy.

Jeremy's eyes were shut tightly. His head was swaying side to side as he felt the groove of the beat. Marcus and I quickly glanced at each other, amused, and then turned our gazes back to Jeremy. Megan was giggling beside him as she watched as well. Jeremy, not knowing that all eyes were on him, continued to sing in a high-pitched tone about never getting back together.

Jeremy eyes flashed open, and he stopped howling in mid-song. His brows bunched together as he studied all the eyes on him. "What? Taylor Swift is hot!"

Marcus snapped his head toward me and with an arched brow said, "This is going to be a long fuckin' drive."

CHAPTER SEVENTEEN

MARCUS

Five and a half hours later, we were back in Boston. Although it had been great to escape, it was also a relief to be home. Jeremy was annoying me during the entire drive. I was glad to have finally dropped his ass off. Megan and Jeremy nagged at each other constantly, which was both amusing and frustrating at the same time. It made me feel a bit more at ease about my relationship with Mia, just knowing that we weren't the only couple that argued all the time. At least when we did, it was for valid reasons, whereas Megan and Jeremy nitpicked at every detail and then joked about it after an unnecessary argument.

Mia dropped her things at her apartment and came home with me. I didn't want to push the issue about moving in together because I knew she wasn't ready for it. She was satisfied with how we sometimes slept over at each other's places, but I wasn't content with it. I wanted her close to me every night. We had put the wedding aside at her request as well. If it had been up to me, I would have married her yesterday. Again, I couldn't force her into any of it. I just had to stand back and wait until she was ready.

As I pulled into the driveway of my home, Mia let out a yawn and stretched. We had left Philly around eleven in the morning and had arrived home close to six that evening. It was a long and exhausting fucking drive. After turning off the ignition, we exited the vehicle, and I grabbed our bags. Mia waited by the passenger side as I made my way toward her from the trunk of the car. She leaned in towards me as I wrapped an arm around her shoulder. "Are you hungry?" I asked as we walked side by side.

"No, I just want to crawl into bed and sleep. I have an early class in the morning."

"Okay, I think I'll join you. I have a deposition at ten tomorrow morning. We can have an early breakfast before your class."

Mia tilted her neck up, and the edge of her lips curled into grin. "What?" I asked matching her smile.

"Nothing. Sometimes you can be sweet, you know?"

"Ha, no, I thought I was an asshole."

"That too, but sweet for the most part."

"I'll take it." I kissed the top of her head as she let out a slight giggle.

We walked up the stairs of the front porch and quickly spotted Jimmie. His head was slumped back against a patio chair with a beer in his hand and a cooler beside his foot. Mia and I glanced at each other skeptically and then went over towards him. Jimmie never drank when he was watching Elle. He said it was a bad example.

As we approached Jimmie, I noticed that his eyes were closed. I wasn't sure if he was asleep, so I tapped his boot with mine. "Hey, Bro."

Jimmie snapped one eye opened. After a few seconds, he collected his thoughts and opened both eyes, "What's up, guys? How was Philly?" He kept his head back against the chair.

"It was good." Mia answered.

I quickly looked around the porch and then back at him, "Where's Elle?"

He let out a heavy sigh, ran a hand over his face, and then sat up straight in his chair. "She's with Mom. She's also mad at me because she's being punished."

Laughing once, I arched a brow, "Your punishment for her was sending her to Mom? Mom spoils her rotten."

He raised both brows as he chugged the rest of the beer. After he finished, he placed it on the floor beside four other empty bottles. Reaching into the cooler, he twisted open another one and leaned back. "Yeah, well, she called Mom after I punished her and said, and I quote, 'Grandma, Daddy is not being a fair father, and I want to run away.'" He took a long pull on the fresh beer and then shrugged, "So, of course, Mom came to the rescue. After Mom and I talked, well, more like argued about my parenting skills, she took Elle out to calm her down. That was forty minutes ago."

"Yep, that sounds like Mom."

Mia bunched her brows together. "Sorry, Jimmie. She'll come around. Little girls can be a bit dramatic."

"You think?"

Mia pulled out from my arm wrapped around her and gripped the bag in my hand, "I'm going up. I'll see you in a bit." She glanced meaningfully at me then tilted her head towards Jimmie, indicating for me to stay and talk with him. I nodded in understanding. "Oh, Jimmie, how about that group date this weekend?"

Jimmie shook his head. "Nah, things didn't work out with Jessica and me."

Mia's face fell sadly. "Oh? I'm sorry."

"It's good."

Mia gently smiled and then made her way into the house after saying her farewells to Jimmie. I was tired, but knowing I'd never seen Jimmie in that state, I reached for a beer and slumped into a chair beside him. We both sipped on Samuel Adams, our gazes straight ahead, overlooking the front landscaping.

The silence lasted long enough. I spoke up first, "Why was Elle punished?"

"She kicked some kid in the balls at the park yesterday." He shook his head when I chuckled.

"What did the kid do?"

"Why does that matter?"

"You know Elle. She's not violent. The kid had to have done something pretty bad to make her go to that extreme. Maybe she was defending herself? Did you ask?"

His jaw slightly tightened as his lips smacked to the side. As if trying to control his anger, he took a long sip on his beer. When his jaw relaxed, his gaze dropped to the bottle in his hand. "The kid asked her where her mom was, and when she told him that she didn't have a mom, that she only had a father, he made fun of her. She got angry and kicked him in the balls."

"Good. The little fucker is lucky I wasn't there. Making fun of my niece? He would have been eating dirt."

Jimmie blew out a heavy sigh. "As a parent, I have to set an example, Marcus. Jeez, I can't let my kid walk all over me."

I didn't understand. Maybe that was a little harsh of me to say, but what the fuck? "Please don't tell me you yelled at her and didn't even talk it out with her?"

"No, first, we started talking. She asked about Cynthia. She wanted to know more about why she was the only kid in her class that didn't have a mom. I told her that her mom was in a better place and that . . ." He paused as he continued to focus on the bottle, twirling it around in his hand. "I didn't know how to tell her that sometimes people in your life, no matter how much you love them, are taken away."

Turning his head toward me, his eyes saddened, he pulled his brows together. "How was I supposed to look into my little girl's eyes and explain something like that? I tried, but then she asked, 'I won't ever lose you, Daddy, right? Promise me.'" As much as he wanted to, I knew he couldn't make a promise like that, especially with the work we did. He tore his eyes away and chugged the rest of his beer. "So, yeah, it didn't go so well. Mom said I should have promised her or told her I wasn't going anywhere, that she's only a little girl and she doesn't understand things like that." He laughed once. "If only she knew . . . Elle's smarter than Mom thinks."

"I know it's not easy with Elle, even though you have Mom and me. I know it's still hard raising a little girl on your own."

"It's not all that bad. I wouldn't trade her for anything in the world, but there are times where I want to rip my hair out. There's going to come a time when she won't be able to talk to me about certain things. And dating? Fuck, when she gets to that age, I'll be hunting dudes down if they get near her."

"I'll be right along with you on that one." We both burst out laughing at the thought. I could just imagine the two us all over Boston, spying as she went on her first date. It would definitely be good times.

After our laughter died down and we finished chatting about what we would do if we were to ever catch a guy touching Elle, we sat in silence and sipped our beers. It was a good silence. I was sure he was reminiscing about Cynthia, and my mind eased for the first time in a long time. Even all the shit I had to deal with in the upcoming week didn't race through my head.

"You know the first exchange at the club is next week, right?" Jimmie poked through my thoughts.

And just like that, within minutes, my eased mind was fucked by Lou, again. "Yep, what are your thoughts on that? You didn't speak up about it when he made the suggestion."

Jimmie raised a brow sarcastically. "We're all screwed anyway. Sooner or later, it'll just come crumbling down, and before we know it, we're all fucked."

"I'm going to need you to hop onto the fuckin' optimistic train. What's gotten into you? You've been acting differently—even before this little shit with Elle." Jimmie burst into a hard full gut belly laugh. "What?" I asked alarmed by his reaction. He laughed even louder at that. Standing up from his chair, he slightly bent over, holding on to his stomach as tears began to form from laughing so hard.

"What's gotten into me?" He barely got that sentence out through his laugh. "Me?" He pointed a thumb at his chest as his laughter erupted throughout the front porch. Like a fucking maniac.

What the fuck?

Then his face fell and his brows narrowed as all the humor washed from his face. "Life, Marcus. Life has gotten into me. Every day is a fuckin' fight—a fight to get out of bed and stand, a fight to push forward. If it weren't for my little girl, I wouldn't give two fucks about any of it. Every night, I fuckin' pray that I can one day make that promise to Elle—that I'll live to see her go to her first day of high school, to see her walk down the aisle, and hopefully one fuckin' day to see her with her own child. I live to protect her from ever falling in love with a man like me, because let's face it, Marcus, we are not good men. Would you want your child with someone like you? Me? Better yet, would you want Elle with someone like us? That's my fuckin' deal." He turned around and stormed over toward the edge of porch. With his hands shoved into his front pockets, he bowed his head and stood silently.

There was nothing I could say to ease the tension because I knew full well that every word Jimmie had just said was true. In silence, I leaned my elbows into my knees and sat there as Jimmie's words sank in deeply. He was right and the fucked-up part of it all? There were only two ways out of this life we'd chosen—death or becoming an informant. Neither one of us was an informant, so I knew what he feared. There was no starting over. That wasn't an option for us.

After fifteen minutes of complete silence, I thought to head back in the house when I heard the sound of a car pulling into the driveway. Jimmie headed toward the edge of the stairway of the porch. The engine shut off and doors slamming shut were heard followed by Elle's voice. "Daddy." Soon afterward, she was climbing the stairs with a pout as she stopped in front of Jimmie, waiting for him to accept her. Jimmie ran his hand over her small face, and she burst into tears. "I'm sorry, Daddy. I didn't mean to kick the boy in the balls. I won't do it again. I promise. Please don't be mad at me." Jimmie chuckled and pulled her in to a tight hug.

"I'm not mad at you, princess."

She tossed her arms over his shoulders as she shut her eyes tightly. "So I'm not punished anymore?"

"Elle, don't push it."

"Okay, Daddy."

"Go in and get ready for bed. You have school in the morning. I'll be up in just a bit." She nodded, pulled away from him, and slowly walked up the steps. Jimmie stood and walked toward the car to our mom.

I headed toward the door. "Hi, Uncle Marc." Elle mumbled as she reached the door. I opened it for her.

Slightly bending, I tugged her chin up, "Hey, I don't get a welcome-home hug?" A soft smile formed along her face.

"Sorry." She said as she reached her hands and wrapped them around my neck. Pulling her in, I whispered, "Oh, and, Elle?"

"Yeah."

"Good job on the balls kicking. Next time, for your sake, tell your dad you tried to aim for the knee and just missed." She giggled with a nod and entered the house.

Jimmie by then ran up the stairs and arched a brow at the grin on my face. "What's up with the smirk?"

"Nothing, man."

He reached for the door and patted my shoulder with his free hand. "Mom's in the car if you want to talk to her."

"She's not coming in?" Jimmie shrugged and went in the house.

Glancing over at driveway, I could see my mother in the driver's seat of her BMW. Her eyes were on me. Although it was darker out, the lights in her vehicle were on. I let out a deep breath and headed towards her. She cut off the ignition and climbed out of the car at that time.

"Hi, baby." She whispered as she reached out and rubbed her hand along my arm. She leaned up to kiss my cheek.

After I returned the gesture, I shoved my hands into my front pockets and then straightened my shoulders. "Hey, Mom."

She dangled the car keys in her hand and bowed her head toward the ground, lost in thought. "How was Philly?" She asked in a low tone and then brought her gaze back to me.

"It was good."

She nodded, pressed her lips together, and then let out a sigh. "Marcus, I really want to talk to you. I know you traveled all day and are probably exhausted, so I won't bother you tonight, but do you think we could meet up for lunch? Tomorrow perhaps? I'll stop by the office. We can eat there or out, whichever you'd like."

"Yeah, sure." She responded to my short answer with a tight smile. I knew I wasn't being exactly cooperative, but I wasn't ready to get into a big emotional scene with her. With just getting back and the whole thing with Jimmie, I just wanted a fucking drama-free night for once.

"Okay, is noon good for you?"

"I have a deposition at ten. Let's make it one to play it safe."

"Okay, that sounds good. Thank you." I nodded in response.

My mother turned on her heels, hopped into her car, and pulled away.

***

When I entered the bedroom, Mia was fast asleep. Not wanting to wake her, I hopped in the shower, dressed, and went back down to my office. I needed to look over the Jefferson file for tomorrow's deposition. It wasn't my case, but I was filling in for another attorney and needed to catch up on the file. I also needed to focus on anything else besides my mother and Lou, the club, and what Jimmie had said. I shoved all of those fucking thoughts to the back of my head and focused on work.

Fingers grazed along my jawline, waking me from my sleep. I knew it was her by the scent of her perfume even before my eyes flashed open. I smiled as she climbed on top of my lap in a straddled position. Her hair was untamed from her sleep. I leaned my head back and watched her for a while as she ran her fingers through my hair. I felt at ease.

"When I woke up, you weren't in bed." Her concerned eyes scanned my face. "Are you okay, baby?"

I reached up and twirled a lock of her hair around my finger. "I was working on a file and fell asleep."

Smiling, she wrapped her hands around the back of my neck. "Mmmh, well, come to bed with me. It's lonely without you."

With my head tilted aside, I watched as her still sleepy eyes studied me with a slight smile. "Move in with me?"

Puzzled by the random question, her brows pressed together, "Huh?"

"Come on, Mia. It just seems right." I grazed her cheek with my fingertips. "I just want to hold you close every night and wake up to this beautiful face every morning."

"Marcus, I . . ." At a loss for words, she lightly shook her head, in an attempt to clear her mind. After she wet her lips, her eyes locked back on mine. "Can I think about it?"

Disappointed by her response, I forced a smile and gave a curt nod. "Of course. Let's go to bed."

"Okay." She whispered as she climbed off my lap and reached her hand out to me. I took it, stood, and we made our way out of my office up the stairs and into my room. I lay in bed more confused than ever as to where she must have seen our relationship going.

CHAPTER EIGHTEEN

MIA

As I lay on my side in bed with the white silk sheets tangled between my legs, wrapped around my torso, and nestled along my arms, I admired Marcus as he dressed for work that morning. I watched as the man before me stood in front of a long mirror with an unreadable expression, yet I knew he was broken in more ways than one.

He was a man with two lives: one that he wanted no part of and another he desperately tried to keep successful. Any man that had to survive the turmoil and struggles that Marcus had in life was usually twice his age. He was a man with many flaws, which haunted his very existence—a man who had held so much hatred in life. Yet, when he loved? It was strong. It was hard. It was passionate. It was without control. And at the end of the day, all this man wanted was *me*.

Marcus caught me staring as his eyes locked with mine in the reflection of the mirror. A soft smile crept along his lips. "You have to go to school soon. Do you still want to have breakfast? I can drive you to campus, and we can stop by the café shop."

"Why can't we just stay in and lie here all day."

A soft chuckled escaped from him as he buttoned the last button of his shirt and tugged the tail of the fabric into his pants. "As much as I would love to, I have this deposition that I promised Peirce I would handle, and you have school."

I let out a pathetic whimper, and knowing that he was right, I stretched and stood up out of the bed. I made my way over to him, pressed my body against his back, and wrapped my arms around him. He grabbed my hand and lifted it, grazing my knuckles along his lips. Then he placed my hand back on his chest as he reached for his tie. "Let me." I asked as I took the silk fabric from his hand. He turned around and looked down at me.

Smiling, I popped his collar up and wrapped the tie around his neck. I felt him staring down at me as I slowly tied a knot, remembering how I did it for my brother. Michael was terrible at tying one. He'd rather put on a clip tie than knot one himself. I softly giggled at the memory, and Marcus gently tilted his head aside. His brown eyes exuded curiosity and humor, and his lopsided grin showed off that adorable dimple I loved so much. He didn't ask what made me laugh; he just continued to watch me.

After I finished knotting the tie and securing it perfectly, I folded down the collar of his shirt. I took a few steps back to admire my masterpiece, and with a big smile, I rocked on my heels and placed my hands behind my back. "All done."

Marcus stood there with a small smile on his lips as his eyes intently focused on mine. Not taking a look in the mirror, he took two steps toward me and gently pressed his lips along my forehead. "Perfect."

"You didn't even take a look." I glanced up at him through my lashes.

He smiled. "I meant you."

With an arched brow, I cocked my head. "Good one. You know you don't have to try so hard with the lines. You'll always get laid."

His laugh surrounded the room. "Yeah, yeah, I'll be downstairs, waiting."

Smiling, I turned on my heels and headed toward the bathroom.

***

"Have you given much thought to what I asked you last night?" Marcus took a bite of his breakfast sandwich. He quickly glanced up from across the small bistro table for two.

"You mean what you asked at two this morning? Which was only a few hours ago? No, I haven't." I teased.

"Well, tell me your thoughts. Why is it such a difficult decision to make?"

With a sigh, I placed my coffee down and focused on him. "Marcus, I'm not sure what it is. On one hand, I really do want to live with you, but then I feel as if something is holding me back. My thoughts keep pulling against each other in a tug of war. I just need time." I lightly shrugged. I wasn't sure why I was having this constant battle between what my heart desired and what my brain advised.

It broke my heart when I saw the same disappointment in Marcus's eyes as I had witnessed a few hours ago. I wanted to jump right on it and say yes. We'd both grown so much, and I knew Marcus was trying hard, but he was still involved with Lou and that criminal lifestyle. As much as I'd tried to put that fact aside, it was something I wanted him to quit. I hadn't told him that because I knew that it would be a major stress and burden to him. Yes, I'd accepted his flaws, but when I thought about having a future with Marcus and starting a family with him, I immediately thought of our children. Marcus became involved in the underground criminal lifestyle because he grew up surrounded by it. Could I live with myself if I allowed my children to grow up in the same environment? I knew I couldn't, because it wasn't a life I knew until I met him.

Maybe I was thinking too far ahead, but I couldn't help it. After what we'd been through in such a short period of time, I wanted to feel secure about our future. Until then, I had to deal with the constant battle between what I *felt* was right and what I *knew* was right.

Marcus simply nodded. "I understand."

He didn't push the issue any further as we continued with our breakfast. After we were finished, he dropped me off at school and drove off to work. With a deep sigh, I prepared for the day ahead.

***

In an empty classroom, I stood before my professor's desk with a shocked expression. His brow lifted, waiting for my response. My stomach knotted as nausea shot through me. "Well, Ms. Sullivan, do you have an explanation?"

"No. I didn't realize I wasn't doing well. I-I . . ." Oh my God, what was I going to do? I couldn't fail this class. My low score on my last exam was threatening my GPA. I swallowed back the lumps that formed in my throat. "What can I do to ensure that I don't fail the class?"

With a smug look, he scribbled something down on a note pad and tore the paper from the binder before handing it to me. I quickly looked at what he gave me. "That's a tutor you can contact. She's really good and could possibly have you back on track before the semester is over. You need to pass the next two exams and the final in order to move forward. I must say, Ms. Sullivan, I'm very disappointed in your lack of dedication. You have to work harder if you want to maintain your GPA."

"You're right; there's no excuse for my lack of commitment. I promise I'll do better. Thank you for this, Professor Barnes."

"I'm sure you will." He went to gather his belongings. Nodding, I turned and walked out of his office. Disappointment burned through me. I'd failed myself. The one part of my life that I should've had under control was falling apart. The hard work I'd put into my studies was what defined me.

Angry with myself, I felt the tears build as I left the building and began my brisk walk home. I wanted to call Marcus and wallow in my self-pity, but he had bigger problems. The last thing I wanted was for him to stress over mine as well. With that, I called the only person I could think of that was used to my whining: Jeremy.

"Oh wow, Mia. Don't cry. I know you're taking this hard, but I know you. You'll get back on track."

Breathing out a heavy sigh as I continued my walk home, I swiped a tear away. "I just can't believe I allowed it to get this far, Jeremy. I don't know what's gotten into me."

"Life. You finally got one. Before, you were so immersed in your studies that you didn't allow anyone or anything else to enter your life. Now, you have Marcus and your mom is back in your life. You've been occupied with them. It's understandable. Don't be so hard on yourself."

"But, this is my future, Jeremy. Without this, I have nothing."

"I know how much it means to you, Mia. From here on out you just need to put everything around you on hold and focus on your studies as you used to do." He was right. There were only a few weeks left in this semester, and I needed to focus all of my attention on studying for my exams. "Mia, you can do this. I know you can."

I can do this.

I can do this.

I can do this.

After repeating it over and over, I felt a bit of relief, "Thank you, Jeremy. Can you do me a favor?"

"Anything."

"Please don't tell Megan. I don't want her to slip and tell Marcus. He has a lot going on right now with work and personal issues; I just don't want him to worry about me as well."

"Sure thing."

CHAPTER NINETEEN

MARCUS

"You were great, Mr. DeLuca." Troy Jefferson exclaimed with a huge grin as he reached out to shake my hand.

"Thank you. You were great as well. You followed the directions and answered all of the questions just as we rehearsed."

"So what happens next?"

"After Peirce handles the defendant's deposition scheduled next week, we'll order the transcripts for both depositions. The opposing counsel and our firm will, of course, go through them. We usually sit back and wait for an offer. If we feel the offer is low, we'll deny it and prepare for trial."

"If we do go to trial, will you be the trial attorney?"

"No, I'm sorry. Peirce is the attorney handling your malpractice claim. He'll be the one at the trial. Don't worry, Mr. Jefferson. You're in good hands."

"I surely don't doubt it. Thank you again." He shook my hand one last time, stood from the chair, and left the conference room.

The deposition took longer than expected, and it was close to one. My mother was due to be at the office soon, which left little time for much else. I quickly gathered the documents, shoved them in the file, and headed toward my office.

When I walked into the office, my mother was already there, early as always, sitting by the bookcase. She was flipping through a magazine. Her head popped up. "Hi honey."

"Hey, I'm just going to use the bathroom, and then we can go. Do you know where you want to have lunch?"

"I thought of the tiny bistro just down the street?"

"Yes, that's fine. Give me a few minutes, and I'll be ready."

"Take your time."

***

We were seated by a private table for two in the far back of the bistro. My mother ordered a glass of wine, and I settled on water. She sipped on her glass as we sat awkwardly in silence. There was a lot I wanted to know, but I wasn't going to push her, so I waited. Hell, I waited until the silence was unbearable. "Mom, you wanted to talk." I reminded her.

She snapped out of her daze, "Yes, honey. I'm sorry. This is just so difficult. I don't know where to begin."

"Try with what began the affair." I suggested in a sarcastic tone.

She wasn't thrilled with my response, but didn't argue against it. Instead, she straightened in her chair and went on after a curt nod. "Marcus, before I explain, you have to understand that I loved your father very much."

"That's very hard to believe."

Her lips quivered at my harsh remark, and then she pressed them together. "Well, I did. It may not seem like it to you now, but I did. There was nothing in the world I wouldn't do for him. He was my first love, my first everything. I knew no one else but him. I was young, naïve, and allowed him to bring me into a way of life that I would be against today. It wasn't easy at first. I accepted it, though, because I loved him, and I was prepared for all of it. At least, I thought I was."

She wiped away a tear that ran down her cheek and then continued, "It wasn't until Jimmie was born that I knew enough was enough. I begged him to leave that lifestyle behind because I didn't want my little boy to be influenced by it. Your father promised me numerous times that he would walk away from it all someday, that he was just waiting for the right time." She slightly shook her head. I listened intently as she continued her confession. "But the right time never came. After I had you, it got even worse. He would use money as a way to justify it all. He said that he wanted a better life for his boys, for me. We constantly argued. I thought we had more than enough money, but to him, it was never enough. I think in the end, because it was the only lifestyle he knew, he didn't want out, because if he really did, he would have left."

"It's not that easy," I blurted, wanting to take it back at that moment. Her head tilted aside, as her eyes grew with curiosity.

"No, no it's not, but there's always a way out, Marcus." She went silent for a moment and then went on. "A couple of months before your father's suicide, he had Lou around you boys and me more often." The sound of his name raked at my skin and boiled my fucking blood. My nostrils flared, and I tried to control the building anger as she continued. "There was a bad exchange. I didn't know much about it, but there was a threat against your father and his family. So Lou was around to protect us, I guess. I wasn't sure how it all began, but it did." A sob escaped her as she confessed to being unfaithful to a man she claimed to love. "Lou satisfied the void that your father failed to fulfill." Tears began to stream down her face as she sniffed a few times. "Oh God, I know it was a terrible and disloyal thing to do. I felt sick about it, and I prayed every single night and day for forgiveness. When your father found out about the affair and then he committed suicide a week later, my heart shattered into a million pieces, Marcus. I blamed myself every single day since his death. *Every day.*" I leaned back in my chair and watched as my mother broke out into soft sobs.

As much as I wanted to be pissed off with her, I couldn't. The fact that she thought she was responsible for my father's death sickened me. I wasn't sure what was behind Lou's reasoning in killing my father, and I wasn't sure that I would ever know. Maybe the affair was one of the many reasons. But if I truly knew Lou, I knew that he was a greedy son of a bitch and desired nothing more than power. He wanted to control it all, and the fact that my father was the one in his way convinced me that had to have been more than just the affair. Seducing my mother was probably some sick fucking twisted plot of his.

I reached out and grabbed my mother's hand. She looked up at me as she dabbed a tissue along her eyes. "Mom, I'm sorry for not hearing you out to begin with, and I'm sorry you had to live with that burden for the last fifteen years, but you must know you were not responsible for Dad's death. You have to let that go and move on with your life."

"One day I will." She sniffed. "Thank you, honey, for understanding."

She pulled out a compact mirror from her bag, and her eyes widened at her reflection, "Oh my, look at me. I have mascara smeared everywhere." She grabbed a fresh tissue and cleaned her face up.

"You still look beautiful, Mom. Don't worry about it."

She laughed at that. "Oh, you not only have your father's looks and traits but his charm as well." Her expression fell as her gaze focused on me from under her lashes. "Marcus, promise me something?"

"Anything, Mom."

"Promise me you'll find a way out."

Puzzled, I tilted my head aside. "What do you mean?"

Her eyes softened. "You know what I mean. Mia's a good woman. Don't put her through what your father put me through.

My heart began to race as my breathing grew rapid. "You know?"

"I've lived that life for almost twenty years. So, yes, I've known. I wasn't thrilled about it. I was hoping you'd find a way out. I wanted to reach out to you, but when I almost did, I thought it was too late. The life sucked you right in. Then, suddenly, out of nowhere you changed. That's when Mia walked into your life. I've loved her from the moment I met her, and I've wanted to thank her. In a way, she's saved you. I've always said people walk into our lives for a reason. She walked into yours to help you break free from all of this, Marcus. Then I thought maybe, just maybe, it's not too late."

Each word she spoke stabbed at my heart. I wasn't sure if it was the talk about my father, about Lou, or even Mia, but something came over me. It felt as if someone had reached deep within me, pulled me out, and jerked me alive.

Fuck it all.

I stood from the table, gave my mother a kiss on the cheek, and left her sitting there with her eyes puzzled and confused by my unexpected departure. Instead of going back to the office, I made a few phone calls to see where *he* was—the fucker I needed to see that fucking moment. After locating him, I jumped into my car and raced there.

During the entire drive, my blood pumped. The reason for being in this entire fucking mess with Michael and Jimmie to begin with had completely vanished. The thought of ever losing Mia and my family or them losing me due to a wrong fucking decision sprinted through my head. Lou could go to fucking hell for all I cared.

I didn't want it anymore.

I didn't care for any of it any fucking more.

Pulling into the driveway of his nephew Gio's home, I hopped out of the car and stormed toward the door. My heart was racing with every step. The adrenaline pumped through my veins. I reached the front door with a clenched fist and repeatedly banged against the wooden surface. Breathing heavily, I rocked in place with my fist secured by my side.

The door finally swung open and a baffled Gio stood on the other end of it. "What are you doing here?"

"Where's Lou?" I sneered as I barged passed him, not waiting for him to invite me in.

"He's in the backyard."

I made an abrupt halt in the foyer when I realized I'd never been here before. I turned back around to face Gio. "Lead the way."

His brows kneaded together. "What's this all about, Marky?"

"That's between Lou and me."

"Hmmm. Really?" He cocked his head aside.

Fuck it. I didn't have time for his fucking games. I turned around and began storming through the house. "Lou!" I yelled as I turned into what seemed to be a family room. Fucker wasn't there. Turning, I went down a hall. "Lou!" I shouted again as I entered a dining area.

"What the fuck, Marky?" Gio followed behind me.

I pushed him aside when I twisted around again and exited the dining room. Heading down another hall, I entered the kitchen. There were sliding doors that led to the backyard. "Lou!" I spat out.

Rushing forward, I slid the door open and stepped into the back yard. There he fucking was. He sat by the pool in a suit. He was engaged in a conversation with two other men. All three looked my way as I rushed over to them. "Lou, we need to talk."

Irritation spread across his face. He must be handling a deal, but I didn't give two fucks. The other two men were not pleased with my interruption, judging from their smug expressions. "Marky, this will have to wait. I'm handling business here."

"Now, Lou." I sneered.

With wide eyes, the veins in his neck bulged as his face turned beet red. Very slowly, he snapped his head side to side, cracking his neck. Lou breathed in trying to calm his nerves as his nostrils flared. "Excuse me, fellas," he said smoothly, although I knew he was boiling inside. Good. I wanted him on my fucking level.

Standing from his chair, he loosened one button from his suit jacket. The entire time his gaze held onto mine. "Marky, this way." He waved his arm back to where I had just come from.

I nodded, and then I quickly went back through the sliding doors and paced in the kitchen as I waited for him. A few seconds later, he closed the door behind him as he entered. "Have you lost your fuckin' mind? Never, ever, barge into a fuckin' meeting like that again. What the fuck is your problem?"

"I'm out."

Confusion shadowed his features. "What the fuck are you talking about?"

"I'm out. I'm done. I don't want it, Lou. I'm finished being your fuckin' puppet. I'm going to live my life my way, and that's without all of this shit." I stretched my arm toward the backyard indicating the jobs, the deals, and the fucking mob.

His mocking laughter erupted in the room. After it subsided, he adjusted his jacket and leaned against the breakfast bar. "I'm sorry to tell you this, but that's not happening."

"And why is that exactly?" I grew more agitated as his cocky fucking grin grew wider.

"Because there are only two reasons why you leave the family." He lifted two fingers, as he referred to the mob as the family. *Family* my fucking ball sack. "One, you turned on us and are a fuckin' rat, or, two, you're a fuckin' pig. Which one is it, Marky?"

"I'm neither. I'm not a fuckin' cop, nor am I a fuckin' snitch. I'm just finished with it all. Done. I'm out, Lou. If you don't like it, then tough shit." I turned my back on him to make my way through the hall. I came to a complete fucking stop at the sound of his gun being cocked. Slowly, I turned around. Lou stood there with his gun pointed directly at me. "You're going to fuckin' shoot me, Lou?" I wasn't surprised, I didn't expect anything less. I still didn't stop as the rage pumped through me. I ripped off my jacket, tossed it on the ground and raised my arms. "Shoot." His eyes grew in amusement as he tilted his head aside. "If you're going to point a gun at me, then use it, Lou. I'm not backing down. If I stay in this shit, I'm a fuckin' dead man anyway, sooner or later. So go the fuck ahead. Shoot."

Laughing once, he slightly jiggled the gun, playing with it, and then he brought his hand down to his side. I dropped my arms, nodded once, and spun back around. "Marky?" I stopped in my tracks but didn't face him again. "I know about your little girlfriend." My heart skipped a beat as I faced him again. He held a smug grin. "The lovely Mia Sullivan, sister of the undercover BPD Michael Sullivan." He cocked his head to the other side. "Oh, did you think I wouldn't figure it out?"

I didn't respond as I bit down, clenching my jaw tight.

"I've had my men all over you and her for weeks now. I know every fuckin' move both of you make. I know Mia's school schedule. I know what she fuckin' ate for breakfast this fuckin' morning. I even know when she last sucked your fuckin' cock." His expression fell as it grew with anger. "Don't fuck with me, you fuckin' bastard. I hold the key to both of your fuckin' lives. I can make one fuckin' phone call, and just like that," he snapped his fingers, "she's dead."

"You fuckin' asshole, if you lay a hand on her . . ." I went to surge toward him but was instantly held back. Arms wrapped around me and pinned me in.

"Not a fuckin' move." Gio growled.

I struggled against him as Lou made his way toward us. "It's fine, Gio. Let him go." Gio was hesitant at first but then released me.

"Fucker." I spat as I shoved Gio against the fucking wall.

Gio swung at me, but I ducked in time and quickly jabbed him in the rib with a tight fist. He winced on contact. I jabbed him again with a right hook, and his head jerked back into the wall. In a matter of seconds, he regained conscious and flung himself at me, wrapping his hands around my neck. Blood. I wanted to see blood. With a white-knuckled tight fist, I slammed it against his fucking nose and continued to slam against his face over and over again. Blood gushed from his face. A bit satisfied and with a sly smile, I shoved him against the wall and continued to pound my fist into him.

BANG!

The sound of a gun going off forced the both of us to stop fighting. Gio and I both turned towards Lou. He held his arm up with the gun in his hand pointed at the ceiling. Debris from the sheetrock drifted to the ground.

"Now, that I have both of you fuckers' attention." I tugged away from Gio and groaned. I could taste the blood from my busted lip.

Gio wiped the back of his hand over his nose.

"Marky, we're still using the fuckin' club. You want out of the jobs, so be it. I don't trust you'll be successful with them anymore anyway, but the trades will still happen in the club with or without your presence."

My chest heaved in and out as I breathed heavily. "And Mia?"

He arched a brow. "Do you agree on the club?"

"You can have the fuckin' club."

"Then Mia is no longer an issue."

That was all I needed to hear. I bent over, grabbed my jacket from the ground, faced Gio with a narrow glare, and got the fuck out of there.

As I entered my car, I reached for my phone and dialed Jimmie's number. He wasn't going to be thrilled with my news.

"What the fuck, Marcus?" Jimmie's voice pierced through the car speakers as I sped down the highway.

"I had enough, Jimmie."

"Did you honestly believe Lou would just let you walk out scot free?"

"No, I don't, but that's where you come in. We need to figure out who was working with Michael. Fast. I can't risk the chances of Mia getting hurt."

Jimmie cursed under his breath. "You just fuckin' signed your death warrant." He blew out through the phone. "I'll see what I can do. At first, I wasn't successful, but I just got some information that may lead me somewhere."

"Good. Oh, and Jimmie, don't mention this to Mia. I don't want to scare her."

"She has to know soon. What if she's confronted by one of Lou's men?"

"I'll take care of that. Just take care of the Michael situation."

"Alright, I'm on it."

***

The scorching water hit my aching muscles. I bowed my head and allowed the steamy water from the shower to drench my skin and seize all of the tension. With a drained sigh, I thought of Mia. I had a busted lip and bruised face. There was no way I could see her that night. She would only question me, and all I wanted to do was to protect her from it all.

I felt as if I were being pulled apart in so many fucking directions: one toward Mia and another toward the dark fucking path my life had been heading before I met her. Mia kept me grounded and at that very moment, there was no room to be weak. I needed to focus on protecting her and bringing down Lou. I had no clue how, but I was starting with Mia. I wasn't sure whom to trust because anyone could be working with Lou.

After my shower, I dressed and drove to Mia's apartment, parked out front, and stayed in the car all night until the early morning. That was all I could do for now.

CHAPTER TWENTY

MIA

For the next couple of weeks, I'd been extremely busy with school, studies, and tutoring. I hadn't had much time for anything else. Literally *nothing* else, not even Marcus. God, I missed him so much. The separation was killing me. He was just as busy with the firm and with all of the jobs lately, so I wasn't sure when we'd have time for just us, until he texted me last night.

> Do you think I can buy some time to spend with my girl? Maybe dinner tomorrow night?

It made me smile and feel guilty at the same time. I knew that if we actually lived together, it would be easier on both of us. What the hell was wrong with me? It was just at that moment when I realized that nothing else mattered as long as I had him close by me always.

I quickly glanced at the bedroom door when I heard a light knock, and Megan poked her head through. "Hey, Mia."

"Megan, hi! Come in."

She padded her way over to my bed and slumped down beside me, tossing her head back onto a pillow. I quickly grabbed some of the notes I'd written from beneath her and secured them under my textbook. My bed had become my fort for the last few days. If I wasn't in the library with my tutor or in class, I was in my bedroom. It was also a mess.

"I feel as if, even though you live here, you've been so absent."

"Yeah, I'm sorry. This class is kicking my ass. With only a few weeks left, I'm really focused and determined to get it over with."

"Yeah, I can see that." She glared at the pile of textbooks, my laptop, and documents spread along my comforter.

"I'm sorry."

"It's okay. Hey, do you want to have a spa day today? You could use a day off from all of this."

"I have dinner plans with Marcus tonight."

She shrugged. "It's only noon, and we'll be back before then. What time is he expected?"

"I believe eight."

She jumped up and grabbed my arm with both hands, pleading with her eyes. "See, we have plenty of time. Please! I miss you."

With an eye roll, I tossed the highlighter in my hand on the bed and agreed. "Fine."

"Yay!" she squealed.

"What's this spa thing I'm hearing about?" Jeremy trudged into the room with a bowl of cereal in his hand. His curly blond hair was tossed in all sorts of directions as his blue sleepy eyes scanned my bed.

"We're getting massages," Megan said with a nod.

Jeremy scrunched his nose and shook his head before dipping the spoon into the bowl of flakes and shoved it in his mouth. After a few chews, he asked, "You like massages?"

"Who doesn't?" Megan shot back.

"I don't." He made another face.

"Had a bad experience before, Jeremy?" I asked, laughing at his face expression.

"Nope, never got one."

Megan arched a brow in confusion. "Then why are you so against it?"

"It puts you in a completely relaxed state."

Both Megan and I were beyond confused, but curious as to what he'd come up with. "Okay, that's kind of the point, Jeremy." I chimed in.

"Exactly." Megan followed.

Jeremy rolled his eyes, "Exactly, my point. Just imagine: your lying there, completely relaxed. Every single muscle has never been so stress-free. Then you have someone pressing down on each part of your body. It feels great, right? But," he held a finger up with wide eyes, "eventually when they push down on your back, you're bound to let one loose."

"What?" I burst out laughing. He was too much. I couldn't take it. My head fell back as I held my stomach trying to control the ache from laughing so hard.

"A fart, Jeremy! Really? That's why you don't like massages!" Megan stood with a hand on her hip as she rolled her eyes. "You're unbelievable!"

He gave a slight shrug. "Don't believe me? Wait and see." He turned on the heels of his bare feet and left the room.

Megan shot me a look when I couldn't control my breathing. "Are you going or not?" She asked with slight annoyance.

"Okay, phew. Okay. I'm going." I calmed myself.

***

Megan and I sat in a small room wrapped in oversized robes as we sipped champagne. The lights were dimmed as soft music played in the background. The scent of lavender filled the room, making it feel like a sanctuary. I was happy that had Megan invited me along. I needed that moment to get away from it all. Deep down, I still felt guilty because I could have been using that time for my studies, but I'd been working my butt off for the past couple of weeks. A few hours wouldn't kill me.

"Ladies, whenever you're ready." A very good-looking man exited one of the rooms. Megan wiggled her brows at me as we both stood and made our way over to him. As we entered the room, there were two massage beds beside each other. It was even darker in that room than it had been in the waiting room. "I'll give you five minutes to get yourselves together. Each of you will lie on the bed face down. Please remove everything except for your underwear." He smiled and left Megan and me alone.

Megan stripped off the robe and lay on the bed to the left. I took the one on the right and nestled in. "This is going to be awesome," she said in a loud whisper.

"I'm glad you talked me into this. I really needed it."

"Of course, now relax and enjoy it." There was a knock at the door, and this time, the man brought a woman with him. She was my masseuse while he worked on Megan.

I wasn't sure how long it was into our massages, because I was in such a daze, when Megan called out for me. It felt amazing as my masseuse worked out all the kinks in my aching and stressed muscles. "Mia," she whispered again.

"Yes," I moaned as the masseuse continued to work her magic.

"Um, I think Jeremy was right."

Oh my God. I snorted, causing both of us to erupt into full-blown laughs. It was so bad that we had to stop the massages early. We couldn't stop laughing.

***

I couldn't control the impulse that came over me. Once I saw Marcus leaning against his car, looking every bit as sexy as he was, I exited the apartment building, and a squeal escaped me as I ran and jumped into Marcus's arms. Nearly knocking him over, I landed wet kisses all over his face. How I had missed that handsome face. He held me tightly against his chest with a smile. "Whoa, is it safe to say that someone missed me?" He flashed a crooked, adorable grin.

"You have no idea." I smashed my lips against his, kissing him over and over again. My eyes flashed opened. "And I'm horny. I'm so horny." I rumbled against his mouth.

Chuckling, he narrowed his glare. "Quite honestly, I'm not sure if I should be thrilled about that or feel offended?" I raised a brow, confused as to why he would feel offended. "Because you see me as your love slave instead of your boyfriend." He winked.

I smiled. "Feel offended, very offended, but whatever you do, just take it out on me in bed."

Marcus tossed his head back and laughed. After he controlled himself, he pulled me in tighter. "Ah, I've missed you."

"So you agree then? We can just ditch dinner and go straight for the car sex?"

"Settle down there." He placed me back down on the ground. "We need to eat first. You'll need plenty of fuel for what I have planned for you."

I snapped my fingers. "Damn it, I was so close."

Shaking his head, he opened the passenger door for me. "Come on my little horny demon. Let's go eat."

"Fine, but if you need me to quickly polish you off on the way to the restaurant, I'm your gal." I winked and hopped into the passenger seat.

"What has gotten into you?" He laughed. "Have I neglected you for that long?"

Innocently, I shrugged and batted my lashes. He laughed again and shut the door.

The entire drive to the restaurant, Marcus and I chatted as if the last two weeks had not even passed. We caught up, sure, but a lot of it was because we had deepened our connection. I told him about Jeremy and the massages, and we couldn't stop laughing about it. I also mentioned that I was taking my studies more seriously because the semester was coming to an end, but I left out the tutoring and possibility of failing my class. We were in such a good spirits, and I didn't want to ruin the moment.

We pulled into a parking lot, and he cut off the ignition. I was still laughing from our goofing around. Calming, I tossed my head against the headrest and ogled him. Marcus leaned back and stared at me as well. He brought the back of his fingers to my face and traced them along my jawline. "You're so beautiful."

"You're quite a catch yourself. I think we make a pretty fine couple, Mr. DeLuca."

His face softened with a sly grin. "I love seeing you like this."

"Like?"

"Happy. Laughing. Just being you."

My heart swelled with so much love for him. "You make me like this."

He leaned in and pressed his lips against the tip of my nose and then trailed his lips down to mine. "Good. I would hate to be responsible for your unhappiness."

"You could never make me unhappy."

Although he nodded at that statement, his eyes filled with doubt.

During the next couple of hours, Marcus and I indulged in good food, wine, and conversation. We discussed the talk he had with his mother and how he felt better afterwards. That was a relief. The issue with his mother was such a huge burden on him, and I was glad that it was finally resolved. It reminded me of something: in life sometimes you don't have second chances, and you shouldn't be scared to just take a chance on something you really want. There could be numerous excuses that you come up with to avoid making that leap of faith. That day, I decided to take a leap for the reason staring right at me.

"Marcus?"

"Yeah?" He ate the last bite of his meal, wiping his plate clean.

"I want to move in."

He looked up from his plate and shot me a slight grin. "You're joking?"

"No, well, not right now. After this semester, during winter break. I can't focus on a move at this moment with my upcoming exams, but definitely when it's all over. That is, if you still want me?"

"Are you kidding? You can move in tonight. Hell, you don't need to move a thing. I'll do it all so you can focus on your studies."

Laughing, I rolled my eyes, "Marcus, you can wait a few more weeks."

"What if I withhold sex from you until you move in? Would that make you move in any faster?"

My jaw dropped open with a gasp. "You wouldn't dare."

With a mischievous grin, he leaned back in his chair, placing both his hands behind his head. "Oh, how the tables have turned. You remember that two-week bet? It'll be a bit similar."

My expression fell. He did not just go there! I reached for the napkin and tossed it at him. He burst out laughing.

"That is so not fair."

"Maybe you're right, but I remember having that same argument about your little arrangement." He winked.

When I went to speak again, his phone beeped. He grabbed it from the table and swiped the screen to read the message. His facial expression went from humorous to unreadable within a matter of seconds. "Everything okay?" My eyes scanned his face.

"Yeah, but I need to get going."

"What? You mean our night is over?"

He glanced at me with apologetic eyes. "Yes, babe, I'm sorry. I have to be somewhere, and it's very important."

"Where do you have to be?"

"I have to meet with Jimmie."

"For what?"

"To collect some information."

"What kind of information?"

Our eyes locked. We were pleading with each other; he was pleading with me to stop the interrogation and I was pleading with him to answer.

"Mia, can you just drop it? The information is confidential."

I dropped my gaze. "Okay. I'm going to use the restroom and then we can go." I stood from my chair and began to briskly pass him when he caught my wrist.

"Mia, just trust me, okay?" I nodded and hurried to the restroom.

After Marcus paid the bill, we jumped in his car and drove in silence back to my apartment. For the entire drive, my mind raced, wondering what the information could be that he claimed was so important. I shouldn't be upset that he was leaving, but in a way, I couldn't help it. I hadn't seen him in over two weeks, and I wanted to be selfish, even if it was for one night.

As he pulled up in front of my building, Marcus tugged at my chin for me to look at him. I tore my gaze from the passenger window and focused on him. "Mia, I'm sorry. I promise we'll have plenty of nights together. I just really need to take care of a few things. I'm working on our future."

What was that supposed to mean? But I knew that questioning him was problematic, so instead, I leaned in and kissed him. "I know you are." I gently smiled. "We have the rest of our lives together, right?"

His eyes gleamed. "Exactly."

CHAPTER TWENTY-ONE

MARCUS

After Mia entered her apartment building, I waited for a few minutes and then sped off. As I kept my eyes focused on the road, I quickly dialed Jimmie's number, only glancing a few times at the screen. On the third ring, he answered, his voice in surround sound coming out of my car speakers. "Are you on your way?" He asked.

"Yeah, you're home, right?"

"Yep."

"Are you going to give me any clue about this urgent info that you retrieved?

"Nope." The information he had must have been intense because he didn't disclose it over the phone.

"Fine, I just dropped Mia off. I should be home in forty minutes."

"See you soon, Bro."

With traffic, it was impossible to go any faster than I was already going. As I ripped through the hectic city of Greater Boston to Back Bay, where trucks double-parked and pedestrians hadn't a care in the world as they risked walking in front of moving vehicles, my mind was immersed in the last couple of weeks. Mia was busy with school, which prevented her from questioning my absence. Jimmie and I had been working hard on trying to find any piece of information that could link us to who Michael was working with. We searched old documents and emails he had sent us.

It was difficult to trust anyone, so we walked on eggshells and were careful with whom we spoke. We knew that any of Lou's men were out of the question. Even if we suspected one of his men, we couldn't risk it. I hadn't spoken to that bastard since our encounter at Gio's home a couple of weeks back. Jimmie wasn't thrilled with it, but it got us away from Lou, for now at least, until we found something to bring the fucker down. Lou used the club last Sunday for the first time. I had heard it was a smooth transaction, but I knew that it wouldn't always be the case. For the life of me, I couldn't figure out his infatuation with the damn club.

After a pain-in-the-ass car ride, I finally reached my home. Hopping out of the car, I hurried into the house, tossed my keys onto the table by the door, and entered the living room area. Jimmie was there with Elle. He nodded in acknowledgment.

"Uncle Marc!" Elle squealed in excitement. I hadn't seen Elle for the past couple of weeks either, with her being in school and with my sleeping in my damn car at night watching Mia's place.

"Hey, sweetheart." Elle ran over to me and pulled me into a hug.

Jimmie stood up from the couch. "Elle, Uncle Marc and I need to talk, and it's past your bedtime. Get ready for bed, and I'll be up in a little while to tuck you in."

"Pfft." She sucked her teeth. Jimmie sent an authoritative glare her way. She slightly pouted and bowed her head. "Sorry, Daddy. Good night, Uncle Marc."

"Night, baby." I waited until she made it up the stairs then shot Jimmie a narrow glare.

"What?"

"Why are you making my little girl pout?" I asked him.

"My little girl, Marcus. Remember that." He shook his head. "She's been giving me a lot of attitude lately. I need to show her who's the parent, or she'll walk all over me, as she does with you."

"Whatever." No point in getting into that. "What's going on?"

He looked over my shoulder and then leaned in to whisper, "I found out who was working with Michael, and you won't fuckin' believe who he is."

"Who?" He nudged his head behind me. I turned to see my office door closed. "He's here?" Jimmie nodded. "What the fuck, Jimmie? Are you sure he's not working with Lou?"

"Marcus, I have evidence: photos of Michael and him together trading information. When I confronted him, he didn't deny it. Marcus, he knew every single detail of the info Michael gave to us. *Everything.*"

With a deep breath, I nodded, spun around, and stormed over to the office door with Jimmie following closely behind me. I wasn't sure who to expect as I opened the door, but once I entered the room, my chest constricted when I saw who it was.

Vinnie, my right hand man when it came to jobs for Lou, was standing by my desk. "Vinnie?"

"What's up, Marky." He nodded his head.

"You were working with Michael? But . . ." I tried to make sense of it. Nothing came up.

"I know it comes as a shock."

"A fuckin' shock is an understatement, don't you think?" I shook off the uneasiness in discovering that bit of information and walked over and grabbed a seat behind my desk and looked over at him. He and Jimmie took a seat in front of me.

"I don't understand. Are you with Boston PD?"

"Nah, I'm actually with the FBI."

I laughed once, but I wasn't the least bit amused. *How the fuck did I miss that?* An agent? I shook my head in disbelief, "For how long?"

He leaned back in his chair lost in thought. "Well, I've been working with the agency for six years now and on the Sorrento case for about three years."

"That's around the time Vinnie became involved with the Sorrentos." Jimmie reminded Marcus.

"Yeah, I remember that," I replied to my brother, then focused my attention back on Vinnie. "So when you began working for Lou, that's when you started the investigation?"

Vinnie nodded. "Yeah, pretty much."

"But, Michael didn't confront us with any information until about a year ago."

"Michael was working with us, trying to bring down any corrupt cops working with the Sorrentos. He was involved with the case from the very beginning, but we needed to get in deeper. What we had wasn't enough. Granted, it takes time to build a case against someone like Lou. I worked on a case before this one in New York, which was a five-year investigation and still ongoing."

Jimmie adjusted in his seat to face Vinnie and asked, "So why were we involved?"

"Bait." Vinnie shrugged. "We knew the two of you were the closest to Lou. He trusted you guys with anything, well, until recently, that is. When he requested information on Mia, we knew you guys were fucked. I was the one he asked to collect info on her. I've had one of my men looking out for her ever since."

Ignoring that, I continued to question him. "Michael said he had evidence and a confession from a source that Lou was the one who killed our father." I leaned into the table, placing both elbows along the wooden surface. "Are you saying that was a lie to get us involved?"

Vinnie let out a heavy breath. "We needed something to lure you guys in. We needed the two of you on our side and against Lou."

"So you're fuckin' saying our father's suicide wasn't a set up?" Jimmie asked to clarify.

Vinnie nodded in response.

What. The. Fuck.

Everything we'd believed the past year was all a fucking lie!

I tossed my head back as a roaring laugh escaped me. Tears began to build from laughing so hard. Jimmie snapped his head at me with a wry expression. Although none of it was funny, not even in the least shape or form, I couldn't stop laughing. It was fucking hilarious how we were led to believe all of it. We were being played as fucking puppets either way. By Lou. By the Feds. My laugh triggered confused looks from both of their faces, as tears built from laughing so hard.

Then I thought of how my life had been turned upside down and ripped apart for the past year: How I wanted to kill Lou with my bare fucking hands because I thought he was responsible for my father's death. How my brother and Michael kept me out of the fucking loop for so long, because they thought I couldn't handle it—thought I would ruin it all. How I went on jobs for that fucking bastard, Lou, wishing that if I didn't live one more day, the last thing I would hope for was to see Lou gasping for air as my hands were wrapped tightly around his neck, squeezing the life out of him. How the stress and pressure built day in and day out, not wanting the life anymore, not caring to live. How for years I hated my father and then felt relieved that he didn't kill himself—that maybe, just fucking maybe, he wasn't a fucking coward—but NOW that was stripped away from me.

"Get out!"

Vinnie eyes widened at my raised voice. Maybe he didn't hear me the first time. Standing from my chair, I hovered over the desk, and with a hard glare, I yelled, "Get the fuck out!"

"Marcus—

"No. Because of this cocksucker, we've been walking around on fuckin' eggshells, wondering what to do next." Straightening, I swung my arms in the air. "We were getting fucked in the ass the entire time, by a fuckin' pig at that!"

"Marky, I'm sorry for how everything went down. I don't mean any disrespect to you or Jimmie, especially with you, Marky, not after what you've done for me."

I reluctantly placed my hands to my hips and tried to calm my breathing as Jimmie asked, "What was that?"

Vinnie went on to answer Jimmie but kept his eyes on me. "He saved my life. It was my first night on a job. We had a trade with a cartel group. I made a mistake by turning my back on a bad trade. Marky warned me before we went in to never turn your back on anyone. I was fuckin' stupid and turned to put the money in the truck, but he shot one of the men before they got me. I remember a loud gun going off, and for a split second, I thought it was me, that I was dead. Then when I came to my senses and turned, Marky was standing behind me with a gun in his hand, and the douchebag he shot was on the fuckin' ground beside me." He shook the memory from his thoughts. "Anyway, what I'm trying to say is that I owe my life to you. I can make it all go away for you guys."

"What are you saying?"

"I'm the lead investigator in the Sorrento case. Due to cuts in funding, I only have two men working under me. There wasn't enough money for wiretapping, so we have to figure out everything from word of mouth or video surveillance, which isn't much. At the end of the day, we write down transcripts on a daily basis. You and Jimmie can easily be erased from those memos."

"But . . ." Jimmie chimed in, knowing that there was a catch.

Vinnie leaned into the desk, adjusting his position so that he could take a good hard look at the both of us. "In two weeks, Lou himself will have his largest trade yet—one hundred pounds of cocaine worth five million dollars."

Jimmie whistled. "With whom?"

"Salvatore Lombardi."

That was fucking huge. *Salvi* was the boss of one of the largest mob organizations in New York. He had been around a lot longer than Lou, knew all the ins and outs of the trade, but they'd remained friendly rivals. The two of them together caught by federal agents would be the largest mob bust in history.

"Do you know what this would mean if we had both Lou and Salvi?"

"Yeah, a fuckin' death wish." I spat as I sank back in my chair.

"Not without help from the two of you."

Jimmie raised a brow at that comment. "And how do you propose we help?"

Vinnie stood and walked around his chair, gripping the back of the seat. "There's surveillance all over the club except for the basement, which is where the trade will occur. We need surveillance in every corner of that area. No blind spots."

"We can do that." Jimmie said with a shrug.

"But I'm sure that's not all you need from us." I added with a raised brow.

Vinnie nodded. "With the low funding, I don't have the pull or power for back up. I only have two men on my team: One is looking after Mia. The other just provides info when needed. The team that's working on the Lombardi case in New York is going to handle this bust with us."

"But?"

"We need someone to make sure it happens, someone to let us know their every move: what time they arrive, when both Lou and Salvi are spotted together, and the time of the exchange."

"You do understand that Lou doesn't trust us now, right?" I leaned back in the chair, placing both of my hands on the back of my head. "How do you expect us to retrieve that info? We didn't even know about the Lombardi trade."

"Lou hasn't trusted you in months, Marky. Ever since he was suspicious of you and found out the info on Mia, he's been watching you. I've been watching *you* for him. We had a meeting a few days back. He took you out as second in command and gave it to Gio, so you know what that means."

I absolutely did. It meant that, if for some reason Lou was killed, the second in command would take over. I was supposed to be the one that would take Lou's position if there was ever a hit on him. I never wanted it to begin with, and it didn't surprise me that Gio took over my position.

"Okay, so the question remains: how do you expect us to retrieve that information? Do you really think he'll let us near the job at this point? No, he won't. His trust in me is shot to hell."

"I just need you to be at the club on the day of the exchange. I don't know for sure what your involvement would entail, but that Sunday morning, we can meet up, probably here, go over all the details with my men, and then move on from there. You have my word. If you two do this for me, you will not be mentioned at all."

Jimmie shook his head in disbelief. "But the bust will take place at the club that Marcus owns. With all the media attention that has occurred in the past couple of years increasing people's suspicions about our involvement with the Sorrentos, how would you pull that off?"

"Well, I've thought of that. Every month there's inventory done at the club?" He raised a brow in question. I nodded in response. "Well, the two of you will be at the club for inventory that week."

"What about the media?" Jimmie questioned.

"We'll take care of them. Granted, no matter what, the media will have their own take on things. Reporters may mention your names, no doubt about it, but if we play it right, we can pull it off."

We sat there for a few moments silently, taking in that bit of information that had been provided. Jimmie turned his head and looked at me with a raised brow. Even though he didn't speak, I knew he was waiting for my take on it. After another few minutes, I nodded my head at him.

He looked at Vinnie and with a shrug said, "Okay, we're in."

CHAPTER TWENTY-TWO

MIA

Two weeks. That's how long it'd been since I'd seen Marcus. He had texted me a few times, but his messages were short. I wasn't bothered by it as much as I thought I'd be, because I knew he was busy with work and I was distracted with school. I aced my last exam, which was a huge stress reliever. My next exam wasn't for another couple of weeks, and then the final was in December. I was certain that if I continued the way I was going, I'd pass the class.

Because I had busted my butt for the past few weeks, I had decided to take Saturday off. I had texted Marcus to see if he wanted to go out to dinner or stay in or just spend some time together, but he was busy that night, which turned into a night of wearing PJ's, eating junk food, and watching old movies. That was until Megan barged out of Jeremy's room.

I jumped at the sound of her slamming his bedroom door behind her. "I can't stand him!" She rushed over and slumped beside me on the couch. With a wrinkled nose, she crossed her arms and huffed.

Before I could ask what happened, Jeremy stormed out of his room and came over to us. "Seriously, Megan? You won't even let me explain anything . . ."

"I'm not speaking to Jeremy at the moment, Mia. Can you please let him know that?" She asked me as she turned her head, looking away from Jeremy.

When my eyes glanced up to Jeremy, he'd rolled his eyes in frustration. "So we're five now? Awesome."

"Shut up, Jeremy!" She angrily wiggled in her seat but kept her glare toward the wall beside her.

Jeremy shot me a look that said, "Can you help me out here?" Since I had no idea what the hell was going on, I shrugged my shoulders in response.

He let out a heavy sigh and tossed his arms in the air. "Fine, act that way, Megan. I'm out!" He turned his back on us, marched toward the door, and grabbed his keys by the table before slamming the door shut behind him.

Megan sucked her teeth. "Can you believe him? Ugh."

Still alarmed by the entire show, I asked, "What happened?"

"It's a long story. Let's go out." She jumped from the couch and reached for my arm. "We'll find something hot to wear and hit Club21."

"Oh, I don't know, Megan I was sort of content with just chillaxing at home."

"Come on, Mia. Please." She pleaded with her big hazel eyes. "I can't stay here, and I need to let out some frustration. Drinks and the dance floor will do the trick, but I need my best girl there. *Please.*" She begged again.

Why I allowed her to influence me in any way was beyond me. Her lips curled into a slight grin, after my nod. "Can I borrow an outfit?"

I rolled my eyes and nodded again. I knew that was coming too.

***

"I'll have a cosmo, please. Thank you." The bartender nodded before heading toward the end of the bar to prepare my drink.

Letting out a deep breath, I sank my chin into my hand. I knew tonight was supposed to be a fun girls' night, but Megan refused to mention what happened between her and Jeremy. It was just the two of us, and I hate to dance, so as Megan demolished the dance floor, I sat by the bar and tried to drink away my boredom.

"Can I buy you a drink?" A deep tone pierced through my thoughts. Turning my head, I was presented with a familiar face. At first, the name didn't dawn on me.

"Gio, right?"

"The one and only." He gave a charming half grin.

"Well, it's nice to see you again. How are you?"

"I'm doing a lot better now." He said in a seductive way and then winked at me.

I felt my cheeks turn a burning red. The bartender brought my drink right on time, allowing me to hide the embarrassment with a few sips of my cosmo. I'd only met him once when he stopped by Marcus's house, but there was something about him that was pleasant. I didn't feel uncomfortable around him. Maybe it was his upbeat persona. Yes, he was a very good-looking man, but I was madly in love with Marcus. Gio didn't compare to Marcus, not in the least. No man could ever win my heart except for Marcus, but I wondered if he still felt the same about me. It was hard not to think that way because he had been so distant lately.

Gio straightened up and ordered a beer before speaking. "So where's your man?"

"I have no clue." Though, I wish did. "I'm here with my cousin, who's out there on the dance floor, sweating off some frustration." He looked over to where I pointed at Megan. She was shaking her hips, swinging her arms, and grooving to "Locked Out Of Heaven" by Bruno Mars. She was also pushing away every man that had tried to dance with her. Megan was beyond angry and needed to let loose. After a few shots, she was doing just that.

"Ah, I must have a talk with Marky. I mean if I had a beautiful woman like you I would never leave your side."

Rolling my eyes, I cocked my head aside and stared at him for a few seconds before replying. "Marcus is a busy man. That's all."

His eyes slightly squinted as if confused by my response. "Busy doing what exactly?"

"On jobs. What else?"

Laughing once, he took a long pull of his beer then placed the bottle on the bar. "Is that what he's been telling you? Marcus hasn't handled a job in the last four weeks. Vinnie and I have been taking care of them."

Staring at Gio in disbelief, my throat closed and instantly felt very dry. All the excuses Marcus had given me sprinted through my mind: he was busy; he couldn't make it; he was sorry, but he needed to work on a few things.

Why would he lie about it all? He promised that he wouldn't keep anything from me. Suddenly, I felt more detached from him than I'd ever felt. "Excuse me, but I have to go." I muttered while grabbing my clutch from the bar. I tried to stand, but Gio put his hands on my shoulders and forced me to sit back down.

Angrily, I snapped my head and glared at him. "What are you doing?" Just because I was a bit comfortable around him, didn't mean he knew me well enough to put his hands on me.

"Look. I'm sorry. I shouldn't have said that to you. Maybe he was given a separate job to handle."

"Bullshit. Don't try and cover his ass now." I crossed my arms while tapping my foot along the leg of the metal barstool in front of me. What was Marcus doing on those nights if he wasn't on a job? Jealous thoughts began to take over, causing my blood pressure to rise.

"Look at you! You're working yourself up over something that's not even an issue. Come on. Let me grab you another drink." Raising a brow, he flashed a wide grin. Maybe he was right. Maybe I was overreacting. He ordered us another round of drinks after I let out a deep breath and nodded.

"You gotta live a little, Mia." He exclaimed as he ruffled a hand through my hair.

"Hey!" I jabbed his shoulder. His mocking wide-eyed expression made us both laugh.

My laughter immediately stopped when I saw Gio stare over my shoulder. He straightened his position as his facial features went from humorous to stern in a nanosecond. Confused by his instant change in demeanor, I turned to see what had caused it. My heart dropped at the sight of Marcus storming across the dance floor. The look on his face caused my body to slightly tremble with fear. I'd never seen him that angry—the grimness in his eyes, the tightening in his jaw, the thin line of his lips, and the command in his stride. With every step he took, my heart pounded just as quickly.

Gio grabbed his beer and leaned back onto the counter smoothly, as if Marcus's behavior didn't intimidate him. I twirled in the barstool to fully face Marcus as he approached. Once he was in front of us, his eyes never left Gio. "Marky." Gio said while lifting the beer bottle in salute and then chugging the rest down. Marcus didn't respond, not even a nod in acknowledgment. He continued to grimace at Gio. Then Marcus slowly tilted his head and looked down at me. My chest heaved in and out from the angry stare-down. Why was he making me feel as if I had done something wrong?

To lighten the mood, I breathed out a smile, stood, and wrapped my arms around his neck. "Hey baby, I've missed you. How was your night?" I tried to sound upbeat and excited, but his continued glare left me uneasy.

He didn't respond; instead, he wrapped his hands around my wrist and pulled my arms away from his neck. Still with a tight grip, Marcus turned and hauled me through a swarm of dancing drunks. He was walking so quickly, winding through the crowd that I had to practically run to keep up. Megan waved at me as we passed her. I didn't have time to wave back as he pulled me up the stairs and toward the second level. The music died down the moment the door closed behind us.

Once we reached the hallway, he let go of my wrist but continued his way down the hall and into the VIP room. Following him, I shut the door behind me. Marcus paced back and forth in the room while staring at the wooden floors the entire time. I didn't know what to do or say, so I leaned against the wall and waited.

Finally, he stopped by the table. Tightly gripping the back of the chair, he shut his eyes as his breathing became heavier. "Why didn't you tell me you were going out?" His voice was in a low cruel tone.

My lips slightly trembled as I let out a shaky break. What brought on this hostility? "It was a sudden decision. I didn't realize I had to keep you posted on my whereabouts."

He laughed with no sound of humor echoing the room. "Here I am busting my fuckin' ass to keep you safe, and I have no right to know your whereabouts? Fuckin' perfect. As I try to better our future, you're over here flirting with him!"

What did he mean keep me safe? When I was going to question him on it, I remembered his last harsh statement. "You cannot be serious about me flirting with Gio?"

"I'm. Completely. Fucking. Serious." He ran a hand over his face in frustration.

"Marcus, I was not flirting with him. Not in the least." I moved toward him until we were a foot away. "He was comforting me."

His head snapped up at me with dark eyes. "Comforting you? Why would he be comforting *my* girl?"

Marcus sarcastic and harsh tone left me uneasy. "He was comforting me because I was extremely angry when I found out *my* boyfriend had been lying to me for the past few weeks." I crossed my arms and dropped a hip, waiting for his response as his mouth slightly opened.

Then his eyes grew angry as his jaw clenched together. "You have no idea what you're talking about."

"No? So you weren't lying to me for the past few weeks? You were, in fact, on jobs for Lou? Or were you so busy at the firm that you had to stay *extra* late hours with Stephanie, I wonder?" I raised my hands in question with a mocking tone.

"You need to stop right there." Marcus sneered as he turned his back on me and walked over to the bar area of the room. Grabbing a glass and a bottle of whisky, he poured a glass.

Anger rushed through me. Storming over toward him, I pulled the drink from his hand and dumped the liquor into the sink.

"What the fuck, Mia!"

I inched in and pointed my finger at his shoulder. "We have not seen each other in two weeks, Marcus. Two whole weeks! We were doing *so* well. Are we back to arguing and not discussing our issues? I know that you're hiding something from me. I can feel it." I reached my hand up to touch his beautiful face and stared into those damaged eyes. With a lower tone I went on, "Why are you not telling me? I don't understand. Are we back to that now?"

He exhaled at my touch and shut his eyes, contemplating, and then he lifted his eyelids open. "Do you trust me?"

With all my heart, I trusted him, but he obviously didn't trust me. "Do you trust me?" I shot back.

His eyes focused on mine as if the question was difficult to answer. I couldn't believe him. I'd never for one second given him a reason not to trust me. I'd stuck by him through all of his decisions, good or bad. I'd accepted his lifestyle, because I knew deep down it wasn't what made him who he was. Whether he believed it or not, he was a good man.

My eyes blurred as he continued to stare at me but didn't answer my question. Removing my hands from his face, I studied his features. "Wow." I couldn't believe it. He didn't utter a word, but, judging from his actions, it was clear that he did not trust me.

"Mia, listen." He reached out to grab my arm.

I pulled away, stepping back. "No. I get it."

"Mia, no, you don't."

"I've done everything in my power, Marcus, to show you what you mean to me—that I love you more than I care to breathe. It hurts me, and I mean a terrible heartrending pain, for you to stand there, look me in the eyes, and basically admit that you don't trust me." Sniffing back, I couldn't keep the hot tears from streaming down my face. His expression broke at my words. "What do you want from me? What else can I give you?"

He leaned into me and stared down. We were so close I could feel the heat from his body against mine. With his unsteady breathing, his tortured eyes danced along my face. For a moment, it looked as if he was going to crack, but then he contained himself, took in one deep breath, and shut his eyes. "I need you to trust me when I say it's important for you to grab Megan and go home." His eyelids opened, and my heart swelled in pain at his words. He reached up and grazed my cheek with the back of his fingers. I was beyond angry. He was pushing me away when he should've been able to confide in me. Before the warmth of his touch seeped through my skin, I tore my face away and stepped back again.

"Mia." He tenderly whispered.

"Whatever you say, Marcus. I'll just go home with Megan and sit around and wait for whenever I get to have *my* Marcus back. Because the one in front me at this very moment . . . I have no idea who he is. I want *my* Marcus: the loving, caring, and passionate one." His face was broken, but I needed to say how I felt. "Let me know when he's back."

With my back turned to him, I stormed out the door, dragged a highly intoxicated Megan off the dance floor, and grabbed a cab.

Something deep down within me knew that Marcus was involved in something deeper than he had disclosed. It left me nervous and unsettled. Guilt began to seep through me as I thought of the way we had left things. I should have kissed him and held him tightly against me. My deepest regret that night was that I didn't pull him in and hold him, even if it was just for a few seconds.

CHAPTER TWENTY-THREE

MARCUS

"Marcus. Marcus. Yo, Marcus!" I broke out of my daze as Jimmie hovered over my desk, snapping his fingers. "What the hell? I've been trying to get your attention for the past five minutes." His brows bunched together, concerned. "You alright, Bro?"

Having had no sleep, I blinked my dry eyes and ran a hand over my face. There was nothing that could rid me of the exhaustion I felt. When Mia left the club the night before, I wanted to tell her everything that was going on, but it was better to keep it from her for now. It was the only way I could keep her away from the Club and the only way I knew to protect her. It was the day of the bust, and I would be fucking lying if I wasn't running all the possible scenarios of what could go wrong through my mind: the thought of possibly not coming out alive, never having a chance to express the love I had for Mia, to show her that it was always true, and that my reason for everything was her.

Then I thought of my niece and mother as I looked into Jimmie's same fearful eyes. "Sorry, Jimmie. When will Vinnie be here?"

He slumped back in the seat of my home office. "Soon. I told Mom that you and I were dealing with inventory at the Club today. She took Elle out for breakfast and then a trip to park since it's nice out." He quickly glanced at his watch. "It's still early, only nine. Vinnie said the bust will happen at two this afternoon." He nervously ran his hands along the thighs of his jeans. "Marcus, I need to ask you something." Jimmie looked up at me. "If anything happens to me, I need you to take—"

"Don't talk like that!" I slammed my hand against the desk in frustration. The last thing I wanted to hear was my brother being weak. "We are going to get out of this. You'll be home with Elle, and I'll be home with Mia. It'll all be okay. We are going to be okay." It felt as if I was trying to convince myself more than him.

His eyes clouded over as he cleared his throat. "You're right."

"Listen, Jimmie, I want you to stay here, okay? There's no need for both of us to be there."

"No." Jimmie shook his head adamantly.

"Jimmie, just stay here."

"I said, 'no.' We got in this together. We're going to leave it together."

"You're a stubborn fuck, you know that?"

"Yeah? Well, it's a trait I picked up from my little brother." He gently laughed and sniffed. Then he stood from his chair as he turned his back to me. He didn't want me to see the emotion prickling his features. "I have to go to the bathroom."

Jimmie walked over to the door of my office. He froze with his hand on the knob. "Marcus?"

"Yeah, Jimmie?"

He bowed his head as he opened the door. "I love you, Bro." He whispered and left the room.

"I love you too." I whispered into an empty room. I let out a heavy breath and sank against the chair.

***

Half an hour later, I had my brother, Vinnie, and his two men in my office. Jimmie stood by the door listening for Elle and our mom. Vinnie's two men, Eric and Liam, sat on the chairs in front of my desk. Vinnie stood beside me hovering over the desk and pointing his finger on a plan that showed the entire layout of Club21.

"Okay, so you see this entrance right here?" He pointed to the left side of the building. I nodded and he continued, "This is where Lou is planning on bringing the shipment in a few hours. Since there are double doors, they open flush against the brick wall outside. Lou plans to have his men back the truck in as close as possible and unload the drugs here." He pointed to the wall inside next to the door. "Once his men unload everything, the truck will leave, and they'll await Salvatore Lombardi and his men."

"When are they expected?" I asked, hovering over the club's layout plan.

"An hour after Lou arrives. He wants to make sure everything is set and ready. Lou will have his men surrounding the building." He pointed two fingers at the entrance. "He'll have Buddy and Rich at the main entrance, fully armed." His fingers traced down the back of the building where the parking lot was. "This is where two of Lou's guys and I will be. My men here," he nudged his head at both Liam and Eric in front of us, "will handle those two; they'll be in custody before the bust begins."

Vinnie straightened his position. "Obviously, Lou will have Gio with him for the exchange, but he's also called in some backup. Lou made an agreement to have some of Rick Boyle's men there."

"What the fuck, Vinnie. How many are there?"

He crossed his arms and pinched his lips together, as if lost in thought or calculating in his head. "I'd say a total of ten, maybe twelve, men of Lou's. Salvi agreed to bring the same amount, not to overpower Lou during the exchange, but if I know Salvi, I'm sure he'll have a few men close by, just in case."

"How many men do you have in your team for the bust? Are we outnumbered?"

"We have enough, Marky."

"Bull fuckin' shit!" Jimmie spat out, all heads turned in his direction. "You expect us to risk our lives out there with only a handful of your men who we don't even fuckin' know? Do you realize who you're fuckin' dealing with here? Lou Sorrento is not some fuckin' Joe from down South, and Salvatore Lombardi? You've all lost your fuckin' minds."

Vinnie grew agitated. With his arms spread wide, he glared at Jimmie. "Maybe we have, but at least we are fuckin' trying. If you ever want to do something in your life, do this, Jimmie. Think of your little girl."

"Don't you ever bring up my fuckin' little girl, you fuckin' bastard. I've been thinking about her since day fuckin' one! We're all signing our death warrants as we march into that fuckin' club, and you know it, Vinnie!" Jimmie pointed, as he tried to catch his breath, his shoulders heaving up and down from his heavy breathing.

"So what? You want out? Just like that? Fine, be a fuckin' coward. The one thing I never expected was a DeLuca brother backing down, especially you, Jimmie."

"You shouldn't set your expectations so fuckin' high, Vinnie. People change all the damn time, especially when it involves possibly never seeing their loved ones again."

Frustrated by the change of events, I spat out, "Okay, enough of this shit." I stood from my chair, "We're doing this, Vinnie." I turned my head toward Jimmie, and his head snapped in my direction. "Yes, Jimmie, we're doing this."

Laughing once, Jimmic waved his arm exaggeratedly and bowed down to me. "Whatever you say, *boss*."

"Come on, Jimmie. Don't be like that. You said it yourself. We started this together, and we're ending it together."

Jimmie stared at me as he took in the words I threw back at him. He leaned back, crossed his arms, lifted one leg, and pressed his foot against the wall to keep balance. After a few minutes, he nodded at me and then at Vinnie to go on.

Vinnie let out a breath in relief and turned back to me. "Okay, you and Jimmie will be in this VIP room." He pointed back to the plan on my desk. "That's where the surveillance will be set up. You two will radio every detail of what's going on: a play-by-play. Once you spot both Salvi and Lou in the same room—the moment Salvi arrives and Lou is there—you let us know and we move in." Vinnie looked around the room at each and every one of us. "Do you all understand the plan?" We all nodded in response. "Good, let's get going. I want you guys set up in the surveillance room before Lou's men show up."

Vinnie and his two men grabbed their things and walked out of the office. I stood up from my chair and adjusted my jacket before reaching into the drawer and removing two guns. I put one in the back of my pants underneath my shirt and the other in the front of my pants, adjusting it by my hip."

I grabbed another two and walked over to Jimmie and handed them to him. "Are you sure you can do this? It's not too late to stay here with Elle and Mom. I can handle this, Jimmie."

He uncrossed his arms and straightened his shoulders. Grabbing the guns from my hand, he adjusted them on him as I did mine. "I'm with you all the way."

Relieved in a way, I bowed my head. "Jimmie, I just want you to know the only reason why I want to go on with this is because of Dad." I looked up at him as his brows pinched together in confusion.

"Don't you see? If we keep on going as he did, little by little we'll break, and before we know it, we'll end up like him. It just proves that there's no easy way out, well, at least not without a fight."

Jimmie's expression relaxed, indicating that he had understood what I had said, and then he gently slapped the side of my face and nodded.

Not another word was spoken as we walked out of the house. We all hopped into the same car and drove off.

CHAPTER TWENTY-FOUR

MIA

All night, I couldn't stop thinking of Marcus and the uneasiness I felt when we had left each other. I wasn't able to take it anymore. I knew it was still early that Sunday, but I had to drive to his house and talk to him. During the entire drive, the past few months sprinted through my head. These last few weeks, we hadn't spent much time together, but I knew it was because of our busy schedules.

I missed falling asleep in his arms and waking up next to him. Maybe waiting until the semester was over to move in with him was ridiculous. I could simply move my clothes over to his house, and everything else could wait. I felt guilty that I might have led him to believe that I didn't love him enough to want to spend every possible minute together.

When Megan and I arrived back at my apartment the night before, Jeremy was there waiting for us. She was completely intoxicated from the tequila shots she'd thrown back. Jeremy guided her into his bedroom and came back out. Then, he filled me in on what happened between the two of them. Apparently, Megan said, "I love you," and it scared Jeremy. He was thrown off by it and wasn't sure how to handle it. Megan had gotten upset because he just froze and didn't respond, which caused her to walk out the door. Jeremy said that, after we left, he took a walk around the neighborhood and that's when it dawned on him that he did love her. When he came back, we were already gone. Needless to say, they were back to being Megan and Jeremy by the morning.

As I pulled into Marcus's driveway, Theresa was pulling in at the same time. I turned off my ignition and hopped out of the car. "Mia!" Elle shouted as she jumped out of the passenger side of Theresa's vehicle. She ran up to me and wrapped her tiny arms around my hip.

"Elle, how are you, honey?"

"I'm good! Did you come to see me?" She spread her lips into a huge grin.

Smiling, I leaned down and kissed her cheek, "Actually, I need to speak to your Uncle Marc. Is he around?"

"I believe you may have just missed him." Theresa proclaimed as she approached us. I straightened to greet her. She pulled me into a hug. "How are you, sweetheart?"

"I'm good." We untangled from our embrace. "Do you know where he might be? I thought he'd be here because it's still so early."

"Inventory." At my puzzled expression, she continued. "The club. It's that time of month for inventory. It's done once a month."

"Ah, so he's there?"

"Yes. I just came back from the park with Elle. Would you like to have lunch with us while you wait for him?"

"Actually, I think I'll just go to the club. I really need to speak with him."

"Everything okay? With the two of you I mean?"

"Oh, yes, I just really need to talk to him." I assured her.

"Okay. I'll see you later?"

"Yes, of course." I leaned in, hugged her and Elle good-bye, and entered my car. Pulling out of the driveway, I turned at the curb and zoomed toward the club.

***

As I pulled into the empty parking lot of Club21, I was concerned that I may have missed Marcus, because I didn't spot his car. There was a huge truck on the side of the building backed up into an entrance, but I didn't see anyone. Looking around before I exited my vehicle, I noticed the back door was wide open. He had to be there. Exiting my car, I made my way toward the door and poked my head in before going in. The hallway was quiet and empty. Shrugging my shoulders, I walked through the hall. Halfway through, I heard a noise coming from one of the side doors, a door that led to the basement. Because the truck on the side of the building led to the basement, it made sense that he was down there. I pulled the door open and walked down the stairs.

I looked around, confused at first, but then, everything started to register. It was a bust. All around the basement were at least twenty to thirty men with their guns drawn on each other. There were men in blue-and-yellow FBI jackets with their guns pointed at some men who I recognized from Marcus's surprise party. They were all a part of the mob. I was sure of it. They had their guns pointed at the federal agents as well. My heart fought against my chest as my eyes scanned the room searching for Marcus. They landed on Vinnie, Marcus's friend, who wore a badge around his neck and locked eyes with mine. "Mia, I want you to stay where you are. Do not move! Do you understand?"

My mind felt as if I nodded, but I wasn't sure if I did. I was in complete shock. Swallowing the huge lump in my throat, I continued to scan the room. I saw more angry men all with guns who cursed and hissed at one other. The moment I realized who was standing beside me, he gripped me against his chest and pressed a gun against my head. "Lou, let her go now!" Vinnie yelled. Everything was happening so fast. My vision blurred as I tried to focus on something—anything. My heart thundered against my chest, my breathing increased, and sweat beaded along my skin.

Lou wrapped his arm around my neck as he pulled me in tighter. My arms reached up and tried to pull at his grip, but his hold was snug under my chin. I whimpered as he traced the tip of the gun down the side of my face and under my jawline. He pinned my head back into his shoulder. His lips grazed the outside of my ear as he harshly whispered, "Your man's not around to save you, huh, princess?" Lou dug his nose in my ear and wildly sniffed in the scent of my shampoo. "I wonder if I should kill you now and make your death fast and easy like your brother's."

My knees buckled and I collapsed into him. My eyes burned as I fought to see past the tears. My nails dug into his hold, but I couldn't pull him away. It was difficult to breathe as I gasped for air. Laughing, he secured his grip on me. "After I'm done with you, I'll make sure we take care of Marky. I have plans for him, though. I'll make sure he dies a slow, tortuous, and painful death." He sneered in my ear.

I broke into uncontrollable sobs.

"Fuck!" Vinnie spat out. "Lou, let her go! You have nowhere to run. This whole place is surrounded."

Lou snapped his head back up to Vinnie. Remembering where we were, he dragged me back with him until he reached the door. He kicked it opened and leaned in as far as he could. "We'll see about that." He pushed me away, turning my entire body to face him. A rush of relief washed through me at the loss of contact and I gulped in air.

With the basement stairway door opened, he leaned in and kept the gun pointed at me. I tried to swallow as he lowered the gun, gave a lopsided grin, and said, "Tell your brother I said, 'Hi.'"

Before I could utter a word, he pulled the trigger, causing a loud noise to echo through the room. My entire body shattered as I felt the bullet bite through my chest. I was frozen. Everything around me stilled. I looked down, and my hand swiped along the burning wound with trembling hands. Dark red blood spread along my palm. A dizzy spell caught me, and as I tried to breathe in, my throat wheezed at the failed attempt. My body fell back as I heard the sounds of gunfire surround me. It all became faint.

I couldn't breathe. My lungs felt as if someone were squeezing every single breath left inside of me. My eyes rolled back, and I focused on the ceiling. With each gasp of air I took in, my mind began to slowly recede. Images of those I loved faded in and out of my mind: my father, Michael, my mother, Jeremy, Megan, and my grandparents. The one I loved more than anything and was willing to give my last breath for, the one that I wanted nothing more than to see his face one last time—Marcus—his was the last image that crossed my mind.

Then I grew hungry—hungry for oxygen—anything to help stop the tortured pain that scorched through my lungs, as I fought for every breath.

CHAPTER TWENTY-FIVE

MARCUS

Ice-covered, I couldn't move. I blinked again to find out if what I saw the first time was real. And it was. Mia had entered the hallway from the back parking lot and had opened the doors to the basement where the bust had just taken place less than five minutes before. I felt my body grow pale as I saw her go down the stairs where it all was taking place.

"What the hell are you doing? Come on!" Jimmie gripped my shoulder and lifted me from my chair, pulling me out of my daze and bringing me back to reality.

Fuck. Fuck. Fuck. My heart pounded against my fucking chest with every step I took. It went with the rhythm of the sound of guns firing.

As we reached the door to the basement, we caught sight of Lou, who was running down the hall. I had a decision to make. Follow him or go see if Mia was alright. "Go! I'll check on Mia." Jimmie shouted over the sound of gunfire. I hesitated. "Go! All of this will be worth nothing if Lou gets away!" He shoved my shoulder. Nodding the moment that I realized he was right, one foot moved in front of the other as I went after Lou.

Everything was happening so fast, but it felt as if I were playing a movie in my head in slow fucking motion. It wasn't happening fast enough.

Once I reached the parking lot, I spotted him by the far end, where a hidden street led behind a group of brick buildings. Picking up the pace, I sprinted towards him. The closer I got to him, the more the adrenaline pumped through me. Reaching for the gun that was pressed against my back, I pulled it out and aimed it at him as I continued running after him. Once I was close behind him, he looked back as he heard footsteps approaching. The moment he locked eyes with mine, he laughed and stopped. He turned around and pointed his gun at me. Breathing out heavily, he said, "You were responsible for all of this, Marky?" His faced was filled with amusement.

With a steady aim on him, I stopped running but continued in a rapid stride toward him. "No, but once I was asked if I wanted to be a part of bringing you down, I didn't have a second thought."

He saw I wasn't stopping, so he cocked back his gun, but before he could pull the trigger, I shot at his hand. His gun, along with a few bloody fingers, fell to the floor. He shrieked as he gripped his wrist in shock. "You fuckin' cock. FUCK!" He huddled over, wincing in pain. I continued running with the gun still aimed at him. Laughing, he stood slanted, squeezing his arm, trying to hold back the rapid bleeding. "You know," he grimaced through clenched teeth as he spat, "I'm glad I pulled that fuckin' trigger on your girl. Now she can fuckin' join that two-faced brother of hers." He spat at the ground and laughed at me as he weakly stumbled back.

Everything around me went red. All I could see was the fuckin' cocky smirk on his face. One foot in front of the other, I charged at him with every quick step I took. I knew I was closer, but it wasn't fast enough. My legs quickened and I sprinted at him. The moment I was close enough, I tightened a fist, cranked my arm back and swung it directly at his face. There was a loud crack as my knuckle smashed against his nose. Lou's head jerked back at the contact, forcing him to stumble a few steps.

With his eyes wide, he snapped his head forward. He glared at me with intense and vicious eyes at the unexpected blow. Blood gushed out of his nose. His jaw tensed, and the veins on his neck popped out in rage. His body shook with adrenaline. "You're a fuckin' dead man, Marky. Dead!" He came after me, but I didn't give him a chance as I smashed my fist against his face again. Crack.

And again.

Crack.

And again.

Crack.

With each blow, he was forced back until he was against the brick wall.

I gripped his neck with one hand, squeezing it tightly, forcing every fucking breath he had out of him. His eyes bulged out of their sockets; he let out a desperate gasp for air. Gripping the sides of his face with both hands, even with the gun I held pressed against the side of his cheek, I began slamming his head against the brick wall. "You're the fuckin' dead man, Lou!" I spat as I cracked his head against the concrete wall. "You'll never see another fuckin' day."

Crack! I grunted as I did it again. Hatred for this man was drilled into every fiber of my being. I wanted nothing more than to suck the life out of him.

His eyes fluttered with each blow of the head, but it didn't deter him from chuckling one last time. "I saw her gasp for air as she took her last breath."

Reaching my boiling point, I lifted my other hand, placed the barrel of the pistol against his lips, and shoved it down his throat, causing his teeth to shatter from the force. "I want to see your fuckin' brain splattered against the fuckin' wall, your blood drenched against my fuckin' skin, and your dead body on the fuckin' ground right along with the scum where you belong. Soon no one will know who the fuck Lou Sorrento ever was!" My finger steadied against the trigger, I breathed out a lopsided smirk, and that was the last image he saw. Without a second thought, I yanked at the trigger.

BANG!

Just like that, the last I saw of Lou Sorrento were his eyes bulging wide open as the bullet pierced his brain and the residue splattered against the wall. His body dropped to the ground the moment I let go of the hold I had on him.

Looking at his lifeless body lying on the ground, I spat on him. All of the rage and disgust I felt for him was displayed in that one final gesture. Turning my back on him, the meaning of his words finally sank in. I ran fast. I ran hard—back to the woman I loved. There was no way she was fucking gone.

As I entered the room, my blood was still pumping with adrenaline from what just happened. I blinked a few times as the cloud of smoke from the gunfire filled the room. My eyes searched for the one person I feared for the most. It was a rampage and guns continued to fire. I quickly ran around searching but could not find that familiar face.

My heart picked up its pace as I hovered over lifeless bodies and held a tight grip on the gun in my hand, ready for anyone who got in the way. As I continued my search, I finally spotted Jimmie. He was kneeling on the ground, hovering over someone. My throat closed, and my entire body stilled as I saw the person before him. For a mere second I grew faint but managed to force my trembling legs toward them.

Jimmie quickly turned and aimed his gun at my approach. His mouth dropped opened in relief at the sight of me. Tears swelled in his bloodshot eyes, and breathing heavily, he stared at me, ready to break. "I'm so sorry. I tried, but I . . . *Fuck! I fuckin' tried . . .*" Immediately, he turned his attention back to the person before him. "Come on, don't do this to me." With bloody hands, he pressed against the wound as he grunted. My body shuddered, terrified as I leaned over his shoulder to have a closer look.

My heart was ripped out of my chest as I gasped. My mind was screaming and yelling, but I stood mute. I collapsed beside Jimmie, and the gun I held dropped onto the cement floor, making a distant clinking noise. Forcing Jimmie aside, I looked down and witnessed the one person that I loved more than anything in the world covered in blood. I couldn't breathe as my beloved was gasping for a last breath. I watched as the face of my truelove turned slightly blue while she continued to gulp for air, and then her eyes locked with mine before her lids shut closed and her jaw spread open.

Traumatized by what I was witnessing, my throat collapsed as fear coursed through my veins. Reaching down, I gathered up her body and pulled it into mine. With a shaky hand, I tried to locate the gunshot wound.

I shook my head viciously. This could not be happening. This had to be another nightmare. *I'm not going to lose you. Come on, wake up. Come on, wake up!* My eyes blurred with tears, and I blinked them away as I brought that face against my chest. "Come on, baby . . . Come on, you need to get up." With bloody hands, I caressed her soft, perfect skin. I tried to wipe the blood off, but it continued to smear along her perfect cheek bones.

I wanted to scream from the top of my lungs as I rocked back and forth, trying to keep myself from breaking down. I wanted so badly to be strong. There wasn't much I could do, but I needed to do something as I pressed my fingers along her soft eyelids. "Come on, baby, open your eyes. Just wake up for me." AHHH! I needed to do something. I was useless! The love of my life was motionless and helpless, and there was nothing I could do about it.

I felt a hand press firmly against my shoulder, pulling me away, telling me that help was close by.

But help wasn't there at that moment. Something needed to be done now! "No, I have to do something. I have to at least try." Still rocking, I pressed my lips against the frigid lips that I had kissed a thousand times before, those perfect lips that used to make all my worry and stress disappear once they touched mine.

In between small gentle kisses, I began CPR. "Come on, baby, don't leave me. I need you."

CHAPTER TWENTY-SIX

MARCUS

"Sir, we need you to step aside." A paramedic shoved at my shoulder as he and his partner hurried to Mia.

With hefty breathing, I stayed kneeling beside Mia as I watched them quickly work on her. They both lifted her body onto a stretcher. One held a hand at the wound while the other placed an oxygen tube against her face. Everything was happening fast as they rushed out of the building. I quickly followed behind as I heard them discussing medical terminology that I couldn't understand. "Hemothorax" and "chest tubes" were mentioned. *What the fuck was going on?*

In the ambulance, the female paramedic quickly lifted Mia's shirt and swiped a cloth along her rib to clean the blood. Then she cut small incisions along the fourth and fifth ribs. The male paramedic handed his partner a couple of tubes. He placed the first tube in one incision and the other tube in the second. Blood drained quickly from one of the tubes. "W-what are you doing?"

The female nodded at her partner, who hopped into the driver's seat. "Sir, I need you to come in or stay back. We have to get to the ER now."

I quickly jumped in and took a seat along the bench. The sirens went on and the ambulance moved at a rapid speed. Mia gasped for air as her chest expanded. My chest expanded along with hers in a sigh of relief. "Is she going to be okay?"

"I don't know, sir. It's hard to determine how severe the injury is at the moment. She's lost a lot of blood. The gunshot appears to have pierced her lung. The tubes right now are helping her breathe. They are removing the blood that filled her lungs as well as pumping in air that she cannot breathe on her own."

"B-but she'll be okay, right?" I couldn't help the desperation in my tone. I just needed to know she'd be okay. I needed to know that she'd wake up in a few hours and I could hold her again. I needed to know that I was not losing her.

I just needed . . . her.

Before I knew it, the ambulance came to a complete stop, the back doors opened wide, and they pulled the stretcher out, rushing her into the hospital. I hurried behind them, but I didn't have a chance to look at her one last time. They were too quick for me as they hurried out the doors. I stood there, breathless, as my entire world came crumbling down.

***

As the minutes ticked by, my desperation increased. My clothes were splattered in blood, and I wasn't sure whose it was anymore. I sat in the waiting room with other families surrounding me, waiting to hear the news about someone they loved as well. Despite all of the hustle and bustle, the only sound I heard was the clock ticking, second by second, minute by minute.

My legs bounced in place. I ripped my nails apart as I chewed at them savagely. The waiting game was excruciating, and I couldn't take it anymore. I was going fucking insane. I plopped my head back against the wall and let out another groan in frustration. It had only been ten minutes since I last asked for an update, but it felt like hours ago. When I thought to ask again, the doors burst open. Glancing over, I saw my mother and Jimmie rush through them.

I stood in place and waited as my mother with teary eyes ran over to me. She threw her arms around me. As she trembled in my arms and sobbed, I tried to keep myself from breaking down. I exhaled deeply and held tightly on to her. I needed to comfort her, to keep myself from joining her in her meltdown. "It's going to be okay, Mom," I whispered.

She pulled back with wide green eyes and sniffed. "She's going to be okay? You've heard from the doctors?" I shut my eyes and breathed slowly and steadily as I shook my head.

"Oh, Marcus . . ." She leaned in and wrapped her arms around me again.

Jimmie approached us. "Any news?" After I shook my head again, he gently nodded to express his understanding, and sat down in one of chairs.

"You must be hungry, baby." My mother pulled away and reached into her purse. After she pulled out a tissue from her bag, she swiped it along her cheekbones. "I'll grab you guys something to eat." She went to turn.

"Mom, please, food is the last thing on my mind. I'm not hungry."

Her eyes saddened. "Marcus, I need to do something. Let me feed my boys." That was her way of keeping her mind occupied, a way to try and soothe the wrong. I nodded, and just like that, she quickly dashed through the doors.

"Vinnie is pissed the hell off." Jimmie said in a harsh whisper as he looked around the room. I sat beside him and ran a frustrating hand down my face.

"The last thing I give two fucks about right now is Vinnie and his fuckin' crew."

"Yeah, well, how are they going to explain a dead fuckin' Lou in the hidden street behind the club? When the surveillance video shows you running after him out of the building and then coming back minutes later with blood all over you?"

I shut my eyes, and through clenched teeth, I spat, "Well, if I recall, brother, you were the one that insisted I fuckin' go after him. What did you expect? For us to come back holding hands singing 'Kumbaya'?"

"This is fuckin' serious, Marcus." He leaned over his thighs, placing his elbows on his knees, shoving his hands over his head. "All of it was worthless. We're fuckin' screwed either way!"

"I'll take care of it."

His head snapped up with wide eyes. "Oh yeah? And how do you expect to do that? By spending the rest of your life locked up?"

"If that's what it takes."

"Jesus, Marcus, what's gotten into you?"

"What's gotten into me, Jimmie? Out of all people, I would think YOU would know what I'm going through right now. After what you went through with Cynthia? My mind is racing thinking that the doctor will come out and tell me that I lost the one person I've ever loved. My heart is shattered at the thought that I may never touch or feel her again. My body is swamped with guilt because, if I'd just told her from the beginning what we were doing, she would have never shown up to the bust, and we would not be here right now. So spare me a fuckin' lecture, Vinnie, about what all the FBI agents or even you think I should have done differently. I'm trying hard as hell to control everything and hold it all in and not break down right now. I'm trying to be strong for her, and if she gets out of this alive, I'm trying to find a way to beg her to forgive me for all that I've done, because in the end she was always too good for me. In the end, I never deserved her. She never deserved any of this. *That's* what's gotten into me."

I stood and walked away, and even though he was calling after me, I kept on going. I needed air. It was hot, and the humidity in the waiting room was suffocating.

***

An hour later, Jeremy, Megan, and Mia's mother had showed up. They asked what happened over and over again. Jimmie explained to them what had occurred and exactly what was reported on the news—everything that had happened, except that we were involved. Apparently, we were actually at the club for fuckin' inventory and walked into the bust. After Jimmie snapped a bit at Jeremy, who was suspicious about the entire incident, there was dead silence.

Just then, all of us jerked our heads at the sound of doors opening. The surgeon walked over to us. "Mia Sullivan's family?" We all nodded. Those who were seated stood, anticipating the results. I had been against the wall but was now by the doctor's side.

"Is she going to be okay?" Sara questioned, with concern haunting her tone.

The doctor nodded. "Yes, she's going to be fine."

My chest expanded as the air of relief filled my lungs. "What happened during surgery?" Megan asked eagerly.

The doctor placed the clipboard under his arm and began using his hands to gesture as he spoke. "In this case, it was a hemothorax. This happens with an open pneumothorax."

"What? English please." Jeremy expressed.

The doctor nodded in apology, "It means that there was an accumulation of blood in the lungs due to the gunshot wound. This caused severe respiratory distress, and the patient presented shallow rapid breathing and oxygen desaturation. We placed a large bore needle in the interpleural space and removed an excess of air and blood. A Heimlich valve was also inserted to evacuate the air from the lung. There was a lot of blood lost, but it was not severe enough to cause hypovolemic shock. So that was a good thing."

"Can we see her?" Jeremy asked.

"Not all of you at the moment. One can stay with her for now, but other than that, we want to keep a close eye on her for the next twenty-four hours. She was sedated, so she won't be awake for another few hours, maybe not even until the morning."

All heads turned to me. "Can I go in and stay with her?" I finally spoke.

"Are you the husband?"

"Fiancé."

"Yes, follow me." He nodded as everyone thanked him.

"Give her a kiss for me." Sara said as she quickly hugged me.

"For us too." Megan added as she reached and grabbed Jeremy's hand. I nodded at them and followed behind the surgeon.

A chill rushed through me as I walked quickly behind him through the cold hospital hallway. We stopped by a door numbered 1020. "She's in here. Please remember she won't wake up anytime soon because she's heavily sedated. Also, be careful with the tubes in her chest."

I nodded. He turned and walked down the hall. I took in a few deep breaths before going through the doors. Not certain what to expect as I entered, my heart clenched as I saw her lying on a small hospital bed, pale and fragile. She looked peaceful but pained as she lay there with her hair disheveled on the pillow.

The sound of the machines beeping forced me back to reality. I swallowed the lump in my throat as I carried myself to her.

After I had reached her side and had seen all the wires and tubes going through her, my entire body winced. I held back the urge to pull her into me. *My poor baby*. I reached my hand out and grazed my fingers along her pale cheek, down her gentle jawline, and across her soft plump lips. I couldn't hold it in any longer. How much stronger could I be? I stood there and watched the one person who had trusted me with everything, even her life, and I had betrayed her. Collapsing, I kneeled down beside her and cradled her hand along the side of my face.

"I'm so sorry, baby." I whispered through a cracked tone. I pulled her hand around and placed her palm along my lips. I patted gentle kisses along her skin and stared at her closed eyes, wishing she'd flash them open and forgive me. I rocked back and forth desperately trying not to break, but as I continued to stare at the only woman I'd ever loved, images of her gasping for her last breath invaded my mind, and I broke down.

I broke down in a way I didn't know a man ever could.

I broke down and cradled her in my arms and kissed her hands, her fingers, her face, her lips, her eyelids, and her jawline. And with each kiss, I begged and prayed for her to wake up and forgive me.

I broke down, and I didn't care how much less of a man it made me, because I wasn't a man at all without her in my life. She made me more of a man than I could ever be. She was the reason that I wanted to start over again and become a better man.

***

"Marcus, honey." At the sound of my mother's voice, I lifted my head from the crook of my arm. I looked around and realized that I was still in the hospital room. My eyes scanned to my side and found that Mia was still asleep. I must have drifted off sometime in the early morning. Yawning, I ran a hand down my face and squeezed my eyes shut. The pounding headache and burning eyes were killing me.

"What time is it?"

"Just past noon. I went home and brought you some things so that you can change out of those bloody clothes."

I looked down at my wardrobe and realized that I was still wearing the same clothing. I hadn't noticed anything that had gone on for the past twenty-four hours. I had been focusing entirely on making sure that Mia was alright before stopping to worry about myself.

"I need coffee." I mumbled.

"I have that too." She lifted her right hand, which held a cup. "Won't you go into the bathroom, freshen up, and come back out and have a good old strong cup?" She nodded. "I even brought you a toothbrush and toothpaste." Hesitant to leave Mia's side, I glanced over at her. "Marcus, she'll be fine. I'll watch her. You'll only be a few feet away."

Taking her advice, I stood from the chair that I had spent the entire night in, lifted Mia's hand that I hadn't let go of yet, and brushed my lips along her knuckles. Then I gently placed her arm back down on the bed. I grabbed the bag my mother had brought for me and entered the bathroom.

I switched the light on and dumped the bag on top of a small table by the sink. Glancing into the mirror, I looked at the man staring back at me. Fuck. He looked like he had been run over by a train and then smashed into a concrete wall.

He looked like shit.

CHAPTER TWENTY-SEVEN

MIA

As I breathed in through my lungs, the air burned against the sensitive muscle. The pain was excruciating, which caused my eyes to flash open and me to wince. Through blurry vision, I glanced around my surroundings. I was in a hospital room. My throat was completely dry. I tried to swallow, but it was a scorching discomfort. The beeping from the machines became clearer as my mind struggled to register it all. After a few seconds, I remembered the reason why I was there and who I was looking for at the time it had all occurred.

Marcus.

Gasping, I forced my body to sit up, but every muscle ached, and my own body fought against every urge to do so. Hell, it hurt to move an inch. *Maybe I should start off slowly.* I carefully lifted my left hand and saw an IV pricked through a vein. Weakly, my hand dropped back down on the bed; it was difficult to do anything. But I needed to know where Marcus was. I needed to get to him. If anything had happened to him, I'd be lost.

A familiar soft face hovered over me as she gasped, "Oh my, Mia, you're awake. How are you feeling, honey?"

I opened my mouth to speak, but nothing would come out. A slight squeak was all that came out as my voice cracked. Frustrated, I slammed my head back against the pillow. Theresa continued to stare at me with concern filling her eyes. I wanted to ask about Marcus. I wanted to know if he was alright or if he was hurt too. When I tried to ask again, the sound of a door creaking open forced me to tilt my head.

There he was, safe and sound. Our eyes locked, and every emotion prickled through me as my heart swelled with relief that he was still here, still with me. His eyes clouded over as he slowly stepped closer toward me. Theresa was in the background mumbling something about going to tell a nurse that I was awake. I may have nodded. I wasn't sure. My focus was solely on Marcus.

The last time I saw him was the night at Club21 when we left on unsettled terms. I remembered going home that night and regretted not pulling him in and holding him tight. I regretted not kissing him or telling him that I loved him before we went our separate ways. I never imagined that the next day could have been my last and I would've never had the chance to hold or kiss him one last time. An overwhelming ache coursed through me. Breaking down, I burst into sobs. He was by my side instantly. Pressing his hand along my cheek, he hushed me. "Don't cry, baby. I'm here." I closed my eyes and leaned my face into his hand. The feeling of his warm touch felt like home as he wiped away my hot tears.

Even though he tried to soothe the pain away, the comfort of having him so close and the thought of ever losing him forced me into a trembling teary frenzy. My body shook uncontrollably. Marcus leaned down and wrapped his arms around me. He was careful not to pull me in too tightly, but the embrace allowed me to go weak in his arms. "I'm so sorry, baby. I will never be able to take away the pain of what you went through, but if you let me, I will try every single day." He whispered into my hair.

Still unable to speak, I nodded into the crook of his neck and continued to allow hot tears to stream down my face.

He held me close until the nurse appeared, and even then, I didn't want to pull away from him. She waited patiently until we were done. Marcus held my hand the entire time as she asked me a few questions and checked my vitals. After she scribbled a few things down, she smiled and informed me that the doctor would be in shortly.

After the nurse had left me alone with Marcus, he pulled a chair up beside me and framed my face. "Do you need me to get you anything? I can stop by your apartment. I can grab you food or water or anything you like." There was nothing I needed but him at that moment. Gently tightening my grip on his hand, I shook my head. "Your throat is sore, huh?" I nodded in response. "Want some ice? Maybe it'll soothe your throat?" I thought it might be a good idea, so I nodded, and he was out the door and back instantly with a cup of ice.

It felt like when I had a terrible sore throat and I tried cough medicine, hot tea, or water to soothe the itching, burning, and rawness. But this was ten times worse. The ice chip helped soothe the pain for about a second until it came back. After a few minutes, I was able to clear my throat and actually speak.

"Better?"

"A little." My voice was barely above a whisper. "It hurts when I breathe."

"Oh, baby, it's going hurt for a while. The bullet grazed your lung."

Wincing at the memory, I leaned back into the pillow. "What happened afterwards?"

"Some people died; some were arrested."

"Lou?"

"He'll never be a bother to you ever again."

"Was he arrested?"

He shook his head, and I knew right then and there that Lou Sorrento was dead.

"Good."

Marcus took the cup of ice I handed to him and placed it on the table beside us. "I'm tired."

Standing, he leaned in and pressed his lips against my forehead. "Get some rest, baby. Your mom, Megan, Jeremy, and your grandparents will be by later on this evening. Do you mind if I stay here?" He pointed to his chair.

I shook my head. "Can you lie with me?"

He tilted his head at the small bed and studied it adorably. I tried to laugh but winced again and slowly slid over to the left side of the bed, making very little room for him. He climbed in next to me and lay on his side, pulling me into his chest. His lips grazed my forehead as he ran his fingers up and down my arm.

"Marcus?" I whispered as I snuggled into his chest.

"Yeah?" He asked in a soft, content tone.

"I love you."

He pulled me in a tighter. "I love you too. More than you'll ever know."

"Is it over?"

Not answering me, he lifted my chin for my eyes to meet his. His eyes scanned my face until they landed on my lips. Gently, he pressed his lips against mine and then laid my head back against his chest.

I held back my tears. I wanted this to be over with, to finally start fresh again in our relationship, but he wouldn't clarify, and I was left again wondering what else could be holding us back. I was too weak to question him; with heavy eyes, I shut my lids and fell asleep in his arms.

***

It'd been a week since I'd been trapped in this hellhole, and I wanted out. I was feeling great, but the doctor said I couldn't be released until sometime next week. Marcus had been out running a few errands, and Megan had stopped by to spend time with me. My hospital room was filled with balloons, flowers, and get well cards.

My mother, grandparents, and Jeremy had visited almost daily. On the first day of their visit, they all asked questions about what had happened. I told them that whatever Marcus told them was what had happened. They were a bit suspicious about it all but didn't continue to push the issue. I believe Jeremy must have put it all together, but when I told him to drop it, he did. The TV was the last thing I wanted to watch as every news channel discussed the bust. Some, as expected, over-exaggerated the events; others were dishing out new conspiracy theories. Only a few got it right.

Lou Sorrento was dead, and so were a few of his men. Gio Sorrento was shot in the arm and leg. After receiving medical attention, he was placed in custody and would be awaiting trial. The other mob leader from New York, Salvatore Lombardi, was arrested along with a few of his men. Others were either injured or dead. A few of the FBI agents were killed in the line of duty. An awards ceremony would be held for them in a couple of weeks.

It all felt unreal. The entire situation played like a movie. I wouldn't have thought that it could actually happen in real life, but it did, and it happened to me.

Marcus had said that he had walked away from his former life completely, but I had to wonder how true that was. Just because Lou was gone didn't mean someone else couldn't take his place. The mob just doesn't disappear. They rebuild their family and continue to go on. There couldn't possibly be any happily-ever-afters when a person gets immersed in that lifestyle. Or could there be?

"I brought a brush with me." Megan sang as she danced her way over to my bed.

"No. Get away from me. You're not touching my hair." I swatted her hands away.

She dropped her hands to her hips and gave me a hard stare, "Mia, your hair is a tangled mess. We need to get it under control."

Blowing out a deep breath as a way of caving in, I scooted toward the front of the bed so that she could kneel behind me. "Fine."

Megan began brushing my hair, "So, where's Marcus?"

"I sent him home."

"How did you manage that? He hasn't left your side since day one."

"I threatened him that if he didn't go home and take a shower I was never going to kiss or sleep with him again."

She let out a giggle. "That worked?"

"If you knew Marcus, you would know that sex is the best way to bribe him."

"You're mean."

"Yeah, I know, but I also wanted him to go out and get some air. Staying in a hospital for several days isn't exactly a spa getaway."

"Like a massage spa getaway?"

We burst out laughing, and I winced as I felt a pain shoot through the side of my rib.

"See. You're not one-hundred percent yet. You can't go home."

"I hate being in here."

"It's a hospital, honey. Everyone does."

She continued to stroke my hair with the brush, and I hated to admit it, but it felt great. Once she was satisfied with the final result, she pulled back to inspect her doing. "Well, it's not exactly how I pictured it, but it'll do until you can wash it."

"Wow, you're such a great friend."

"I'm honest."

Marcus came through the doors with a huge flower arrangement and a smile. "Hello, beautiful."

"Awww!" Megan squealed.

"Marcus, you do not have to bring flowers every single day. What am I going to do with all of these?" I spread my arms around the room.

He shrugged as he found a spot by the corner window seal and set the vase down. "Get used to it."

My lips curled into a crooked smile. "Are you going to buy me flowers every day for the rest of our lives?"

"Yes, I am. Every single day." Playfully, I rolled my eyes at him and he chuckled. "I can see your attitude is back. That should be a great sign that you'll be home early."

"Actually, the doctor said that I won't go home until sometime next week." I crossed my arms across my chest with a huff and leaned back into the bed. The mattress was adjusted into an upright position so that I could sit up and not lie down on it.

"Well, I'd love to stay and chat, but I have to be at work in a few hours. I'll stop by tomorrow." Megan leaned in and kissed my cheek.

"Thank you for stopping by, Megan, and for doing my hair." Marcus bunched his brows together as he tilted his head and stared at my head. I guess there wasn't much of a difference.

"Anytime! Maybe tomorrow I can do your makeup." Her smile was so enthusiastic I couldn't help but nod in response. How could you turn down someone who only wanted to help?

Just like that, with a single wave of her hand, she was gone and out the door.

"What are the plans for today?" I turned my head to Marcus.

"Well, there's the lovely game of Scrabble again." He reached for the game that lay on the table beside the bed. "Or crossword puzzles." He waved the book with a huge grin and a mocking brow wiggle. "And then there's the fine game of Go Fish 'cause you don't know any other card games." He sat in the chair beside me.

"I know 'I declare war.'"

"Not a real card game, babe. Pick a game."

With a hand to my chest, I widened my eyes. "Oh how shall I ever choose with such a huge selection?"

He flashed a wide-dimpled grin. "Or I can go out and buy a few more games if you like."

"No, Scrabble is fine."

"Atta girl." He reached up and lightly tugged at my chin.

During the next hour, Marcus and I were still on our first game of Scrabble, which I was winning, of course, when we heard a knock at the door. Vinnie walked in and my entire body froze. I hadn't seen him since the day of the shooting. Marcus told me that he was fine, but just seeing Vinnie in person made it all come back.

"Mia, how you feeling?" Vinnie asked as he slowly approached the hospital bed.

"I'm good, better than good. How are you?"

"I'm glad you're doin' well. I'm doing well too. Hey, Marky." He nodded over at Marcus who returned the gesture. Marcus exhaled and stood. "No, no, please sit. I don't want to intrude. I just wanted to say a few things."

"Alright." Marcus said cautiously as he slowly sat back down.

"I just wanted to let the both of you know that I'm sorry for what happened and how everything went down. Especially for you, Mia. You shouldn't have walked into that."

"It's not your fault. I was at the wrong place at the wrong time."

"Still it wasn't right, so I'm sorry." Smiling at him, I nodded. "And, Marky, just so you know, there was glitch with the surveillance camera videos after Lou left the building, if you know what I mean."

I turned my head toward Marcus, who wore a baffled expression. "So just like that. Everything is good?" His tone screamed with uncertainly.

Vinnie nodded. "I told you I owed you one, so yeah, just like that."

"But how?"

"Like I said, there was a glitch."

Marcus stood up from the chair walked over toward Vinnie and offered his hand. "Thank you."

Vinnie took it and shook Marcus's hand. They exchanged a quick manly hug, and once Vinnie pulled away, he smiled at me, turned, and walked out the room.

"What was all that about, Marcus?" I asked him the moment Vinnie was out the door.

He shook his head in disbelief. "That was my out."

"Seriously?" My heart fluttered in anticipation.

He nodded. "Yeah. It's over." I reached my arms out, and in a few strides, he was beside me. He kissed my forehead and pulled me into a tight embrace.

We could finally start reclaiming our lives.

CHAPTER TWENTY-EIGHT

THREE MONTHS LATER

MARCUS

Fingers traced along my arm, toward my shoulder, and across my chest. Once at the middle of my chest, the fingers glided down my torso and stopped at the edge of my briefs. A finger hooked its way in and played along the rim of the cotton fabric. "Wake up, my sleepy man." Her voice was a whisper along my ear.

I moaned and adjusted my arm around her to pull her in closer. With my eyes still closed, I smiled at her giggle. She continued to play with the rim of my boxers. I caught her wrist and pushed her hands down. She giggled again as she gripped my length and began stroking it up and down. "I didn't wake you for this." She teased as she went on with her gentle strokes.

"Well, why else would you wake me?" I slightly stretched underneath her and smiled as she leaned in and grazed her lips along my jawline and toward my ear.

"Today is a good day." She mumbled as she sucked in my earlobe.

"Oh, yeah? What's today?"

"I need you to wake up so I can tell you."

"I'm up, baby. Don't you feel the hard on? I'm wide awake."

Another soft laugh escaped her. "Open your eyes for me."

Just like that, I did as I was told, flashing my eyes open. I had the privilege to wake to that beautiful face every morning. She bit her lip as a thrill of excitement filled her eyes. She was so happy with whatever she wanted to tell me that the vibe was transferring onto me. "You're killing me here, Mia. What do you have to tell me?"

She kneeled up on the bed and wrapped her legs around my hips to straddle me. I placed my hands on her waist and stared up at the most beautiful sight I'd ever seen. Her hair, long and wavy, was draped down the front of her shoulders and down toward the middle of her torso. Her soft face radiated a glow that would lighten a room, and those big emerald sparkling eyes, that I fell in love with the moment I saw them, weakened me every time. I raised my brows, waiting for her to respond.

"Well . . ." She looked down at me. Her smile softened as if she were unsure of why she'd awoken me, and then she blurted, "I'm pregnant."

My mouth dropped open and then turned into the biggest grin. "What?!"

She nodded adamantly. "I know. It's crazy, right? I mean we've done everything backwards. Moved in together, pregnancy, and then marriage, but even though it's not in the order everyone expects it to be, I'm okay with that. I'm not sure . . ."

I gripped her face and brought her down, shutting off the rambling that she always did when she was nervous. I smashed my lips against hers. She weakened in my hold and moaned against my mouth. Slowly pulling her away, I stared into her eyes. "Who cares if it's backwards? Who said there was a rule of how to plan your life? Are you happy?"

Her eyes filled with tears as she forced a smile and nodded. "I'm so happy, but I feel guilty for feeling *this* happy."

Puzzled by what she meant, I traced the back of my fingers along the side of her soft cheeks. "Explain that to me."

"Well, every time I begin to feel like my life is finally taking off, that nothing could change the pattern of how great things are going, just like that," she snapped her fingers, "it's taken away from me, as if I don't deserve for once to just be happy."

"Baby." I pulled her in against my chest and ran my fingers through her soft brown hair. "I can't promise you that life won't try to take a stab at you, that you won't run through a few obstacles, and that you won't feel like quitting at times. But I can promise you that, with each stab, I'll be there to heal the wound. With each obstacle, I'll be running right beside you. And every time you fall, I'll be right there to pick you up. We're in this together, always, and no matter how many times it feels like a struggle, we'll fight through it together because we deserve to be happy. *You* deserve all the happiness life can bring."

I tugged at her chin and lifted her wet face from my chest. A soft smile formed on her lips as she swiped away the tears. "Well, be prepared because life is going to bring you a moody, hormonal, and very sensitive pregnant woman for the next few months."

Laughing, I framed her face and grazed my thumb along her cheekbones. "It's worth it; everything with you is worth every bit." I lifted her hand, the one with the engagement ring she had accepted again the moment we moved in together, and played with it around her finger. With a smile, I traced my eyes from her hand to her face. "You've made me happier than you'll ever know."

Mia breathed out a smile, leaned down, and pressed her lips against mine—those lips that I had the pleasure to kiss every day for the rest of my life.

Yes, it was exactly then that I knew, without a doubt, that I was the luckiest man alive.

EPILOGUE

ONE YEAR LATER

MIA

I stared at my reflection in the long mirror before me, and a smile crept along my lips as I admired the beauty in white. The long strapless gown hugged my body flawlessly. The diamond necklace and matching drop earrings were simple but elegant. My hair was pinned into a low bun and covered with a long veil that draped down my back. Gathering my bouquet from the table by the vanity, I held the beautiful yellow roses in front of me and took one last glance at the reflection.

This was the day that I'd walk down the aisle and forever be known as Mrs. Marcus DeLuca. Tears filled my eyes as the thought crossed my mind of spending the rest of my life with the one man I loved. Marcus and I had traveled a path that was dangerous, heart wrenching, and tremendously insane. We also had a life full of love, laughter, and happiness. Even through all the bad times, I couldn't picture my life without him. We had fought for each other tooth and nail. Yes, ours was a flawed relationship, but when we loved each other as deeply as we did, no one could ever take that away from us.

We were meant for each other in every way, and I didn't care how others perceived our relationship. None of that mattered because I was going to spend life with the one person that truly counted.

"Are you ready, sweetheart?" My grandfather popped his head in the door and froze as he set eyes on me. "Well, I'll be . . ." Tears began to fill his eyes. Bowing his head, he walked over to me and pulled me into a hug. "You are the most beautiful bride I've ever seen." He whispered, "Don't tell your grandmother I said that. She'll kill me."

Laughing, I tightened my arms around him. "Thank you so much, and thank you for walking me down the aisle."

"Are you kidding? I'm honored." He pulled back as his eyes danced around my face. "Are you ready to become a married woman?"

"As ready as I'll ever be."

He nodded, stepped aside, and bent his arm. I nestled my hand through the crook of it and looked up at him with a smile. "Let's do this."

We walked out of the hotel room and down the hall. My heart fluttered as I anticipated seeing Marcus. I wondered if he was just as nervous and anxious as I was. As we waited for the elevators, I heard Megan squealing as she ran down the hall. Her long light yellow silk gown with a white sash swayed as she darted my way. It was the perfect gown for a spring wedding.

"You look amazing." She breathed out as she tried to catch her breath.

"You do too." We quickly hugged and walked into the elevator as it opened.

We traveled down to the lobby and headed to where the ceremony was held. Once we reached the doors, the wedding planner pulled me aside against the wall. "No peeking. We wouldn't want the groom to see you early." I nodded and began fidgeting with my hands as my breathing grew unsteady.

After a few minutes, I was able to calm my breathing. Then I caught sight of Elle running down the hall toward me. She was absolutely beautiful in a white dress with a red sash. The basket she held was filled with yellow rose petals. Once she approached me, her eyes glistened as her lips curled into a huge smile. "Wow, Mia. You look like a princess."

I laughed and leaned down to pull her into a hug. "No, you look like a princess. You're beautiful."

"Thank you. I'm here to perform the flower girl duties. Daddy said it's a very important job."

I burst into laughter. "Oh yes, very important. Without the flower girl, the wedding would be a catastrophe."

With a hand on her hip, she nodded. "Yes, we can't let that happen."

"Alright, everyone in place. The wedding will begin in a few seconds." The wedding planner clapped his hands together.

I straightened at his announcement and wrapped my hand snugly through my grandfather's crooked arm.

Right on time, the planner hurried Elle along the aisle. Before walking down the aisle, she winked at me, adjusted her shoulders, and smiled brightly for the guests.

I loved that little girl.

Megan was up next. "See you in a few!" She squealed and waved her hand, showing off her diamond engagement ring, and headed down the same path as Elle. In a few months, she and Jeremy would be reciting their own vows. I couldn't have been happier for them.

"Okay, in about ten seconds, the wedding bells will go off, and then you can walk down."

I nodded at the planner and took in another deep breath.

Right on time, I heard the bells go off. My grandfather moved forward, and I followed beside him as he guided me down the aisle. My head was bowed at first. I heard shoes shuffling as the guests stood the moment we entered. As we continued in a slow pace down the aisle, in the midst of it all, I had the courage to finally look up.

First, I saw my mother standing beside my grandmother with their eyes filled with joyous tears. Second, Jeremy, with a wide smile, gave me one nod. I returned the gesture and then let out a soft laugh. Third, I saw Theresa. She was beautiful in a cream silk gown as her eyes glowed at the sight of me. I looked straight ahead and found Jimmie as the best man with his smile wide and bright. I remembered the talk I had with him the previous night, when he told me that he couldn't have picked a more suitable wife for his brother. I told him one day he'd find love and that, when it came, it would hit him hard. He disagreed, but I knew one day he would.

After I smiled at Jimmie, I turned my head slightly to the left, and then I saw him: my soon-to-be husband. My heart expanded with more love than I ever thought possible. Marcus stood at the other end of the aisle, looking more handsome than ever in a black tuxedo. With a wide dimpled smile, he tilted his arm so I could get a better look of our six-month-old baby boy he held. Michael was dressed in a matching tiny tux. My eyes swelled as I saw my two boys waiting for me at the end of the aisle. I laughed as tears escaped me when Marcus lifted our baby's tiny hand to wave at me.

Once I made my way up to them, Marcus leaned in and kissed my forehead. "You look so beautiful."

"You too." I whispered through my cracked voice.

Marcus chuckled and kissed our baby boy's soft head before handing him over to me. I grabbed him and looked down at the big brown eyes and tiny lips that curled into a small grin, which showed off his dimple just like his daddy's. It was right then that I knew I wouldn't change any of the past couple of years. I'd never been happier. My life was complete as I held my baby and looked up at the man that gave me more than just happiness. He gave me love and a life full of unexpected turns that brought us to where we were now—a life that only a few could dream of, but this wasn't a fantasy. This was real.

We stood before all of our family and friends and promised to love, trust, and be honest for the rest of our lives. There might be rocky times, but we would get past them together and never give up, because love—and not just any love, but *our* love—was worth fighting for.

He leaned down and gave me my first kiss as Mrs. Marcus DeLuca.

THE END

ACKNOWLEDGMENTS

First and foremost, I want to thank my readers. I didn't think anyone would actually like my first book, *Disastrous*, let alone fall in love with the characters. Thank you for the support and love you've given me. If it weren't for your continued support, *Cautious* would've never met its deadline. You guys are the reason why I'll continue my passion. I have so much more and can't wait to give you.

To my husband, Alex, words cannot express how much I love you. Although, we're not perfect, (What relationship is?) I can't picture life without you. Thank you for always supporting me, for being there when I cried because I thought I couldn't meet my deadline, and for picking-up laundry duty along with the take-out dinners. I know you haven't had a good home-cooked meal in months. I owe you one or a few. ;-) Love you, babe.

To my family and friends, I'm sorry I haven't been around as much as I used to. I was always a phone call away or jumped in my car when I was needed, but you still stuck by me and supported me the entire way! I love you all! Seriously, from the bottom of my heart, thank you! <3

Mom! You're the reason for all of this. It'll never get old for me to remind you! Thank you for pushing me to publish *Disastrous;* it started my new beginning. Love you!

To Christine Martinez, thank you for sending me different medical terms to help with the "shooting scene." You're the best!

To my beta readers, Jennifer Diaz, Lori Francis, and Karinna Baez, thank you ladies for the feedback and for going through this process with me. *Heart hand motions*

To Jennifer Wolfel, you're simply awesome. Thank you for dealing with my anxiety and slapping me a few times to get me out of my depression. Your honest feedback helped improve my story, so thank you for that as well!

To Ashley Hartigan Tkachyk, AHH! I love you! I'm so happy you stalked me *inside joke* because we would've never become great friends. I'm certain if you were not with me throughout this entire process *Cautious* would not be what it is and I probably would've been admitted into an insane asylum. Also, thank you for listening to me cry and whine over the phone or through private message. I know you rolled your eyes a few times, even though you said you didn't. LOL. You're the best, and your feedback on *Cautious* was amazing.

To Melissa L. Delgado, are there enough words to express to my CP/soul sister/awesome sauce friend how much I love her? Nope, not enough words! Melis, thank you so much, for everything. Not just for the feedback on *Cautious* but for being a friend. You showed me that there are still sincere and genuine people out there. *Ending a Broken Journey* is going to touch so many readers, and I can't wait to ride that journey with you! Love you, honey bunny! ;-)

To Becca Manuel, thank you for the amazing Cautious trailer; you're very talented. I can't wait to see you shoot for the stars. Also, thank you for being simply sweet!

To David Goldhahn, again thanks for a wonderful job on the cover. I can't wait to continue to work with you on my future covers.

Theresa Wegand, it was amazing working with you again. Thank you for beta reading, editing, and formatting *Cautious*.

To Miranda Petrillo, wow, you did such an amazing job proofreading *Cautious!* I couldn't be happier with the end result and will be working with you in the future! Thank you so much for your hard work.

To all book bloggers, there are so many of you that it would have taken ten pages, but I just want to say thank you so much, from the bottom of my heart. You take time out of your work life, family life, and personal life to support and spread the word of your favorite authors. I'm in *awe* of you, for just being so committed and loving a story that has touched you and all you want to do is simply share your passion about the story with others. Thank you for that! If not for you, many readers would lose out on the opportunity of finding a story that they might fall in love with as well. Thank you!

Last, but certainly not least, to my author group; you girls keep me sane. Seriously, you girls made me laugh when I wanted to cry, allowed me to feel pride when I was discouraged, and allowed me to believe in myself when I had doubts. A special thank you to Syreeta, Gail, Madeline, Claire, Cindy, Trevlyn, Karina and Laura—you girls rock! Thank you for listening to my everyday rants. <3

COMING SOON

By E.L. Montes

PERFECTLY DAMAGED

This is a standalone scheduled to be released: Fall 2013/Spring 2014

Sometimes in life we are confronted by unforeseen hurdles. Other times there are people introduced in our lives for unexpected reasons: reasons beyond our control or desire. No matter the differences, sometimes two people find one another when they are most needed, even when not searching.

When Jenna McDaniel meets Josh Lewis, she begins to slowly discover herself. Josh Lewis wasn't looking for love or even a girlfriend. Trying to make ends meet and help care for his nephew, his already screwed up-life goes downhill the moment he is confronted by Jenna.

No one deserves to be alone, no one deserves to be judged, and no one certainly deserves to be unloved. For more reasons than one, sometimes we find something perfect—even when it has flaws.

Beaten, stomped, or simply thrown away, anything could be perfect even when damaged.

FIGHTING TO STAND (a novella)

This is a spin off from the *Disastrous* Series—Jimmie DeLuca's story.

To be released: Fall 2013/Spring 2014

Synopsis coming soon.

ABOUT THE AUTHOR

Emmy Montes was born in Puerto Rico but was raised in Philadelphia, Pennsylvania. She currently resides in Philadelphia with her husband, Alex, and their English bulldog. She has a Bachelor of Science degree in Legal Studies. She works full time as a paralegal for a mid-sized law firm. Although she loves the legal field, writing was always her passion.

Her love for books began with the Goosebumps series as a child. After that, she read anything and everything from poetry to short stories. She was passionate about the fictional world and intrigued by the way an author could pull you into a story with just simple words. As a hobby, she started writing her own poetry, daily journal entries, and short stories.

She actually dreamed of being a journalist and even went as far as researching colleges to earn a degree in Journalism. At the time, major newspaper companies and magazines were having budgets cut, and after careful thought, she settled on another major. When she finished her degree, she felt as if something were missing. She continued to write for several years, working on different story ideas, but never finished. *Disastrous* was her first completed novel.

Connect with Me Online

Email: auth.el.montes@gmail.com

Facebook: E.L. Montes

Goodreads: E.L. Montes